DEATH
COMES TO
KURLAND HALL

Center Point
Large Print

Also by Catherine Lloyd and available from Center Point Large Print:

The Kurland St. Mary Mysteries
Death Comes to the Village
Death Comes to London

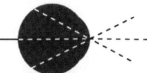

DEATH COMES TO KURLAND HALL

CATHERINE LLOYD

CENTER POINT LARGE PRINT
THORNDIKE, MAINE

This Center Point Large Print edition
is published in the year 2017 by arrangement with
Kensington Publishing Corp.

The text of this Large Print edition is unabridged.
In other aspects, this book may vary
from the original edition.
Printed in the United States of America
on permanent paper.
Set in 16-point Times New Roman type.

ISBN: 978-1-68324-518-6

Library of Congress Cataloging-in-Publication Data

Names: Lloyd, Catherine, 1963– author.
Title: Death comes to Kurland Hall / Catherine Lloyd.
Description: Center Point Large Print edition. | Thorndike, Maine :
    Center Point
    Large Print, 2017.
Identifiers: LCCN 2017026493 | ISBN 9781683245186
    (hardcover : alk. paper)
Subjects: LCSH: Murder—Investigation—Fiction. | England—Social life
    and customs—19th century—Fiction. | Large type books. | GSAFD:
    Mystery fiction. | Regency fiction.
Classification: LCC PS3616.E246 D426 2017 | DDC 813/.6—dc23
LC record available at https://lccn.loc.gov/2017026493

This one is for Sophia Rose Catherine.
My favorite and only daughter.

Acknowledgments

Big thanks to Ruth Long and Tony Mozingo for reading the manuscript and pointing out all the mistakes, especially the big ones. Also thanks to Kat Cantrell for finding the most accurate Bible verses to help the plot along, which saved me a lot of time. All other mistakes are my own.

Chapter 1

"Lucy, my dear, you cannot ignore Major Kurland forever."

"I know that."

Lucy Harrington sighed and turned away from the window where she had just watched the major retreat down the tree-lined drive in his carriage. He'd sat with Sophia for a correct fifteen minutes, while Lucy had hidden cravenly in the library until she was certain he had gone.

"In a village as small as this, I am already finding it difficult to avoid him. When I return to the rectory, I'll be right next door to Kurland Hall."

Sophia patted her dog and then looked up at Lucy. "I still don't understand what he did to provoke such a response from you." She hesitated. "Did something happen on the way back from London? You barely spoke to each other for the entire journey. I ended up chattering all the time just to fill the silence. Major Kurland probably thinks I am an absolute fool."

"I'm sure he doesn't. I hoped you wouldn't notice that we were at odds."

"It was rather difficult to miss. You do tend to provoke each other, but you are rarely silent about it. I'm not sure which is worse, the bickering or the sulking." Sophia sighed. "I do hope you will mend your fences soon, or my wedding is going to be very difficult indeed. Andrew asked Major Kurland to stand up with him and be his chief supporter at the altar. That's what he came to tell me today."

Lucy sat on the couch beside Sophia, almost dislodging Hunter, the dog, who ceded his place with obvious reluctance. "I swear I will not do anything to adversely affect your wedding. If that means treating Major Sir Robert Kurland, baronet, as if he was the Prince Regent himself, I will do it." She squeezed Sophia's hand. "I never meant for you to suffer from my stupidity."

"*Your* stupidity?" Sophia raised her eyebrows. "What on earth did you do, Lucy? *Throw* yourself at him?"

"Ha! I almost threw *something* at him." Lucy rose and paced the carpet, her hands locked together at her waist. "He . . . asked me to marry him."

"Good Lord!" Sophia chuckled. "I thought his broken engagement with Miss Chingford had put that notion out of his head for good. What did you say?"

"What do you think? As you pointed out, we

were hardly smelling of April and May for the remainder of the journey, were we?"

"You declined his offer?"

Lucy raised her chin. "Obviously, seeing as it was made under duress."

"Someone held a gun to his head?"

"Of course not." She fixed her friend with a severe glance. "Only a *metaphorical* pistol, in that my uncle asked Major Kurland to declare his intentions toward me."

"I suppose the earl was trying to do his duty when your own father was absent. Major Kurland was rather *particular* in his attentions to you. Many people remarked on it."

Lucy took another agitated turn around the room. "You know why he sought my company. It was everything to do with solving a murder, and nothing to do with him having any romantical notions about me whatsoever."

Sophia patted the seat beside her. "Do sit down, Lucy, dear. You are giving me a headache with all that pacing. I assume Major Kurland made no effort to *be* romantic when he proposed?"

"As if I would've believed him if he had." Lucy sat down again with a thump. "In truth, he suggested that he *owed* me an offer of marriage."

"Oh dear."

"He sounded as if he was being led to the gallows and had accepted that his fate was to hang."

Sophia stifled a sound behind her hand.

Lucy frowned at her. "Are you laughing at me?"

"I . . . am trying not to. I can just picture Major Kurland saying those words. I'm surprised you *didn't* throw something at him."

"I thought about it, but I was reluctant to cause a scene at the inn."

Sophia angled her head to one side and observed Lucy rather too closely. "You don't find it amusing, do you?"

"No. It was hideously embarrassing."

"Then I'm sorry I laughed," Sophia said contritely. "Perhaps if he had presented his case in a different way, you—"

Lucy shot to her feet as the butler entered the room and bowed.

"Mr. Stanford is here, ma'am. Do you wish to see him?"

"That would be delightful. Please send him in." Sophia's pleasure in the arrival of her intended shone in her face. At one point Lucy had wondered if Andrew Stanford would make *her* a good husband. After discovering he meant to reside mainly in London—a city she couldn't bear to live in permanently—she was almost relieved when she discovered he had fallen in love with Sophia.

His ready smile widened when he came into the drawing room and saw Lucy.

"Miss Harrington, what a surprise! When I passed Robert on the drive, he told me you were not at home."

Lucy felt herself blush. "I just returned from a walk, Mr. Stanford."

"So I see." His amused gaze swept over her gauzy morning dress and thin slippers, attire that was hardly suitable for a trip outside. "Did you hide in the attics to avoid the wretched man?"

"Andrew! Don't tease dear Lucy," Sophia said.

"Well, it is rather amusing to see Robert balked of his prey. Whatever did he do to deserve such treatment, Miss Harrington?"

Lucy forced a smile. "Major Kurland has done nothing wrong. Please excuse me. I have to go and finish packing." She nodded at Sophia. "I will be back tomorrow to help you with the last of the invitations, but it might not be until the afternoon. I'm sure my father will have a thousand things he wishes me to do for him."

"I'm sure he will." Sophia made a sympathetic face. "My mother will be here in a day or so, which will make matters proceed far more speedily."

Lucy curtsied to Mr. Stanford and made her way up to her bedchamber, which faced the home park of Hathaway House. Her bags were already packed, but she'd wanted to get away from the affianced couple before Sophia felt obliged to tell Mr. Stanford exactly what Major Kurland had

11

done. Sophia was normally very discreet, but she seemed incapable of keeping anything from Mr. Stanford, which was perhaps as it should be.

As it was a pleasant afternoon, Lucy decided to walk over to the rectory instead of riding in the cart with her bags. She'd already sent a note to her rather peevish father to reassure him that after two weeks with Sophia, she was finally coming home. She'd decided it was good for him to feel a certain sense of uncertainty about her whereabouts, because she no longer intended to be taken quite so much for granted at the rectory.

After consulting with the butler about the removal of her bags and boxes, she put on her stoutest boots and the old bonnet that matched her favorite blue pelisse and went down the stairs and out into the park beyond. As she walked, she took deep breaths of the clean country air, which was so much more invigorating than the sooty, smelly haze of London. Cutting across the corner of the park, she came out on the country lane and turned right.

She was glad to be home. It was unfortunate that Major Kurland had proven to be right about her ability to survive in London. As she stomped along, she reminded herself that he hadn't been right about everything. It wasn't her inability to secure a husband that had drawn her home to Kurland St. Mary, but lack of freedom and pure boredom.

Behind her, she heard a horse and moved closer to the hedge, glancing over her shoulder to see who was driving by.

"Miss Harrington." Major Kurland's voice was used to carrying on battlefields and couldn't be ignored. "Miss *Harrington.*"

Lucy stopped walking and waited for the gig to pull up alongside her.

"Good afternoon, Miss Harrington. May I offer you a lift?"

She kept her gaze straight ahead. "There is no need, Major Kurland. I am almost at the village."

"But I do believe it is going to rain. I couldn't leave you to struggle through a storm."

There was an implacable note in the major's voice that she knew all too well.

She sighed. "Thank you."

He leaned across and opened the door for her. Gathering her skirts, she stepped up and sat opposite him, her gaze fixed firmly on her lap.

With a jerk, the gig moved off, the sides brushing against the cow parsley that grew in the ditches on either side of the lane.

"You do realize that you are being ridiculous, Miss Harrington?"

"I wasn't aware of that, Major, or that your opinion of me mattered in the slightest."

His gloved hand tightened on his cane. "I suppose you expect me to apologize to you again."

"Like you *supposed* I expected you to propose to me?" Lucy gave a gasp and slapped her gloved hand over her mouth. "I do beg your pardon. That was quite inexcusable."

"For God's sake, don't apologize for the first honest answer you've given me in weeks."

Lucy cast an anguished glance at the back of the groom managing the horses.

"Don't worry about old Reg. He's as deaf as a post." Major Kurland eased forward in his seat. "Let me make myself clear. I apologize unreservedly for proposing to you. I wish I'd never said anything, and I want to continue our friendship. I don't want to spoil the upcoming wedding, an event we will both be heavily involved in."

"Neither do I."

"Then perhaps we should declare a truce. I'll refrain from embarrassing you with any more marriage proposals, and perhaps you will stop treating me like a leper."

"I wasn't embarrassed."

He sighed. "Angry then. But will you at least agree to let the past go?"

She studied the shine on his top boots for a long while. He seemed oblivious to the notion that his proposal might have hurt her feelings. But had it? Had she truly believed he might consider her as a suitable wife, after all? If he'd come to her on bended knee and sworn that he loved her, she wouldn't have believed him. She was well aware that managing females such as herself rarely raised such passionate feelings in a gentleman. They preferred women who treated them like demigods.

She raised her eyes to meet his irascible dark blue gaze. "For Sophia and Mr. Stanford's sake, I am prepared to let the past go."

"Thank goodness for that." Major Kurland sat back against the seat. "Now on to more important matters. I want to offer Kurland Hall as the venue for the breakfast and the evening party after the wedding. It is far larger than Hathaway House and can accommodate all the expected guests."

"I think Mrs. Hathaway would be delighted to accept your kind offer. She and Sophia have been wondering how to manage such a large crowd."

"Then I will consult with her when she returns home. I'm also . . ."

Major Kurland talked on, and Lucy nodded at the appropriate places and silently marveled at the changes in him. A year ago he'd been bedridden and making everyone pay for it. Now he was emerging as a formidable organizer and local leader, which was excellent news for everyone who depended on the Kurland estate for their living. She also wasn't sure how she viewed his ability to move on so easily from their unfortunate disagreement over marriage.

"Are you listening to me, Miss Harrington?"

"Yes, Major."

He frowned. "But you aren't interrupting."

"That's because I have nothing to suggest. You seem to have everything well in hand."

He looked slightly embarrassed. "That's because of Thomas Fairfax, my new estate manager. He keeps me on task."

"I cannot wait to meet this paragon."

"You'll like him. He's intelligent, hardworking, and adept at managing me." His rare smile flashed out. "Rather like you, actually." His gaze shifted to the approaching village, and he raised his voice. "Stop at the rectory for Miss Harrington, Reg." He turned back to Lucy. "Is your father expecting you?"

"I told him I would be back today." Lucy gathered her skirts and found her reticule as Reg came around to open the carriage door for her. Major Kurland alighted first and held out his hand to her.

"You don't need to come in, Major Kurland."

"I most certainly do. I have instructions from Andrew about the wedding ceremony to deliver to your father. Didn't Mrs. Giffin tell you that was one of the reasons I asked about you when I called? I always intended to offer you a lift home."

"Sophia didn't mention it."

Lucy took his hand and descended from the carriage. In truth, having Major Kurland with her

16

when she entered the rectory might work to her advantage and stop her father from quizzing her about her sudden return from London.

Within moments, despite her determined attempts to disengage herself from her companion's side, they were both seated in the rector's study while Major Kurland explained his errand and passed over Mr. Stanford's letter. Lucy knew her father disliked officiating at weddings, and wondered how he would react to being given orders by the groom. He seemed very amiable, and Lucy began to relax.

"Mr. Stanford and Mrs. Giffin also asked me to inquire if you might be prepared to accommodate a couple of wedding guests if Hathaway House and Kurland Hall are full."

The rector looked at Lucy. "Do we have space for guests, my dear?"

Lucy considered. "We have at least four vacant bedchambers until my siblings return home." She missed the twins; her sister, Anna; and her brother Anthony quite dreadfully. It would be pleasant to have the rectory full of people again for a week or so.

The rector rubbed his hands together and smiled. "Then we shall look forward to greeting our new guests and becoming acquainted with them. It can be dull here without the pleasure of new company. Not all of us are able to gad about and go off to London on a whim, are we,

Major?" His gaze rested on Lucy. "Or come back when we realize our father's predictions of our lack of success were correct." He chuckled. "I'm sure Lucy will be more than willing to settle back down to the tasks God obviously designed her for. Home and family must come first."

Lucy stiffened, but Major Kurland spoke over her.

"From what I could tell when I was briefly in London myself, sir, your eldest daughter was much admired and sought after. I suspect she left more than one broken heart behind when she decided to come home and help Mrs. Giffin organize her wedding."

"So I understand." Her father's expression became serious. "Lucy, my dear, perhaps you might go and find out what has happened to our promised pot of tea."

After Miss Harrington reluctantly left, the rector glanced down at a letter on his desk. "My brother says that both my daughters were successful in attracting the attention of suitable men. He mentioned your particular attentions to Lucy, Major."

"He did?" Robert tried to look surprised. "I certainly enjoyed Miss Harrington's company. We are old friends."

"My brother believed it ran deeper than that, but then he is somewhat of a stickler for society's more archaic rules." The rector took off his spectacles, his gaze considering. "Is there something you wish to ask me?"

There was a second of silence, broken by the chiming of the quarter hour by the clock on the mantelpiece. Robert made himself look the rector in the eye.

"If matters do develop between Miss Harrington and myself, sir, you will be the first to know."

"I'm glad to hear that, Major. A woman's reputation is a precious and fragile thing." He folded up the letter. "Although the idea of a man in your new position courting my Lucy is somewhat unlikely."

"I understand that, sir." Robert used his cane to rise out of his chair. "I am far beneath her touch. I must be getting on. Mr. Stanford's children are arriving today, and I promised to be there to greet them."

"How delightful." The rector rose, too, and came around to shake Robert's hand. "What an occasion for our village, eh? A *grand ton* wedding."

"And a lot of extra work and worry for all of us," Robert couldn't help but remark. He still wasn't happy with having his peace disturbed, especially in the countryside, where his inability to join in any gentlemanly sports would be glaringly obvious.

"I believe most of the work and the excitement will be generated by our womenfolk, Major Kurland, which leaves us men with more time to hunt and fish. All you and Mr. Stanford have to do is remember to turn up at the church at the correct time." The rector chuckled at his own joke and held the door open for Robert to depart. "Good afternoon, Major."

As Robert climbed back up into the gig and Reg set off toward Kurland Hall, it finally started to rain. He glanced up at the leaden sky and grimaced. His land-draining schemes were only drawings at the moment, which meant that if the rain kept up all month, his lower pasturelands would be flooded again.

When he reached his home, he went straight to his study and asked Foley to send Thomas Fairfax in to him immediately. The rain made his damaged left leg ache abominably, so he stayed on his feet and close to the fire while he waited.

"You wished to see me, Major?"

He turned to greet his land agent. "Ah, Thomas, we'll have to move the cattle out of—"

"I've already sent down the order to the home farm, sir." Thomas smiled. "I knew you would be worried about the state of the ground."

"Thank you." Robert limped over to his desk and sat down.

"Major . . ." Thomas hesitated and removed a folded piece of parchment from his coat pocket.

"I hate to bother you with such a personal matter, but I received a letter today from my father's wife."

"Your stepmother?"

"I'm illegitimate, sir, so we are not formally related. I do know her quite well, as she occasionally consulted me about estate matters before my father died."

Robert grimaced. "Has Mrs. Fairfax changed her mind? Has she realized what a jewel she allowed to slip through her fingers? I suppose she wants you to return and manage her son's future and her widow's estate. I do hope not. I'd hate to lose you when we've just got started on our plans for this place."

Thomas glanced down at the open letter. "I'm not quite sure what she wants, Major. She says that she will be traveling down from London to see me."

"Then please tell her that she is welcome to stay here at the manor."

Thomas frowned. "Are you sure, sir? Her visit might coincide with Mrs. Giffin and Mr. Stanford's wedding."

"All the more reason for her to come, then. I'll be too busy offering my support to Mr. Stanford to do much with the estate, which will give you time to sort out your personal affairs."

"That is very kind of you, sir." Thomas folded up the letter and hesitated. "Are you sure we can accommodate her?" He picked up the guest list from Robert's desk and studied it. "If Mrs. Fairfax *does* stay here, we will need to alter the sleeping arrangements for one of the other guests. Did the rector offer any further accommodation?"

"He did, so there is no danger of anyone having to sleep in the stables," Robert said. The clock chimed twice, and he glanced outside the window. "Mr. Stanford will be back soon, and his children are set to arrive this afternoon. Perhaps we should finish our work before that happens?"

"Yes, indeed, Major. Speaking of the stables, I was hoping to discuss the current management of them with you . . ."

Chapter 2

A h, Lucy, there you are."

"Good afternoon, Father." Lucy entered the hallway of the rectory and went to remove her bonnet and cloak.

"We have visitors in the drawing room." He beckoned imperiously to her. "Mr. Thomas Fairfax accompanied them."

"They must be the wedding guests we were told to expect."

Lucy smoothed down her skirts and followed her father into the drawing room. An unknown man bowed to her, but she hardly saw him, because sitting together on the couch were Miss Penelope Chingford, her mother, and one of her younger sisters.

Her father smiled. "Mrs. Chingford and her daughters will be staying with us during the wedding festivities. I believe you made their acquaintance in London, Lucy." He gave Mrs. Chingford a small bow. "I, of course, knew this lady when she was Miss Flood and a beautiful young debutante."

"Oh, Mr. Harrington, you quite put me to blush!" cried Mrs. Chingford as she patted her cheek and fluttered her eyelashes. "I am surprised you remember me at all."

"How could I forget such grace and charm?"

Lucy managed to keep her smile in place as she studied Miss Chingford, who looked just as unimpressed with her parent's antics as Lucy was. She turned her attention to the young man who stood slightly to the rear of the couch and was observing the ponderous gallantries of her father and Mrs. Chingford's flustered replies with what looked like concealed amusement. He had brown hair and hazel eyes and an unremarkable face. His clothing was well made yet fashionably restrained, as befitting his status as a land agent.

"Mr. Fairfax?"

He stepped forward to take her hand. "Miss Harrington. It is a pleasure to meet you at last. I believe you were instrumental in bringing me to Major Kurland's attention."

"I wouldn't quite say that, Mr. Fairfax, although I did pass your excellent references along to the major for his consideration."

"Well, I thank you. I am enjoying working here very much."

"I'm glad to hear it. Not many men can stand up to Major Kurland's rather forceful personality."

He smiled then, which made her revise her opinion of his attractiveness. "The major says it is rather like dealing with you, which he assures me is a huge compliment."

She smiled back and heard a sharp cough to her right, which she attempted to ignore.

"Miss Harrington!"

With some reluctance, Lucy turned away from Mr. Fairfax and faced Miss Chingford. She looked remarkably pretty in a mauve pelisse and matching feathered bonnet.

"Miss Chingford, I wasn't aware that your slight acquaintance with Mrs. Giffin qualified you to be invited to her wedding."

"I hardly know Mrs. Giffin. My mother is distantly related to Mr. Stanford." Miss Chingford lowered her voice. "We were *supposed* to be staying at Kurland Hall."

"I'm sure we can make you and your family very comfortable here. The bedrooms at Kurland Hall tend to be very drafty."

"I am well aware of that. Unlike you, I have stayed there."

Lucy gave her a sweet smile. "I do apologize. I had forgotten that when you were betrothed to Major Kurland, you once viewed Kurland Hall as your future home." She paused. "Perhaps Major Kurland thought it would pain you to reside under his roof again."

"He has no such regard for my feelings." Miss Chingford snorted. "It was my mother who offered to move down here. She said she had always wanted to renew her acquaintance with your father."

They both turned to look at their respective parents, who were happily reminiscing about their first meeting at a London ball. The younger Miss Chingford stifled a yawn and looked longingly at the door as the rector leaned over to whisper in her mother's ear.

"Perhaps you and Dorothea would like to see your room? We have put you next door to your mother," Lucy said loudly.

Her father waved at her to proceed, keeping Mrs. Chingford chatting as Lucy thanked Mr. Fairfax for bringing the Chingfords down from the manor house. He departed soon afterward, and she led the two ladies up the stairs.

"We shall dine at six. If you need anything, please ring the bell." Lucy drew the curtains wide to let the sunlight illuminate the guest bedroom. "Your boxes have already been brought up, so I shall leave you to settle in."

"Thank you." Miss Chingford surveyed the charming guest room as though she'd been escorted to a cell in a debtors' prison. "I'm sure we will be . . . very comfortable in here."

Lucy headed for the door. "I'll send Betty up right away to help you unpack."

She escaped down the stairs and went into the kitchen, where Betty and Cook were sharing a pot of tea at the table. With a sigh, she sat down and helped herself, as well.

"Our guests have arrived. Betty, will you go up and help them unpack? And, Mrs. Fielding, we will have three extra for dinner tonight."

"The rector already informed me of that, Miss Harrington." The glum reply wasn't a surprise. Mrs. Fielding rarely liked anything Lucy said to her, preferring instead to receive her orders directly from the rector before she was willing to even consider carrying them out.

Lucy took another fortifying gulp of the strong tea. "I'll go and see if Mrs. Chingford is ready to be taken up to her room. My father is in danger of monopolizing her attention."

"Is he now?"

There was an ominous note in the cook's voice, which Lucy couldn't help but secretly revel in.

"Yes. Apparently, they are old friends. He seems very taken with her."

Mrs. Fielding snorted and turned her attention to the stove, banging the pots and pans around. If Mrs. Chingford wasn't careful, she might find herself being poisoned by the jealous cook, who considered the rector her personal property. The thought of poison reminded Lucy of her recent sojourn in London, and she shuddered. She returned to the drawing room, where her father most uncharacteristically lingered with Mrs. Chingford.

"Your daughters are both settled in, Mrs. Chingford, and George awaits you in your study, Father. He says you are meant to be reviewing the Sunday sermon with him."

Her father sighed and then bent to kiss Mrs.

Chingford's hand in a most dashing way. "Duty calls. I look forward to seeing you at the dinner table this evening, ma'am."

Mrs. Chingford positively bridled. "I look forward to it, sir."

Lucy waited until her father disappeared into his study to consult with his new curate, and then turned back to Mrs. Chingford, whose smile had vanished. She was still a handsome woman with a classic profile her daughter had inherited. She had risen from her chair and appeared to be studying the china on the mantelpiece.

"Is this a portrait of your late mother, Miss Harrington?"

"Indeed it is." Lucy paused to admire her mother's serene smile. "It was painted just before she had the twins."

Mrs. Chingford angled her head to one side and clicked her tongue. "She looks frail. I'm not surprised she didn't survive the birth."

"My mother was never an invalid, Mrs. Chingford. Her death was quite unexpected." Lucy tried to sound calm.

"How old are the twins now?"

"Eight. They are at school."

"Where they should be." Mrs. Chingford gave a mock shudder. "I am so glad I had girls. They are far more biddable."

"I'm sure they are. Would you like me to

take you up to your bedchamber?" Lucy started walking simply to get Mrs. Chingford away from the portrait. "The twins were certainly boisterous at times, but—"

"You brought them up?"

"Naturally." Lucy continued to climb the stairs and spoke over her shoulder. "As the eldest daughter of the family, my father expected me to do my duty. And it was no hardship. They are quite delightful." Which wasn't true, but something in Mrs. Chingford's tone was beginning to annoy Lucy.

She opened the door into the best bedchamber and waited as Mrs. Chingford moved past her, fingering the curtains and the bed hangings and then studying the embroidered cushions that lined the daybed set by the window.

"This is a handsome room."

"It was my mother's." Lucy curtsied. "Now I will leave you in peace to unpack. I'll send Alice up to help you."

Mrs. Chingford swung around to face Lucy. "There's no need to sound so defensive whenever I ask you a question, my dear."

"I beg your pardon?"

"No one is suggesting that you haven't done a fine job taking care of your siblings and your father for all these years."

"As far as I am concerned, no one has ever suggested any such thing." Lucy raised an eyebrow. "Is there something in particular you wish to say to me, Mrs. Chingford?"

"Whatever do you mean?" Mrs. Chingford opened her blue eyes wide, and her voice became caressing. "One must hope that you won't turn into one of those *elderly* spinsters who sees her widowed father as her property. That is always so *sad,* isn't it?"

"Trust me, ma'am, if my father wishes to find a new wife, I would be delighted to relinquish all my responsibilities to her." Lucy paused. "But with all due respect, he loved my mother so much that he has never looked at another woman since." She curtsied again. "Good afternoon, Mrs. Chingford."

She made her way down the stairs, wondering what it was about the woman that made her hackles rise. How was she supposed to deal with someone who asked the most outrageous questions with a smile on her face? She could only pray her father wouldn't be taken in by the sweetness for too long before he discovered the sour underneath. But then men often seemed incapable of seeing much at all. . . .

"And, as I said to my dear friend, the rector . . ."

Lucy slipped out of her chair and walked the length of the picture gallery to the other end, where she hoped Mrs. Chingford's voice would be fainter. They'd come to the manor to pay a call on the major and the other wedding guests. Mrs. Chingford hadn't stopped talking for at least a quarter of an hour. From the expressions on some of the other ladies' faces, Lucy reckoned she wasn't the only one who found Mrs. Chingford's rather pointed conversation objectionable.

After two days of enduring Mrs. Chingford at the rectory and watching her father bloom and preen with all the attention lavished on him, Lucy was glad to be out of the house. Unfortunately, she'd had to bring the Chingfords with her. She stared down at the formal knot garden Major Kurland was having restored behind the Tudor wing of the manor. The orderly clipped hedges and symmetrical patterns soothed her a little.

"Are you avoiding Mrs. Chingford?" A voice at her elbow made her jump. "She really is insufferable, isn't she?"

Lucy turned to look at the indignant face of one of Mr. Stanford's aunts.

"I hardly know her, Mrs. Green."

Her companion snorted. "It's like picking up a hedgehog. Hundreds of tiny spines just waiting to pierce your skin, and while you're distracted, one long barb is left quivering in your heart." Mrs. Green lowered her voice. "That's why she's rusticating at this wedding. She's offended far too many of society's notables during her relentless drive to marry off her wretched daughters." The glance she shot at Mrs. Chingford was pure

31

venom. "I've also heard rumors that she is in debt and on the lookout for a new husband."

Lucy immediately thought of her father and then relaxed. He had an easy competence from his father's estate, but since his brother had a son, he was no longer the heir to the earldom. In Mrs. Chingford's eyes, he was probably a nonentity.

As if echoing her thoughts, Mrs. Green poked her with her fan. "You'd better watch that handsome father of yours, my girl. He seems quite smitten."

"Smitten with whom?" Major Kurland appeared at Lucy's side and bowed to both ladies. He was still using his walking cane, his black hair was disheveled, and his cheeks were slightly reddened from the wind. "I apologize for not being here when you arrived, Miss Harrington. I was down at the home farm."

Mrs. Green curtsied. "I'll leave Miss Harrington to explain. I've had just about enough of listening to Maria Chingford holding court!"

Major Kurland frowned down at Lucy as Mrs. Green stalked out of the room. "Whatever is wrong with her? She was positively bristling with indignation."

"She doesn't like Mrs. Chingford, and she told me to warn my father off."

"She believes Mrs. Chingford has set her cap at the rector?"

Lucy shrugged. "She might be right."

"That's excellent news." His expression relaxed. "If she takes your father off your hands, you'll be free."

"And homeless. I couldn't abide sharing a house with her and Miss Chingford for more than two weeks."

He grimaced and scratched the back of his neck. "I apologize for that. I wasn't intending for the Chingfords to descend on you, but somehow it was all arranged without my knowledge. Thomas didn't know about my previous connection with Miss Chingford."

"It's all right. Miss Chingford said her mother was rather keen to stay at the rectory so that she could renew her acquaintance with my father."

Major Kurland turned slightly away from the group settled around Mrs. Chingford. "You don't like her very much, do you?"

"She isn't very nice." Lucy wished she could say more, but her feelings about Mrs. Chingford were too complicated to put in words. "She . . . twists everything you say and uses it against you."

"I hadn't noticed myself."

"That's because she values your good opinion and would hesitate to offend you."

"And perhaps sees you as a rival for your father's affections?" Major Kurland patted her hand and placed it on his sleeve. "Mayhap she is jealous of you?"

"I suppose that could be it, but—" Lucy stopped speaking as the major drew her toward the group clustered around the fire. Voices were raised, and there appeared to be some kind of argument in progress between a sweetly smiling Mrs. Chingford and Mr. Stanford's sister.

"That is untrue, Mrs. Chingford." Miss Stanford rose to her feet. "Such gossip should not be repeated—especially now, when my brother is about to marry again."

"I do beg your pardon, my dear." Mrs. Chingford fluttered her fan. "I didn't realize that my silly little remark would upset you." She glanced over at Sophia, who was frowning. "And to you, Mrs. Giffin, I do apologize. I *assumed* Mr. Stanford would have *mentioned* the rumors surrounding his wife's premature death."

Major Kurland cleared his throat. "I'm sure everyone will forgive you, Mrs. Chingford. Now, perhaps you might like to take advantage of the sunshine and enjoy a tour of my new garden?"

As the other ladies rose like a flock of birds to accept the major's invitation, Lucy disengaged herself from Major Kurland and went over to where Sophia remained sitting by the fire, her gloved hands clasped tightly in her lap. Lucy sat next to her and lowered her voice.

"Don't listen to Mrs. Chingford, Sophia. She just has to meddle in everything. I'm sure there is no truth in what she said."

Sophia gave a tremulous smile. "I must admit, she did sound rather convincing."

"Then ask Mr. Stanford. I'm sure he will tell you everything you need to know. Where is he?"

"I believe he is settling his children in the nursery. Perhaps I should go up and . . . speak to him."

Lucy squeezed Sophia's hand. "I would. I'm convinced there is nothing to worry about at all."

"Then why spread such malicious rumors?"

"Sophia, some people just can't resist stirring the pot like the witches in *Macbeth*. Mrs. Chingford appears to be one of them. Go and find Mr. Stanford."

Sophia rose and, with a brisk nod, headed for the main staircase. Lucy followed her out more slowly and took the more convenient servants' corridor, which led directly out to the side of the house and the gardens. The stone-flagged and timbered passageway was part of the original Tudor mansion and was quite dark in some places. Ahead of her, Lucy heard the murmur of voices and instinctively slowed her step.

"Don't be a fool."

Lucy slowed down even further as she recognized Mrs. Chingford's voice.

"I hate you, Mother. I hate the way you treat people, and I wish you were dead."

Was that Penelope speaking? Lucy frowned.

No, it was Dorothea Chingford, the younger daughter.

"You silly little girl, with your silly little *tendre* for Mr. Stanford. Do you think you ever stood a chance with him? He never even noticed your existence! You should be pleased that I am exposing him for the murderer he surely is."

"That's *completely* untrue, Mother. He's—" The sound of a slap echoed down the hall, and Dorothea choked back a cry.

"He's not interested in you. Stop defending him. It makes you look even more pathetic than you normally are." Mrs. Chingford's voice was harsh. "Get along with you. We need to join the others in the garden."

Lucy stayed where she was until the mother and daughter reached the end of the corridor and went out of the door. What a truly detestable woman. For the first time in her life, Lucy actually felt sorry for the Chingford sisters. It seemed their mother enjoyed spreading rumor and innuendo like some scandalous weekly broadsheet. Raising her chin, she made her way out to the garden. It was up to her to make sure her father didn't succumb to Mrs. Chingford's charms.

Robert watched as his guests strolled around his newly restored herb garden, and did his best to be cordial and answer questions. Poor Mrs. Chingford seemed to have a knack for saying the

36

wrong thing. She had attached herself to him and now promenaded at his side, her hand tucked in the crook of his elbow.

"I knew you would understand my position, Major, because you are quite a blunt man yourself, aren't you?" She sighed. "Women are not allowed to be honest. It is seen as being cold and callous toward one's own sex. I am treated quite dreadfully."

"If you say so, ma'am." Robert looked desperately back at the house, but there was no sign of Thomas or Miss Harrington coming to rescue him. "Would you care to sit and admire the view? It is quite remarkable from here."

To his relief, he spotted Thomas approaching, with a slight figure dressed in stark black on his arm. He raised his hand and beckoned his land agent to approach.

"There you are, Thomas."

"Major Kurland. May I present Mrs. Emily Fairfax?"

Robert took the lady's gloved hand and bowed over it. "A pleasure, Mrs. Fairfax. I do hope you enjoy your stay."

The widow raised her black veil, and Robert was treated to the sight of a far more beautiful and younger woman than he had anticipated. She looked not much older than he was. He reminded himself that she was the second wife of Thomas's father.

"Major Kurland, it is so kind of you to receive me when Thomas tells me that you are in the midst of preparations for a wedding. I can assure you that I will keep out of the way."

She had a breathy little voice that was hard to hear. "Do whatever you are comfortable with, Mrs. Fairfax. Are you familiar with this part of the country? There are some quaint towns and villages to explore if you feel like venturing farther afield."

"I am quite familiar with the area, Major. I grew up in the neighboring county of Essex before I moved up north to marry my beloved Mr. Fairfax." Her lip trembled.

Robert bowed. "My condolences on your loss, ma'am."

"Thank you." She raised eyes full of tears to his. "I loved my husband very much."

Beside him, Mrs. Chingford gave a delicate snort. "From all accounts, Mrs. Fairfax, your husband drank too much. It's a shame you didn't love him enough to prevent *that*."

Mrs. Fairfax gave a tiny gasp and pressed a black lace handkerchief to her lips. Thomas stepped between her and Mrs. Chingford and placed his stepmother's hand on his arm.

"I'll take Mrs. Fairfax up to her room, Major," he said.

"Thank you." Robert waited until the pair was out of sight before turning back to Mrs.

Chingford, who was staring after the couple, her expression intent. "May I help you with something, ma'am?"

She finally tore her gaze away and looked at Robert. "That girl looks familiar."

"Are you referring to Mrs. Fairfax?"

"Is that what she calls herself now?" Mrs. Chingford sniffed. "I must try to remember where I have seen her before." Her smile returned, and she looked up at him. "Never mind that, Major. I am so glad we had this chance to reconnect after my daughter's woeful decision to end your betrothal. I have to tell you, sir, I was most displeased with her."

Robert inclined his head an inch. "It was for the best, Mrs. Chingford, and it was a mutual decision. We have both changed considerably in the past five years. We were no longer suited. It was very brave of Miss Chingford to realize that."

"I agree it would have been awful for her to be married to a cripple who has to remain hidden in the countryside." She gave him a pitying smile and patted his arm. "But we don't always get what we wish for in life, do we, Major?"

He took that direct hit without flinching. "Indeed, ma'am. I'd rather not *be* a cripple, but I've had to come to terms with it."

She prodded him with her fan. "Good Lord, Major, there's no need to poker up. I was speaking *metaphorically,* of course."

Robert bowed. "Of course." He spotted Miss Harrington moving purposefully toward him. "Will you excuse me?"

He walked away before Mrs. Chingford gave her permission, but she didn't pursue him. It seemed that Miss Harrington was correct. Mrs. Chingford clearly believed that killing with kindness was an acceptable way to behave. From all accounts, on her first visit to his house she'd managed to upset at least three people, if not more.

He bowed and took Miss Harrington's elbow in a firm grip and drew her away from the rest of his guests.

"Your Mrs. Chingford has a knack for upsetting people, doesn't she?"

Her gaze sharpened. "What did she say to you?"

"Nothing that bears repeating, but I think you are right to be wary of her."

"She certainly upset Sophia. Were there really rumors that Mr. Stanford did something to cause his wife's death?"

Robert hesitated. "There was some . . . gossip at the time, but I can assure you that Andrew did nothing wrong. His wife's mind never fully recovered from the birth of their second child. She became very withdrawn and unlike herself. Andrew tried everything to help her, but nothing seemed to work." He lowered his voice. "She

40

took her own life. That isn't widely known. I wonder how Mrs. Chingford came to hear about the problems within that marriage."

"She is the kind of woman who is attracted to gossip like a bee to pollen." Miss Harrington shivered. "And the thing is, her gossip and innuendo always has that element of truth to it that makes it very hard to ignore."

"I'll tell Andrew to be on his guard."

She raised her chin to look directly up at him. "And tell him to be honest with Sophia. She deserves to know the truth."

"I agree." He smiled at her, and she immediately looked away. "Cheer up, Miss Harrington. In a few days the wedding will be over, and we can all return to a more peaceful existence."

"I sincerely hope so, sir." Miss Harrington cast a look over her shoulder at Mrs. Chingford. "Because I have to admit that my store of Christian charity is running rather low."

Chapter 3

Lucy accepted Major Kurland's arm and followed the now married couple back down the aisle, toward the open church doors. The major wore the full dress uniform of the Prince of Wales 10th Hussars and looked very well in it. He was still using his cane to aid his walking but had improved his gait remarkably. She'd chosen to wear one of her London gowns and felt almost equal to his magnificence.

"Thank goodness that's over," he murmured as they came out into the sunlight. "Weddings give me the shivers."

"So I've noticed, Major." Lucy kept her gaze on the bride, who was smiling up at her bridegroom. She wore a cream gown with Brussels lace at the neck and on the sleeves and as a trim on the hem. "But Mr. Stanford and Sophia look remarkably happy about the whole affair."

"They do. It almost makes one believe in love, doesn't it?"

She looked up into his face, but he didn't appear to be making a joke. "I believe in love. My parents loved each other very much."

"So did mine." His smile was fond. "My father married out of his class, and he didn't care what anyone thought of him. At the time he had no idea

42

my mother was the heiress of a brewer and would bring him a dowry equal to a king's ransom."

"Then he was a very lucky man."

Major Kurland chuckled. "Indeed. Love and money. Who could ask for more?"

She found herself smiling back at him and then hastily re-collected herself. "I must go and assist Sophia with her gown."

"And I should help Andrew." He touched the brim of his hat. "A pleasure, Miss Harrington."

She curtsied and watched him make his slow way over to the carriage to speak to the coachman. The wedding breakfast was being held at Kurland Hall, so most of the guests would be able to walk from the church to the manor house without much difficulty.

Reaching Sophia, she smiled and took her hands. "I'm so happy for you, my dearest friend."

"Thank you." Sophia kissed her cheek. "I hope Charlie understands." She searched Lucy's face, her voice suddenly uncertain. "He would want me to be happy, wouldn't he?"

"I'm quite certain he would approve of Mr. Stanford."

Sophia exhaled. "Thank you. Now, will you come in the carriage with Mama, the children, and me? They are rather overexcited, and I'm afraid they won't sit still."

"Of course I will." Lucy bent to gather up

Sophia's train. "Let me help you ascend without treading on your hem."

Anna had arrived back from London for the wedding, and Lucy had spent the previous evening unburdening herself of her growing dislike for Mrs. Chingford and detailing all the people who had been offended by their unwelcome guest so far. Anna had added a few stories of her own about Mrs. Chingford's behavior in London, and the sisters had agreed to try to be nicer to Penelope and Dorothea, who obviously had a lot to bear.

As the carriage swept out of the church gates, Lucy caught a glimpse of Mrs. Chingford walking with her father. Miss Chingford followed along behind, in earnest conversation with George Culpepper, the new curate. Dorothea brought up the rear, a scowl on her face. She reminded Lucy of Anthony at that age, but her efforts to befriend the girl had so far been in vain.

Ahead of them lay Kurland Hall and the rest of the wedding celebrations to get through. Squaring her shoulders, Lucy fixed her gaze on the diamond-paned windows of the long gallery and resolved to do her best to give her friends the most splendid and trouble-free wedding day she could contrive.

After the celebratory breakfast, Major Kurland gave a surprisingly witty speech and sat down to wide applause. The groom stood to thank him and to toast his new wife and her maids of honor. Lucy allowed herself a second glass of wine and smiled benevolently around her. Thomas Fairfax had done an excellent job preparing the manor for the wedding and had consulted Lucy on several occasions as to exactly how things should be done. She liked him very much, although the appearance of his former employer dressed in black at the wedding seemed rather inappropriate, but she supposed he could hardly turn her away.

Her father rose to his feet and cleared his throat. "Mr. and Mrs. Stanford, Sir Robert, Lord and Lady Teasdale, and fellow guests, may I have your attention for one moment?"

Lucy slowly put her glass back on the table and studied her father, who was looking remarkably pleased with himself.

"Firstly, I would like to wish the newly married couple a long and prosperous life together." He raised his glass to the Stanfords. "And secondly, it is a well-known fact that one wedding leads to another." His smile became smug. "Which is why I am delighted to tell you that Mrs. Maria Chingford has consented to become my wife."

Lucy's horrified gaze locked with that of Miss Chingford, whose mouth was open, as if she was ready to shout the denial that crowded Lucy's throat.

"No!" Dorothea leapt to her feet, her fists

clenched and her eyes blazing attrition. "You cannot mean this!"

Luckily for Dorothea, the roar of surprise and clapping almost drowned out her words. Lucy saw her spin around, her hand pressed to her mouth, and run out of the room. Miss Chingford went after her sister, leaving Lucy and Anna staring at each other in consternation. Anna slipped into the seat beside Lucy and leaned close.

"They do say weddings beget other weddings. If this one comes to pass, I reckon you and I will both have to follow suit simply to avoid living at the rectory."

A little while later, Lucy managed to corner her father in the drawing room while he enjoyed another glass of wine and happily accepted the felicitations of his fellow guests, as though he himself were the bridegroom of the hour.

"Father, why didn't you tell me about your intention to marry Mrs. Chingford?"

He raised an eyebrow. "Because not everything is your concern, Lucy."

"Surely I am allowed to have an interest in who replaces my mother."

"Your mother is irreplaceable, you know that." He hesitated. "I've spent the past eight years alone. I think I deserve the chance to find another to share my life with, don't you?"

"But Mrs. Chingford—"

"Has been widowed like me, with children who still need her. What better for both families than to combine so that we can offer all our children the benefit of our experience?"

"But she—"

Her father held up his finger. "Lucy, please do not spoil this. I know you must be jealous that my affections have been bestowed on another, but trust that I will not allow it to have any bearing on my fondness for you. Maria has recently pointed out how very *possessive* you can be of me, and I fear she is right. You will come to love your new mama and will gladly cede your authority to her. I am quite sure of it."

Lucy opened her mouth to argue and then closed it again. He did deserve some happiness in his life. "If you say so, Father." She stood on tiptoe to kiss his cheek. "If this truly makes you happy, then I am most pleased for you."

"Thank you, my dear." He patted her shoulder. "I knew I could rely on your good sense."

Lucy turned away and headed back toward the main hall, where she could see Sophia about to ascend the stairs to change before she left on her honeymoon. There was no point in remonstrating with her father. When he made his mind up to do something, he was impossible. She supposed it behooved her to go and congratulate her future stepmama. . . .

Mrs. Chingford was also in the hall and

appeared to be in conversation with the widowed Mrs. Fairfax. There was still no sign of Dorothea and Miss Chingford, which wasn't surprising. Despite her reservations about the Chingford sisters, Lucy was fairly certain they would agree to form an alliance with the Harringtons to prevent the unfortunate marriage ever taking place—although quite *how* they would stop it, Lucy wasn't yet sure.

A light touch on her elbow drew her attention to Mr. Fairfax at her side. He lowered his voice.

"I was somewhat surprised to hear that the rector was intending to marry again."

Lucy grimaced. She had grown to know him quite well during the weeks organizing the wedding and had found nothing in his character to dislike.

"I had no idea, either, Mr. Fairfax."

"I should imagine it would make things rather difficult for you. You have my sympathy. I know how it feels to be forced out of one's home." He placed her hand on his sleeve. "My stepmother is beckoning to me. Shall we approach and release her from Mrs. Chingford's curiosity?"

"I'm sure she would appreciate it. I have never met a woman who enjoys poking her nose in other people's business as much as Mrs. Chingford." She glanced up at Mr. Fairfax as she spoke to find his frowning gaze fixed on Mrs. Fairfax. "She seems to ferret out all kinds of secrets and then inadvertently lets them slip at the most inopportune of moments." Lucy felt herself blush. "Forgive me. That was most unchristian of me to besmirch the reputation of another."

"You are forgiven, Miss Harrington. I cannot disagree with you. I am just wondering why she is talking to Mrs. Fairfax. I wasn't even aware that they were acquainted."

"Mrs. Chingford mentioned that she thought she had met Mrs. Fairfax before she was married, and was determined to remember when that was. Perhaps she has worked it out and is sharing the memory."

"I doubt they have many friends in common. From what I know, Mrs. Fairfax comes from a modest, hardworking family who would not have moved in the same social circles as Mrs. Chingford."

"And yet they seem to be conversing quite animatedly," Lucy observed. "Does Mrs. Fairfax wish you to return and manage her estates?"

He sighed. "She has suggested it. I am not sure what I should do. She didn't make me feel welcome when my father was alive. I'm not sure if I wish to be used and then discarded again when it suits her."

"Then stay here. Major Kurland would be delighted to keep you."

His rare smile flashed out, and he bowed. "Thank you for the vote of confidence, Miss

49

Harrington. I must admit that I am enjoying working with the major. His plans for the estate are all encompassing and excellently thought out."

"Major Kurland is a man of many talents," Lucy said diplomatically. "Mrs. Fairfax has finished her conversation and is searching for you. I must go and offer Mrs. Chingford my felicitations."

Mr. Fairfax took her hand and kissed it. "You are a brave woman, Miss Harrington, but then I would have expected nothing less of you."

From the heat on her cheeks, Lucy assumed she must be blushing and hastily disengaged her hand. She smiled as Mrs. Fairfax came toward them.

"Good afternoon, ma'am. Are you enjoying the wedding?"

"It reminds me rather too much of my own, Miss Harrington." A black lace handkerchief appeared and was applied to the beautiful widow's tear-filled eyes. Lucy fought back a spurt of irritation. If the widow was so affected, why had she decided to insert herself into the wedding party at all? "I miss my husband very much."

Mr. Fairfax patted the widow's gloved hand. "I'm sure you would like to retire to your room now, wouldn't you? I shall escort you upstairs." He bowed. "Your servant, Miss Harrington."

Lucy watched them leave, the widow leaning heavily on her previously despised husband's bastard's arm. Stiffening her spine, she turned back to Mrs. Chingford, only to see that Miss Stanford had got in before her and was having a somewhat heated discussion with her smiling companion.

It seemed that even in her moment of triumph Mrs. Chingford couldn't stop herself from getting into an argument. And yet listening to her talk, one would assume that she was the one who was being wounded or attacked by unfeeling people. Miss Stanford was beginning to raise her voice, and the people around her had started to notice. Lucy hurried over, determined that nothing else would disturb the happiness of Sophia and Mr. Stanford's wedding.

"Miss Stanford." Lucy insinuated herself between the two women and caught Miss Stanford's eye. "Your new sister was asking if you would accompany her upstairs to change."

For a second, Miss Stanford hesitated, and then she poked her finger in Mrs. Chingford's face. "You are an abominable woman. One day you will go too far, and believe me, no one will rejoice at your demise more than me."

Mrs. Chingford gasped and placed a quivering hand on her bosom. "Such venom, Miss Stanford. How could you be so unkind?"

"Because I dislike you intensely, and I hope

51

never to see you again." Miss Stanford turned on her heel and nodded at Lucy. "I would love to aid Sophia."

"She is in the great hall. Please tell her I will join you all very shortly."

"Indeed."

Miss Stanford stalked off, leaving Lucy with Mrs. Chingford, who sighed.

"Some women cannot bear to hear a word said against their menfolk, can they?"

"One might consider such loyalty admirable."

"Not if it is misplaced, Miss Harrington." Mrs. Chingford leaned close. "There are several ladies here today who need to hear the *truth,* and to be reminded of their station in life. It is unfortunate that sometimes I have to be honest, but that is my way."

"Perhaps honesty should be tempered with mercy and tact, ma'am."

"Oh, I don't think so." Mrs. Chingford used her fan. "You, for instance. The entire village is aware that you are desperate to wed Major Kurland. Subtle hints don't seem to work on you, so perhaps as your future stepmama, I should be blunt. He will never marry you. If he wasn't happy with my daughter, he'll never settle for someone of your social standing now that he's a baronet."

All thoughts of offering her stilted congratulations to Mrs. Chingford fled Lucy's mind.

"You are quite mistaken, ma'am. Major Kurland has already *asked* me to marry him, and I declined." She managed an airy smile. "As the niece of an earl, I'm not sure Major Kurland is good enough for *me*."

"It appears that you consider no one good enough for you." Mrs. Chingford lowered her voice. "But I'll give you fair warning, Miss Harrington. When I am mistress of the rectory, both you and that obnoxious cook will have to relinquish all notions of being in charge."

"I can't wait." Lucy curtsied. "In truth, I am very willing to leave the rectory, but I wish you joy in removing Mrs. Fielding. She considers my father her sole property. I must go and help Sophia change, Mrs. Chingford. Such a pleasure conversing with you."

She walked away, her gaze fixed on the hallway, and almost growled when someone stepped into her path.

"Miss Harrington? Are you feeling quite well?" Major Kurland asked.

Lucy took a deep, shuddering breath. "No, I am not 'quite well,' Major. I am contemplating murder."

He drew her to one side of the salon, his gaze questioning. "Whatever has happened to upset you?"

"Mrs. Chingford . . ."

"Ah, you are angry because she is to marry your

father? But have you thought of the benefits to yourself? If she takes him in hand, and I believe she is a very managing woman, your time will be your own."

"And I'll have to go and live with my uncle and aunt in London, because she is determined to push me out."

"Surely not, Miss Harrington." He hesitated. "I know that she can sometimes seem a little insensitive, but—"

"*Insensitive?* She uses words like weapons and doesn't care how many people she hurts or maligns, because she believes in being honest."

"I cannot criticize her for choosing to be honest. It is something of a fault of mine, too."

"You are different. You don't intentionally mean to hurt with your words."

His smile was rueful. "Sometimes I do, and sometimes I hear myself speak and then regret every syllable I've uttered. You have cause to know that all too well."

She held his gaze for far too long and then had to look away. "I must go to Sophia."

He brought her hand to his lips and kissed it. "Yes. Andrew is awaiting her reappearance with great impatience."

Lucy picked up the skirts of her blue silk gown and went up the main staircase to the bedchamber where Sophia was changing out of her wedding dress and into something more suitable for travel.

Fixing a smile firmly on her face, Lucy went over to Sophia and embraced her.

"You look beautiful. Mr. Stanford is a lucky man."

Sophia kissed her. "No, I am the lucky one. And just think, if we hadn't gone to London and become involved with the Broughtons, none of this would've happened."

"I suppose you did get to know Mr. Stanford rather well while I was investigating with the major."

"I did indeed, and I liked him immediately." Sophia turned to the chair and dislodged her dog from her pelisse. "Hunter is going to stay here with Andrew's children until we return. They already love him and have promised to take him for walks and to play with him."

"That is very kind of them. They also seem more than willing to accept you as their mother."

Sophia sighed. "I know. Isn't it *wonderful?* I cannot wait until we are all under one roof and can begin our family life together." She stepped back to stare into Lucy's eyes. "And if Mrs. Chingford becomes unbearable, you know that my home is always open to you. I have already told Andrew this, and he quite agrees."

Lucy smiled at her best friend. It must be pleasant to have men falling over themselves to do one's bidding. It was a trick that she had never mastered but that Sophia and Anna excelled at.

Sophia put on her pelisse, and Lucy handed her the new bonnet that went with it.

"Thank you." Sophia looked around. "Now, where did I put my wedding posy? I wanted to deliver it right into your hands."

"You cannot do that, Sophia. Think of all the disappointment! Perhaps you should aim it squarely at Mrs. Chingford's head."

Sophia shuddered. "That horrible woman. She upset Melissa Stanford again today. She was quite incandescent with rage. Not content with suggesting that Andrew was somehow responsible for his wife's death, she insinuated that Melissa's betrothed was a well-known cheat at cards. Surely your father will see the error of his ways and will not go through with such a ridiculous marriage."

"I can only hope so, but he is remarkably stubborn when he makes his mind up about something," Lucy said gloomily and then re-collected herself. She would not spoil Sophia's wedding day. "Have you seen Miss Chingford or her sister? I don't think they are any happier at the news than I am."

"I haven't seen them since we finished our meal. I do hope they are all right. Dorothea seemed very upset about the news. One would've thought that their mother would have mentioned the matter to them before the announcement."

"Maybe Mrs. Chingford wasn't aware that my father intended to propose so publicly."

There was a knock on the door, and Foley, the major's butler, came in and bowed.

"Mrs. Stanford? Mr. Stanford was asking after you, ma'am." Foley lowered his voice. "In fact, he's fretting himself to the bone and pacing the hall below just like a lovesick bridegroom ought to be doing."

Sophia laughed and tied the ribbons on her bonnet. "Then we should certainly go down and put him out of his misery."

Lucy followed her out onto the landing, and a cheer went up from the assembled wedding party below. When Mr. Stanford caught sight of his bride, his whole face lit up and he held out his hand and bowed.

Sophia went gracefully down the stairs to a roar of approval. She paused on the bottom step to throw her bouquet, and there was delighted applause when Anna caught it. From her vantage point at the top of the stairs, Lucy noticed that Nicholas Jenkins was right behind Anna and that he was smiling down at her. It seemed he still hadn't given up his hopes of marrying her sister, despite Anna's popularity in London.

Lucy also noticed Miss Chingford and Dorothea in an intense conversation with their mother that did not look very cordial. But Mrs. Chingford was amicable only to men and those who she thought could aid her. Everyone else, even poor widowed Mrs. Fairfax, was fair game.

Major Kurland was smiling at his friend and then looked up, caught her eye, and winked. She didn't think she'd ever seen him being so relaxed and charming before. She almost preferred it when he scowled. Andrew's children, a boy and a girl, stood close to the major. The boy now held Hunter's leash in a firm grip as the dog whined and panted after its mistress.

Within moments, the happy couple had gone in a flurry of good-byes and flower petals, leaving the wedding party to partake of the supper Foley and his staff were laying out in the dining room. There was musical entertainment, and some thoughts that the younger members of the wedding party might want to dance had dictated the removal of the carpet in the long gallery.

As she came down the stairs, Lucy mentally checked off exactly what still needed to be done and realized there was nothing. If he thought to turn his hand to it, Mr. Fairfax would make the major an excellent secretary, as well as a land agent. She wasn't really needed here at the manor anymore, what with Major Kurland's resurgence and Mr. Fairfax's efficiency.

It would have to be London, then. If her father did marry Mrs. Chingford, she would have to move out of the rectory. Her hand lingered on the smoothness of the wooden stair rail. If she'd ignored her feelings and accepted Major Kurland's marriage proposal for what it was, she would now be mistress of Kurland Hall. . . . She almost regretted her decision at this moment, when all around her seemed to be heading for matrimony without having to think about it at all.

Mayhap she was too fussy, just as Mrs. Chingford had suggested.

The sound of instruments tuning up in the gallery caught her attention, and she turned toward the throng of wedding guests making their way through the hall. A flash of yellow in the gallery above her made her look up to see Dorothea Chingford peering down at the assembled guests. As if she realized Lucy had seen her, she ran off again toward the bedchambers.

Lucy cast one more glance down at the dancing and then went after Dorothea. Even though the bride and groom had departed, she didn't want any more scenes to disrupt the celebration. Following the sound of footsteps and banging doors, Lucy found herself in the oldest part of the house, which was a warren of smaller rooms, too many staircases, and ancient oak beams reportedly reused from the demolition of King Henry VIII's navy, which would certainly account for their bowed shapes. It was hard to see in the narrow passageways, and Lucy almost lost her way and banged her head on a low beam at least twice.

Suddenly there was a screech and a series of

loud thumps. Lucy picked up her skirts and ran toward the sound. By the time she arrived, there was no sign of anyone. She hesitated by the servants' staircase and then looked down to see a crumpled heap of . . . something at the bottom. Had Dorothea fallen in her haste to get away from Lucy? Holding her breath, Lucy crept down the stairs and knelt beside the recumbent form.

Halting footsteps sounded behind her, and she went still.

"Miss Harrington? Whatever are you doing?"

She lifted her head to see Major Kurland coming toward her.

"Thank goodness it's you, Major. There's been a terrible accident. I think Mrs. Chingford is dead!"

Chapter 4

Robert took his time kneeling beside Miss Harrington and attempted a nonjudgmental tone.

"Did you mean to kill her?"

"Good Lord, Major Kurland, I didn't *kill* her. I just found her like this. I think she fell down the stairs," Miss Harrington said impatiently as she touched Mrs. Chingford's throat. "She doesn't appear to be breathing."

"I just wondered if perhaps you had been in an argument and had accidentally pushed her. You know how these things happen in moments of passion."

She fixed him with her hardest stare. "Major Kurland, I did not kill her. Why on earth would I do that?"

"Because she was about to become your stepmother?"

"I would hardly resort to murder." She snorted. "And there are plenty of other people at this wedding who would be delighted to see the end of this woman. In fact, I—" She paused. "I was attempting to catch up with Dorothea Chingford. That's why I ended up at the top of this staircase."

"And I saw someone disappearing into the

servants' hallways and came to direct them back to the wedding party."

"Was it a man or a woman?"

Robert frowned. "I believe it was a woman, but it might have been a man wearing a cloak." He studied the still figure. In repose, Mrs. Chingford looked remarkably like her daughter Penelope. "Are you quite sure she is dead?"

"As certain as I can be. Is our new doctor attending the wedding?"

"Yes, he is, and as he's an old army colleague of mine, I can count on his discretion. Shall I go and find him?" Robert tried to stand and had to use the stairs for support. "Will you stay with her?"

"Of course I will. There is one thing. . . ."

"What?"

She indicated the position of the body. "If she did trip and fall, she managed to crawl a few feet away from the stairs before she actually died."

Robert grabbed his cane. "It's not unusual for a body to keep moving after death. It seems to take a moment for the conscious self to realize it is no more. I've seen soldiers continue a charge with half their heads blown off and . . ." He re-collected himself and bowed. "I'll go and fetch Dr. Fletcher."

While the major went to find the doctor, Lucy sat on the dusty wooden floorboards beside Mrs. Chingford. It was strange to see her so still and silent. She had always been in motion, like a rather annoying wasp. Lucy glanced up the steep stairwell, but all was quiet. Beams of light from the diamond-paned windows above sent bars of brightness down the wooden stairs. It would be all too easy to catch one's foot in the hem of one's gown and fall. Perhaps it had truly been an accident and Mrs. Chingford had turned to speak to her younger daughter and had missed her footing.

The sound of approaching male voices had Lucy looking back toward the main hall. Major Kurland was talking quietly to the man behind him, who nodded as he walked. He'd also brought more light.

"Ah, Miss Harrington. Not the most pleasant of places to find you, but be that as it may."

"Dr. Fletcher." Lucy waited until he set the lantern on the stairs and crouched beside the body. "I think Mrs. Chingford fell down the stairs."

"I should imagine she did." His gentle fingers moved over Mrs. Chingford's still form, then lingered at her throat.

"Did she break her neck?" Major Kurland asked.

Dr. Fletcher frowned and leaned closer. "Her neck is definitely broken."

Lucy peered through the uncertain light. "It also seems to be bruised."

"Yes. That could happen because of the way she fell. I won't be able to tell exactly *what* is broken until I get a closer look at her." The doctor gazed up at Major Kurland. "Do you think the family would object if we had her transported to my house? There isn't a morgue nearby, and my practice is the quietest place in the village, seeing as no one trusts me to administer to their ills yet."

Major Kurland nodded. "That's an excellent idea. Could you organize the removal of the body without the rest of my guests knowing what is going on?"

"Certainly, if you get Foley to help me."

Lucy closed the dead woman's eyes. "I'll find Miss Chingford and Dorothea and tell them what has happened."

Dr. Fletcher stood and brushed down his buckskin breeches. He had a lilting Irish accent that was very soothing. Lucy imagined that unlike the brusque Dr. Baker, he would be comforting to have at one's bedside. "That would be most kind of you, Miss Harrington. I can lay out the body properly and arrange for them to see their mother whenever they are ready."

As Lucy attempted to make the body look decent before it stiffened, she noticed something caught between Mrs. Chingford's fingers. Lucy eased the chain free and found a gold locket strung on it that was badly dented. She took

64

another glance at the dead woman's throat. Mrs. Chingford was wearing jewelry of far greater value than the simple locket. She'd never seen the rather vain Mrs. Chingford wear such a plain trinket.

"May I help you, Miss Harrington?" Major Kurland had returned from seeing Dr. Fletcher out and offered her his hand. After slipping the locket into her pocket, she accepted his help to rise and stood, smoothing down her now dusty silk skirts.

"Thank you."

"Bring Miss Chingford and her sister into my study. That will give you some privacy when you break the bad news." He paused. "Perhaps I should be the one to tell your father?"

"Yes, please," Lucy said fervently. "I'd quite forgotten about him."

"Then I shall willingly relieve you of that burden." He shook his head. "This is a shockingly bad thing to happen at a wedding."

Lucy hesitated. "Do you think it would be better to wait until the party is over to inform everyone else?"

He walked with her toward the hall door. "You might think me a coward, but I'd rather not have to stand up in front of everyone and tell them such bad news. By the time we have informed the Chingfords and your father of this tragedy, I suspect the evening will be nearly over, anyway."

"I agree." She almost smiled. "And in a village as small as this, everyone will know by morning, anyway."

They emerged into the brightly lit hall, and Lucy blinked at the sudden infusion of light and noise. It was strange how even when one life ended, the world still went on.

"Thank you for your help, Major." Lucy firmly disengaged her arm from her companion's. "I'll go and find Miss Chingford and bring her and her sister to your study."

"And I will seek out your father." He squeezed her fingers. "Good luck, Miss Harrington."

Several hours later, after dealing with Miss Chingford's uncomprehending fury and Dorothea's hysterics, Lucy almost wished she had chosen to tell her father and had left Major Kurland to deal with the sisters. According to the major, her father had taken the news remarkably well and had retired to his study with a bottle of brandy. Lucy closed the Chingfords' bedroom door and went slowly down the stairs.

She and Major Kurland had accompanied the sisters to Dr. Fletcher's to see their mother's body and had eventually persuaded them to come back to the rectory. She had given them all her handkerchiefs and eventually dosed them both with laudanum to help them sleep. Straightening her shoulders, she stepped into the small back parlor, where she'd left Anna entertaining Major Kurland.

He stood when she entered, his gaze fixed on her face. "Is everything all right?"

She sank down gratefully on the couch. "They are both sleeping. Dorothea hasn't stopped crying long enough to form a sentence, and Miss Chingford is simply angry and asking me a thousand questions I cannot answer." Lucy sighed and pushed a stray pin back into place in her hair. "At least Sophia and Mr. Stanford were able to get away before their whole wedding was ruined."

"I'll write to Andrew and tell him what has occurred, but I'll make sure he understands that we are more than capable of dealing with it." Major Kurland sat down again. "I don't want him to feel as if he has to rush back here. But I also don't want him to read about this in a newspaper and be taken by surprise."

"Lucy, you look exhausted. Let me go and fetch you a cup of tea." Anna leapt to her feet. "Would you like some tea, Major?"

"As the rector has taken all the brandy, I suppose tea will have to do." He hesitated and made as if to rise. "Unless you wish to be alone, Miss Harrington? I'm sure Foley can take care of my needs if I go back to the manor."

Lucy waved him back to his seat. "No, please stay. I wanted to ask your opinion on this matter."

"My opinion?" Major Kurland sat back as Anna whisked herself out of the door in a swirl of petticoats.

"Does it not seem very *convenient* to you that Mrs. Chingford fell down the stairs?" Lucy asked.

"In what way?"

"Don't you remember your history? Robert Dudley was desperate to marry Queen Elizabeth the First, but he couldn't, because he was already married."

"And what exactly does this have to do with Mrs. Chingford?"

"Amy Dudley, Robert's wife, was mysteriously found dead at the bottom of a flight of stairs at their country home while he was busy cavorting with the queen in London. Opinion at the time was divided between those who thought Dudley had ordered his wife's death in order to free himself to marry the queen, and those who believed Dudley's enemies had done it to discredit him, because how could a queen marry a man under the suspicion of murdering his own wife?"

"But the queen didn't marry him."

"Exactly."

"I fail to see your point."

Lucy sighed. "Mrs. Chingford liked to stir up trouble. One has to wonder whether someone decided she had gone too far and took the opportunity to get rid of her."

"Following your interesting logic, one would assume that the only people who would want to stop the marriage and murder Mrs. Chingford would be you, your sister, or the Chingford ladies."

"Well, it wasn't me or Anna or my father. But you do have a point. I wonder if Dorothea met her mother at the top of the stairs and had an argument with her. It might explain her current state of hysteria."

"Or Mrs. Chingford simply caught her heel in her gown and fell."

"Her gown wasn't damaged at the hem. I checked. If she'd caught her heel in it that badly, there should have been some ripped fabric." Lucy sat forward and stared at the major's skeptical face. "It just doesn't seem quite right to me."

"And yet you have no proof that anyone was even in the vicinity when the accident occurred."

"It is true that I was close enough to *hear* her fall and yet saw no one when I arrived at the stairwell, but that doesn't mean she was alone." She took the locket and chain out of her pocket and held it up. "She had this clutched in her hand."

He leaned forward to take it from her. "Perhaps it came off her neck when she fell."

"She was wearing a rather nice set of rubies to match her gown. I doubt she would've worn a cheap item such as this unless it held some sentimental value to her."

"She didn't strike me as a sentimental woman." Major Kurland attempted to open the locket, but it was badly dented. He handed it back to her. "So you suspect she tore this off her assailant's throat as she tumbled down the stairs?"

"It's possible."

"It also means we're probably looking for a woman."

"Men do wear lockets sometimes, Major."

"But they are usually secreted beneath a man's shirt, not hanging out for all the world to see."

"True." Lucy frowned and slid the locket back into her pocket. "If the locket did come from around someone's throat, that person might have a red mark from the force of its removal." She smothered a yawn just as Anna reappeared with the tea tray, and she quickly changed the subject.

After a couple of sips of tea, Major Kurland stood and bowed to Lucy and Anna.

"I must go home and attend to my remaining guests. Thank you for your hospitality, Miss Harrington, Miss Anna."

Lucy met his gaze. "Are you planning on visiting Dr. Fletcher tomorrow?"

"I had thought of it."

"Then perhaps you could take me up in your carriage when you pass our door."

"If you wish." He studied her intently. "You

70

look tired. I won't call for you until at least noon."

"Thank you."

He took hold of her hand "Please don't worry yourself into a state about this. It might just be an unfortunate accident."

"I do hope you are right. I assure you, Major, that I don't *wish* to spend my time chasing murderers."

"Neither do I, although we seem to have an uncanny knack of attracting them." He kissed her fingers and bowed. "Good night, Miss Harrington. Sleep well."

Deep in thought, after sending Anna up to bed, Lucy took the tea tray back to the kitchen. To her surprise, Mrs. Fielding sat at the long pine table, helping herself to one of the cut-glass decanters that usually resided on the dining room table.

"Miss Harrington?" The cook smiled at her. "You should share a glass of port with me."

"And why is that, Mrs. Fielding?"

"Because Mrs. Chingford is dead. I was helping up at the manor, and I heard the news." A satisfied smirk crossed the cook's face. "She won't get her hands on my kitchen or the rector now, will she?"

"I suppose not." Lucy paused. Judging from the two bright red spots on Mrs. Fielding's cheeks, this wasn't the first glass of port she had consumed. "You were at Kurland Hall?"

"Yes. Mrs. High and Mighty ordered me to go and help. She threatened to have me dismissed for pilfering." Mrs. Fielding's eyes flashed. "As if me giving my nephew the odd piece of meat for a stew is a crime!"

"It certainly isn't. We all know that you support your sister's family to the best of your ability."

"I do my duty, Miss Harrington, and for that old harridan to suggest that the rector would dismiss me just for that was ridiculous. And I told her so, and she threatened to tell him about—" Mrs. Fielding stopped speaking and busied herself with finishing the port in her glass.

"About what?"

Cook stood and drew the tea tray toward her. "Good night, Miss Harrington. I'm sure we will have a busy day tomorrow, what with dealing with all the callers to the Miss Chingfords. I'll have to bake some more cake and funeral meats."

"Good night, Mrs. Fielding."

Lucy turned and reversed direction to the hall. She paused for a moment outside her father's study, but there was no sound from within, and she didn't have anything to say that he wouldn't misconstrue and make her feel guilty about. Picking up her skirts, she headed up the stairs. It seemed that Mrs. Chingford had even found out something detrimental about the rectory cook. And Cook had been at Kurland manor all day. . . .

The trouble was, Lucy could easily imagine Mrs. Fielding losing her temper and pushing Mrs. Chingford down the stairs. She had long considered Lucy's father her own personal property both in bed and out of it, and the rector had seemed quite happy to accept the arrangement. Until he'd met Mrs. Chingford, who had threatened to dismiss Mrs. Fielding at the earliest opportunity.

But what was Mrs. Fielding concealing from her father? Was it possible that she was considering leaving the rectory for another position or, even worse, another man? Lucy made a mental note to ask Betty for any new scandalous details about Cook's love life.

Lucy caught a yawn behind her hand and decided to undress herself rather than call for her maid. There was much to arrange on the morrow. The Chingfords needed help to organize their mother's burial rites, and the entire village would probably insist on descending on the rectory to find out exactly what was going on. It would make the day difficult, but it would give her an opportunity to study the other wedding guests to see if any of them had red marks on their necks or admitted to losing a piece of jewelry.

Major Kurland would probably tell her to curb her imagination and stick to the facts. In her experience, getting involved in investigating a murder often led to the murderer having designs on oneself. She really ought to learn to let things be.

As she undressed, she rediscovered the battered locket and placed it beside her bed. If the locket didn't exist, she might be more willing to listen to the major's advice. But someone owned it, and she'd wager a hundred pounds that it wasn't Mrs. Chingford.

Chapter 5

G ood afternoon, Miss Harrington, Major Kurland. Do come in."

Dr. Fletcher opened the door to his house himself and ushered them inside. Instead of steering them toward the front parlor, he indicated that they should follow him to the back of the house, where, Lucy knew, there was a separate entrance to his medical practice.

The faint smell of chemicals and harsh cleaning agents made her fumble for her handkerchief and press it to her nose. The last time she'd been in a scientific laboratory, someone had died horribly.

"You don't have to go in there, Miss Harrington," Major Kurland said quietly. "You can wait for us in the kitchen."

Lucy stiffened her spine. "I'm quite all right, Major."

He looked down at her and then stepped aside. "Stubborn as ever, I see."

She ignored him and swept past him, all too aware of the still figure laid out on the cold marble slab in the center of the room. Gathering her courage, she approached Dr. Fletcher, who was writing a note in a large book.

"Did you discover the cause of Mrs. Chingford's death?"

He looked over the book at her. "Her neck was broken."

"By the fall?"

"I'm not sure." He put the book down and approached the dead woman, then pulled the sheet down slightly to expose her throat. "Her throat is very bruised. That could be because of the way the bones broke, pushing outward and into the flesh or . . ."

"It could be because someone strangled her," Major Kurland said.

Lucy looked around, startled at his blunt words. "Why do you say that?"

His mouth twisted in distaste. "I've seen such injuries before. I dealt with several unpleasant and unexplained deaths in the army. At least three of them involved soldiers strangling women."

Lucy's fingers crept to her own throat. "If she was strangled, then one must assume that someone wanted her dead."

"Yes." Major Kurland turned to the doctor, who was following their conversation intently. "Is it possible?"

"That she was strangled? I was an army surgeon. I've seen the same sights as you have, Major." He shrugged. "Those marks could easily be fingers. The thing is, she might have died just from the fall itself. It is impossible to tell."

"Perhaps someone wanted to make sure that she was dead," Lucy commented.

"Well, they certainly succeeded." Major Kurland moved away from the body, and Dr. Fletcher covered it with the sheet. "I have a favor to ask of you, Doctor."

"And what would that be?"

"I'd appreciate it if you kept this information to yourself. I'd prefer the wedding guests and villagers to assume Mrs. Chingford died from a tragic accident."

Dr. Fletcher's green eyes narrowed. "I won't lie for you."

"I understand that. But if Miss Harrington and I are going to catch a murderer, we will require your discretion."

"That I can manage. If anyone asks me directly how she died, I will simply say that she broke her neck. That covers all eventualities." Dr. Fletcher went to the door and held it open for Lucy and the major to pass through. "Do you really believe you can find out who did this?"

Major Kurland looked down at Lucy. "Miss Harrington and I are becoming rather accomplished at discovering murderers. If we can't bring this off, I doubt anyone can."

After bidding Dr. Fletcher a subdued good-bye, Lucy allowed the major to accompany her back to the carriage and then suddenly stopped.

"Could we walk for a while?"

"If you wish." He gestured at his damaged leg. "I doubt I can make it the whole way home, but I will do my best." He shouted to Reg. "Wait for me in the village square."

"All right, sir."

The carriage moved off. It was a cloudy day, but there was no hint of rain as they walked together down the narrow country road toward the center of Kurland St. Mary.

"So what shall we do now?" Lucy asked.

"Our best to discover a murderer." He sighed. "What an appalling thing to happen on Andrew's wedding day."

"Perhaps we should start by listing those who might have wished Mrs. Chingford dead, or at least might have become involved in an argument with her, resulting in an untimely fall," Lucy said. "One would assume that if it had been an *accident,* then someone would have come forward by now, or at least remained with the body and raised the alarm."

"You'd be surprised how people behave in such situations. Even if it was an accident, the person might not even have realized Mrs. Chingford had fallen so badly. They might have gone on their way, thinking they'd taught her a lesson."

"But now we all know she is dead."

"And whoever did it might be too frightened

to confess or might have left the wedding immediately afterward and returned home, none the wiser."

Lucy glanced up. "You have a very jaundiced view of people's morals, Major."

"I was in the army. I know all too well that civilized behavior is a very thin veneer. It doesn't take much to make otherwise perfectly decent men behave like savages."

They continued for a moment in silence, the only sound the tap of the major's cane on the hardened mud.

Lucy considered as she walked. "Dorothea Chingford seemed at odds with her mother, Mrs. Fielding disliked her immensely, as did Mr. Stanford's sister and Mrs. Green, and . . ."

"And you. Don't forget to put yourself on that list. Has it occurred to you that as you found the body, gossip might assume you are the guilty party?"

Lucy stopped walking to meet his level gaze. "You know I wouldn't have killed her."

"Yes, but I'm not everyone. You also had a very good reason to dislike her. No woman likes to be replaced."

"You are quite wrong about that, sir. I cannot begrudge my father another chance at happiness and would never stand in the way of him acquiring a new wife." She hesitated. "In truth, I would be delighted to relinquish his care into another woman's hands, just not into Mrs. Chingford's."

"Others might not believe that," he said flatly.

"You truly believe I might be implicated in Mrs. Chingford's death?"

"I would almost guarantee it, Miss Harrington." He hesitated. "If you feel threatened in any way, please be assured that I will stand your friend."

"I appreciate that, Major, but I doubt I will have need of you." She continued walking, and after a moment he joined her. "As far as I know, everyone considers Mrs. Chingford's death a tragic accident rather than a murder."

"Then let's hope it remains that way," he muttered as they reached the village square. "Now, how can we keep the wedding guests here in Kurland St. Mary so we can investigate this matter properly?"

"I had a thought about that." Lucy was relieved that his attention had moved on from her. "I wonder if the Chingfords could be persuaded to hold the funeral at our church."

"That's an excellent idea. Perhaps I should be the one to mention it to the rector. I can suggest to my guests that they are welcome to stay on at Kurland Hall for the funeral." Major Kurland glanced down at her as they approached the carriage. "You will be careful, Miss Harrington, won't you?"

"Of course, sir." She bobbed a curtsy. "I'll walk

to the rectory from here. Thank you for taking me to see Dr. Fletcher. He seems a most agreeable man."

"He's certainly just the kind of man one needs in a crisis. If it hadn't been for him, they would've amputated my leg to free me from under my horse." He saluted and got up into the gig. "Good day, Miss Harrington."

Robert arrived back in the stable yard just as his groom sat Andrew's son on the back of the oldest and most reliable mare in his stables. He still wanted to warn the boy to be careful— that horses were unpredictable beasts and could behave in ways no one expected. Despite the warmth of the sun, his skin was clammy, and he shivered.

"Are you all right, sir?"

He turned to see Thomas Fairfax and the widow, who had come down the path from the house to the stables.

"I'm a little cold." Robert eased a step away from the oncoming horse. Andrew's son, Terence, was smiling and gripping the reins with great gusto.

"Look at me, Major Kurland! Look at me!"

Robert forced himself to acknowledge the boy and flinched when something touched his leg. Looking down, he saw Andrew's five-year-old daughter, Charlotte, staring up at him. She tugged on his breeches again, and he bent his head to her.

"I don't like horses, either, sir," she whispered. "Don't tell Terence. He laughs at me."

Robert patted her head. "I won't laugh, but you must remember that if you take care around a horse, it will never hurt you."

They both took several nervous steps back as the groom encouraged the horse into a trot. Reaching down, Robert picked Charlotte up, placed her on the low stone wall, and then leaned against it beside her.

"That's not true is it, sir?"

"What isn't?" Robert said.

"That horses can't hurt you. Papa said your horse fell on top of you and hurt you very badly."

Robert glanced down at his shattered leg. "That was slightly different. I was in the middle of a battlefield, and the enemy was shooting at us. It wasn't really my horse's fault that he panicked when he was hit."

Charlotte patted his knee. "But it still hurt."

"Yes, it did." Robert held her gaze. "But I haven't let it stop me from . . ." He paused as he considered his current aversion to his own horses. "I'm not going to let it make me afraid that every horse will do that to me."

Her smile was sweet. "Papa said you were very brave, and now I know why." She sighed. "I wish I was brave."

"I have an idea." Robert picked her up and balanced her on his good hip. "Let's go on a visit." As he passed Thomas, he nodded at him. "Can you keep an eye on Terence while I show Miss Charlotte something?"

"Of course, Major."

Robert walked on into the stables, inhaling the familiar scent of horse manure, straw, and leather, which had once been his entire military existence. Now he came here only if he had to. Charlotte had made him think about his aversion to the place and question it anew.

There was a young boy stationed outside the closed door of the stall at the end of the row, and he stood up when Robert approached.

"Morning, sir."

"Good morning, Arthur. Will you open the top door please so that Miss Charlotte and I can look inside, please?"

Charlotte's fingers tightened painfully around his neck, and he smiled at her. "Don't worry. There is nothing to be afraid of." He said the words as much for himself as for her.

Arthur opened the door, and they both peered in.

"Oh . . . ," Charlotte breathed. "It's a mother and her *baby*."

"A foal that was born last night," Robert said softly. "Isn't he beautiful?"

"Can I pet him?" She almost wiggled out of his arms in her efforts to get closer.

"Not yet. We can come back tomorrow if you like."

She grabbed his ears and kissed his forehead. "Yes, please!" She touched her nose to his and stared deeply into his eyes. "You aren't scared of him, are you?"

"No, I am not."

"Neither am I."

They smiled at each other, in complete accord. She slid down his body, put her hand in his, and skipped back out into the paddock. While he walked, Robert took a moment to wonder how Miss Harrington was faring at the rectory and if she had had any success in identifying the owner of the locket. He had spent a surreptitious and uncomfortable few moments at the breakfast table, scanning his female guests' décolletages for signs of redness, and had seen nothing.

He'd also spoken to Mrs. Green, who had been very forthright in her opinion that Mrs. Chingford was better off dead and hadn't cared who heard her say it. She hadn't gone quite so far as to say she wished she'd done the deed herself, but she had come quite close. Either she was a master manipulator or she hadn't been anywhere near Mrs. Chingford when the event happened.

"Major Kurland?"

He looked up to find Mrs. Fairfax standing beside the carriage that had just been brought back into the stable yard with fresh horses.

"Good morning, ma'am. Are you taking the air? Splendid."

Thomas bowed. "I'm taking Mrs. Fairfax down to the rectory to express her condolences to the Chingfords. I promise I won't be long."

Robert patted his pocket. "Take your time. I wish to go over our plans for the stable expansion. I'll have my thoughts ready when you return."

Lucy continued walking through the village, mentally cataloguing the wedding guests and their interactions with Mrs. Chingford. She would have to speak to Miss Stanford, Mrs. Green, and Dorothea. She almost hoped one of them would break down and confess all but considered it unlikely. In truth, if everyone assumed Mrs. Chingford had died from a tragic fall, there was no need to say anything. Perhaps it was a case of letting sleeping dogs lie. . . .

But what if the person who owned the locket realized it was missing?

She entered the rectory and dealt with a couple of unimportant domestic issues in the kitchen before climbing up the stairs to Mrs. Chingford's bedchamber. After ascertaining that neither of the Chingford sisters was up and about, she opened the door and closed it quietly behind her. A waft of stale perfume rose to greet her as she tiptoed across the carpet.

The room had been untouched since the

morning of the wedding and was a veritable mess of abandoned clothing, beauty aids, and the other feminine jumble. Lucy stripped the sheets from the bed and bundled them up by the door for washing. She picked up and carefully folded all Mrs. Chingford's discarded clothing, searching the pockets before putting each garment in a pile on the bed.

The large trunk was open, its contents spilling out onto the floor. Lucy knelt and checked what else was in there before replacing the assortment of footwear at the bottom and adding the folded clothes. She finally turned her attention to the dressing table, gathering the powders, creams, and lip tints into a large enameled box. Mrs. Chingford's jewelry case was nowhere in sight. Lucy could only assume Penelope had taken charge of it.

All was still quiet, so Lucy moved across to her mother's old desk, where a large leather writing case lay open. An inkpot and a pen were balanced precariously on top of a pile of letters. It appeared as if Mrs. Chingford had been an avid correspondent. Lucy closed the inkpot and laid the pen down on the blotter, her gaze caught by a half-finished letter in what she assumed was Mrs. Chingford's hand. The names Miss Stanford and Mrs. Fairfax were quite legible. Holding her breath, Lucy leaned closer and put on her reading glasses.

"Can I help you with something, Miss Harrington?"

Concealing her start of surprise, Lucy picked up the inkpot and turned toward Miss Chingford. Her old nemesis didn't look very well, her skin pale and her eyes shadowed. She was dressed in a black dress she had borrowed from Anna.

"Good afternoon, Miss Chingford. I do hope you slept well." Lucy slipped the letter into her pocket and placed the inkpot and the pen in one of the desk's pigeonholes. "I came to strip the bed."

"And pry?"

Lucy raised her eyebrows. "Into what, exactly?"

"Intimate details of my mother's life to share with your village friends?"

"I would never to do that," Lucy replied as gently as she could.

"Then did your father ask you to come up here?" Miss Chingford sank down into the nearest chair, her expression hard. "He and my mother were arguing at the wedding."

Lucy took the seat opposite her. "What were they arguing about?"

"My mother didn't appreciate him sharing the news of their supposed betrothal to the masses."

"I did wonder about the wisdom of that," Lucy admitted.

Miss Chingford dabbed at her eyes with one of Lucy's handkerchiefs. "I don't think she had any intention of marrying him. She just wanted to return to London with that news to use as a threat to ensnare the man she really wanted."

"I assume she didn't tell my father that."

Miss Chingford snorted. "Who knows? Perhaps she did. She had a sharp tongue. She called it being honest. I often suspected her 'honesty' came with a healthy dose of malice. Your father was very angry with her."

"He hates being embarrassed." Lucy collected her thoughts. "When did they fight?"

"I told you, at the wedding, just before she—" Miss Chingford pressed the handkerchief to her lips. "I disliked her intensely, Miss Harrington, but I can't seem to stop crying."

"She was your mother. It is quite understandable." Lucy handed over her last clean handkerchief. "How is Dorothea bearing up?"

"I can't get a word of sense out of her. She didn't like our mother, either, and was arguing with her about the intended marriage at the wedding." Miss Chingford sighed. "*Everyone* was arguing with her about something, and she seemed to be enjoying it. She loved being at the center of things. After my father's death she lost her social position and would try anything to reclaim it."

She paused and shot Lucy a suspicious look. "Why are you being so nice to me?"

"Because you and your sister have just suffered

a grievous loss," Lucy said. "I lost my own mother eight years ago. I know how hard it was."

"By all accounts, your mother was a saint." Miss Chingford blew her nose with great force. "My mother was immensely disliked, and for very good reason."

Lucy rose. "I made a start at packing up your mother's things, but you might wish to finish the task yourself. I do hope you have your mother's jewelry case?"

"Yes. I took in into my room last night to put the rubies back in their box."

"Did she own a locket?" Lucy asked. "I found one at the wedding, and I've been searching for the owner."

"Not to my knowledge. She preferred gemstones to simple trinkets."

"Do you or Dorothea remember losing one?"

"I certainly did not. You will have to ask Dorothea herself. I do believe she has a locket that contains a lock of our father's hair. I have no idea why she idolized him so when he couldn't even tell us apart."

Lucy placed another box of lotions and perfume in the trunk, keeping her back to her companion. "I hesitate to ask you such a personal question, Miss Chingford—Penelope, if I may—but do you have family to help you manage this unfortunate situation?"

"My mother managed to alienate almost everyone. And, as she didn't produce a male heir, even our house will revert to one of our Stanford cousins."

"Then where do you think you will live?"

Penelope shrugged. "You know how it is, Miss Harrington. Someone in the family will take pity on us, will give us a home, and then will expect us to be grateful for the rest of our lives."

There was a bitter sound to her words, but Lucy couldn't blame her. Unwanted or unwed female relatives had very few options if their menfolk died. She had always known that if she didn't marry, Anthony or her younger siblings would give her a home where she would be valued. But many women weren't so lucky and became unpaid drudges to their richer relatives.

The sound of a carriage stopping outside the rectory brought Penelope to her feet. "I suppose I'd better go and finish dressing before the vultures descend to offer their condolences."

"Will Dorothea be well enough to come down?" Lucy moved toward the door and picked up the bundle of dirty bedclothes.

"I don't think so."

"Then I will go and greet our callers." Lucy hesitated. "If you don't wish to speak to anyone, Penelope, no one will fault you for it."

"Yes they will. They will think I am too ashamed of my own mother to face them, but

I have done nothing wrong, and I refuse to be cowed."

She swept past Lucy and went into her bedchamber, closing the door behind her with a definite bang.

On the landing Lucy almost ran into Betty, who had been coming to fetch her down to the parlor. She thrust the washing into the maid's arms and patted her own hair before descending the stairs. She suspected the rectory would soon be awash with villagers and wedding guests eager to see the Chingfords and relive the tragedy over tea and cake. Luckily, Mrs. Fielding had baked enough for a hundred such visitors.

Would her father emerge to accept the condolences of his parishioners, or would he continue to hide himself away in his study? And was his nonappearance due to grief, anger, or regret? She hated to consider her father amongst those who had argued with Mrs. Chingford on that fateful day, but she couldn't allow her prejudices to cloud her judgment.

Opening the door into the parlor, she surveyed the early visitors, who were mainly the elderly village busybodies who prided themselves on finding out all the juicy gossip first. Also present was the new curate, George, who was handing round cake and chatting with his parishioners Mr. Thomas Fairfax and Mrs. Fairfax.

She went over to Mr. Fairfax, and he bowed.

"Good afternoon, Miss Harrington. Mrs. Fairfax wished to visit to offer her condolences to you and the Chingford family."

Lucy waited for the widow to draw back her veil and was surprised to see real tears on her cheeks.

"I am so sorry," she choked out in a small whisper. "Your poor, dear papa. I had to come. . . ." She gripped Lucy's hand very tightly between her own. "The Chingford ladies must be devastated."

"Is Miss Chingford coming down today?" Mr. Fairfax made a slight movement forward and gently disengaged the widow's gloved fingers from Lucy's wrist. "If she isn't, I'll take Mrs. Fairfax back to the manor house, and we can call another day."

His worried gaze met Lucy's over his ex-employer's head, as if he was trying to apologize to her. He lowered his voice. "Being so recently bereaved herself, Mrs. Fairfax takes these matters to heart."

"Which is very considerate of her." Lucy guided the weeping widow to a chair. "If you will just rest for a moment, ma'am, I'll go and see if Miss Chingford is available."

She turned toward the door, only to see that Miss Chingford had entered the room, her head held high, her gaze challenging anyone to feel sorry for her. Her black garb did nothing to distract from her frozen blond beauty. The curate almost dropped the plate of scones he was handing around, and Mr. Fairfax went still, his gaze fixed on Miss Chingford's pale face. For a moment, Lucy found herself admiring her former foe, whose future was now so precarious.

"Ah, Miss Chingford." Lucy met her gaze. "Have you made the acquaintance of Mrs. Fairfax and Mr. Thomas Fairfax? They called to offer their condolences for your loss."

Miss Chingford's arrival caused a second wave of weeping from the widow, which made Lucy cravenly withdraw from her side and circulate amongst the other guests. As the gossips left, Miss Stanford arrived, and Lucy hastened to greet her and offer some refreshment. After a while, Lucy managed to find a seat beside Miss Stanford as she handed her a cup of tea.

"Thank you, Miss Harrington." The teacup rattled on the saucer as Miss Stanford placed it on the table beside her.

"Are you quite well, Miss Stanford?" Lucy asked quietly.

"As well as can be expected, seeing as my brother got married yesterday and the woman who threatened to destroy that marriage and his reputation died."

Her forthright manner reminded Lucy of Major Kurland and made her feel rather more hopeful that some direct questions might yield answers.

"I doubt Mrs. Chingford could have done much damage to your brother or your family, Miss Stanford."

"You'd be surprised. She told me quite openly that she was paid by some of the newspapers and scandal sheets to provide gossip about the *ton*." Miss Stanford's mouth twisted. "My brother is a lawyer. He cannot afford to have his reputation brought into question. She also told me that she had already sent a letter about his new marriage to all her sources."

Lucy remembered the vast amount of correspondence she'd discovered in Mrs. Chingford's bedchamber. She certainly had a wide acquaintance, and now it appeared that some of it was for personal gain.

"But Mrs. Chingford is dead now," Lucy reminded her companion. "She can no longer persecute or gossip about anyone."

"That's true." Miss Stanford bit down on her lip. "I just feel so terribly guilty."

Lucy held her breath as she surreptitiously offered the other woman a handkerchief. "Why would you feel like that? From what I observed, you simply stood up for your brother. That was an admirable thing to do."

Miss Stanford shuddered. "And I argued with Mrs. Chingford just before she apparently died. Perhaps it was my harsh words that made her forget to pay attention on the stairs and lose her footing." She sighed. "And now I cannot take those words back."

"With all due respect, Miss Stanford, unless you were actually present in the moment Mrs. Chingford fell, you can hardly consider yourself responsible." Lucy watched carefully to see how Miss Stanford reacted to her honesty, but detected nothing untoward.

"I thought about following Mrs. Chingford and having it out with her in private, but in the end, thanks to your timely intervention, I went upstairs to help Sophia change into her traveling dress."

Lucy tried to recall if she had seen Miss Stanford with Sophia, but had no recollection of her being present.

"So you have nothing to feel guilty for."

"Only my bad temper." Miss Stanford bit her lip.

"One doesn't wish to speak ill of the dead, but in my opinion, Mrs. Chingford was a difficult woman *not* to argue with," Lucy murmured. "In truth, she seemed to be at odds with half the wedding party. You were not the only person who was annoyed with her on that day."

Miss Stanford reached over and took Lucy's hand. "Thank you, Miss Harrington. You have made me feel so much better about my behavior. Robert *said* you were a remarkable woman."

Lucy had no answer to that. Major Kurland

thought her remarkable? It appeared he had some very peculiar notions in his head about everything at the moment.

"You are most welcome, Miss Stanford. We all have regrets, but I wouldn't allow your remorse to overcome you." Lucy hesitated. "If you wish to make amends, you might consider asking your family whether there is a place for the Chingford sisters within their ranks. Not only have they lost their mother, but they will also lose their home to a male relative in the very near future."

"I will speak to my brother when he returns. At least in that way I can make amends for my temper." Miss Stanford took a deep breath. "Now I will go and speak to Miss Chingford."

Chapter 6

If the Chingford family wishes it, Major Kurland, I would be more than willing to conduct the funeral service in our church." The rector paused. "It would be a fitting way to bid adieu to the woman who had promised to be my wife."

"Indeed, sir." Robert nodded. "It would be most fitting. I believe Miss Harrington has already spoken to Miss Chingford about this matter, and she is happy for you to lead the service."

The rector lowered his voice. "Is there a family vault to which the body should be conveyed after the funeral?"

"No. I believe Mrs. Chingford can be buried here at St. Mary's." Before the rector could start speaking again, Robert continued. "I will, of course, cover all the costs of the burial and other funeral expenses."

"That is very good of you, Major."

"As she died when she was a guest at my house, I feel somewhat responsible." Robert rose to his feet. "Do you think you could have everything organized within a week or so? I'm sure we can persuade some of our guests to remain here for another few days."

The rector bent to consult his diary. "I'll have

George contact the church warden and the grave diggers to find out exactly when I can conduct the burial service. I usually advise that a body is buried sooner rather than later."

"Thank you." Robert shook away the memories of bodies strewn over battlefields and instead shook the rector's hand. "Are the ladies at home? I wish to confirm the plans with Miss Chingford."

"I believe they are in the back parlor, sir. I'll take you to them."

Robert followed the rector through the hallways until he could hear the unmistakable sound of female voices.

"Ah, Anna, Miss Chingford. Major Kurland is here."

Anna Harrington came across the room to greet him with her usual charming smile. "Major Kurland, how good of you to call."

"Miss Anna." He bowed over her hand as the rector disappeared, murmuring something about tea and fetching Lucy. "Miss Chingford."

His former betrothed raised her head and studied him. "Major Kurland. Did you settle matters with the rector?"

He took the seat opposite her and rested his cane against the chair leg. "I did, Miss Chingford. Hopefully, the funeral will take place a week from Saturday, and your mother can be buried in the graveyard here."

"I suppose I should thank you."

"There is no need. As I said to the rector, your mother died in my house. I feel somewhat responsible for that."

"Responsible enough to marry me?"

Robert jerked to attention. "I beg your pardon?"

Miss Chingford didn't appear to be jesting, her blue eyes sharp. "With my mother gone, my sister and I are dependent on our distant family to provide us with a home and a dowry. I need to marry to prevent that."

"We have already decided we would not suit." Robert eased a finger into his collar. Was it getting hot in the room?

"There is also the matter of your understanding with my sister, Major, isn't there?" Anna Harrington said, intervening, her voice sweet and very welcome, until he realized she intended to rescue him from the pot by throwing him into the fire.

"My father did speak to you about your intentions, didn't he?" Anna continued.

"He certainly did, but—"

Anna smiled at him and then more sympathetically at Miss Chingford. "So you see, your suggestion wouldn't work at all. There are several other gentlemen of our acquaintance who would make you an excellent husband. We can discuss the matter after the major has gone."

"Please do," Robert muttered as the door opened

to admit one of the maids with the promised tea. Where the devil was Miss Harrington?

Lucy sat on the bed and smoothed Dorothea's tangled hair away from her cheek.

"You really should get up, Dorothea. You cannot stay in bed forever."

Dorothea didn't speak and turned her face deeper into the covers, making Lucy sigh.

"Your mother's funeral will be soon. Do you think it is fair to place the entire burden for this matter onto Penelope's shoulders? She needs your support."

"She doesn't need anything. She's just like her."

"By *her*, I assume you mean your mother."

There was no answer, so Lucy tried another tack. "At the wedding, I saw you watching from the minstrels' gallery above the hall. Did you hear me call you?"

Beneath her fingers Dorothea went still, and Lucy carried on speaking. "Did you see your mother up there as you ran away? I should imagine you wished to speak to her about the news of her impending marriage."

"She would never have married him."

"Why do you say that?"

She jumped as Dorothea suddenly sat up, throwing off the blankets. "Because she *wouldn't* have! Because she was a liar and . . ." Dorothea stopped speaking and glared at Lucy. "Go *away!*"

Too used to the tactics of younger siblings to be put off by Dorothea's sudden rage, Lucy stared right back at her. "What are you so angry about? Did you see your mother fall?"

"I said, go away!"

"If you saw anything or know what happened, *tell* me," Lucy said firmly. "We can sort this out. We—"

"We can do *nothing!* We cannot bring my mother back to life." Dorothea turned away and curled up in a little ball before dragging the covers back over her head.

Lucy waited another minute but knew she wouldn't be granted any more insights. She patted the lump under the blankets. "If you wish to talk about anything, you know where to find me. You cannot keep grieving like this, Dorothea, and you cannot hide yourself away forever."

Leaving the room, Lucy made her way down the stairs and saw Betty coming out of the back parlor.

"Do we have visitors?"

Betty nodded. "Just your Major Kurland, Miss Harrington. He came to talk to the rector about the arrangements for the poor lady's funeral. I just took him in some tea."

Lucy continued down the stairs. Just when had he become *her* Major Kurland? She didn't think he would appreciate being considered someone's property. The mere thought of it made her smile, and she had to fight to conceal it as she entered the room. The major stood and bowed to her.

"Miss Harrington. I was hoping you would be here today. I wanted to ask your advice about something."

He stared at her so intently that she blinked. "I'm always willing to aid you, sir. How may I help?"

Even as she sat down, Penelope stood and left the room with an audible sniff. Lucy looked uncertainly from the major to Anna.

"Is everything all right?"

"I believe so." Major Kurland raised an eyebrow. "Why do you ask?"

"Miss Chingford seemed upset. Did she not wish for the funeral to be held here, after all?"

"Oh no. She was perfectly content with that," Anna said. "But she *was* quite annoyed when Major Kurland declined her offer to marry him."

The major shifted uneasily in his seat. "It was hardly that, Miss Anna. I think Miss Chingford was joking."

Anna winked at Lucy. "I don't think she was, but you handled it very well, Major." Leaning over, she picked up the teapot. "I will ask Betty to refresh the pot for your tea, Lucy. Excuse me a moment."

Silence filled the parlor after Anna left. Major Kurland fiddled with his pocket watch, and

Lucy tried to make sense of what was going on.

"Did she really expect you to marry her?" Lucy asked the question before she could stop herself.

"She suggested that I owed her a proposal because her mother had died on my property. *I* suggested that we had already agreed that we would not suit, and that was the end of it."

"Poor Miss Chingford." Lucy sighed. "She must be feeling quite desperate if she considered marrying you again."

"Thank you, Miss Harrington. I suppose I deserved that."

"You know that wasn't what I meant. Her circumstances have changed considerably for the worse. She truly believes that there is no one willing to look out for her interests, particularly her marital prospects. That is rather sad."

"I suppose it is, but I didn't come here today to discuss Miss Chingford's wedding prospects. I came to ask you whether you had discovered the owner of the locket yet."

Quite willing to be distracted from the uncomfortable topic of Miss Chingford, Lucy marshaled her thoughts.

"No one has openly claimed the locket or even asked about it. I suppose if they believe they lost it at Kurland Hall, they might be more inclined to ask you. Has anyone mentioned it to you or your staff?"

"No one so far."

"Or has Foley noticed anyone looking for anything?"

"Not to my knowledge." He sighed. "So we are at an impasse."

"Not quite an impasse, Major." Lucy drew the half-written letter out of her pocket. "Miss Stanford told me that Mrs. Chingford admitted to selling gossip about the *ton* to the scandal sheets. It was one of the reasons why she continued to argue with Mrs. Chingford about her brother's reputation. She was afraid that Mrs. Chingford's ability to publicly destroy Mr. Stanford was considerable."

Major Kurland raised an eyebrow. "Scandal sheets pay money for the ridiculous gossip they publish? I assumed they made it all up."

"But you can understand why Miss Stanford was determined that her brother's name and character should not be smeared by lies and conjecture."

"Miss Harrington, Andrew is a lawyer. If anyone could defend himself against such accusations, it would be him. His sister doesn't need to protect him at all. She should know that."

"Didn't Mrs. Chingford say something about Miss Stanford's fiancé, as well?"

"I don't recall anything specific."

Lucy frowned. "There was definitely some mention of him. Perhaps Miss Stanford decided that having to defend two people justified her actions."

"You've decided that Miss Stanford is a murderer, then?"

"Not quite." She handed Major Kurland the letter. "I found this in Mrs. Chingford's room. She isn't the only person mentioned in the letter."

Major Kurland frowned. "I do wish you wouldn't talk in circles, Miss Harrington." Lucy handed him her reading glasses as he squinted at the letter. "Thank you. Ah, you mean Miss Stanford is mentioned in this letter, as is her brother, her fiancé, and . . ." He flipped the letter over. "Mrs. Fairfax." He raised his head to stare at Lucy. "Now, why was Mrs. Chingford interested in her?"

"They were definitely acquainted. I saw them talking at the wedding." Lucy took the letter back. "Mr. Fairfax was puzzled as to how they knew each other."

"Who would know?" Major Kurland frowned. "Mrs. Chingford mentioned to me that she thought she had met the widow before, but she didn't know when. Perhaps she was attempting to find out more in this letter."

"The letter is addressed to a lady called Madge."

"Then it might be helpful to discover who Madge is."

Lucy nodded. "I will find a way to ask Penelope

105

about her. I will also ask if she remembers anything her mother said about Mrs. Fairfax."

"And if you will trust me with the locket, I shall have Foley inquire of my guests and the household staff if it belongs to anyone. He can say it was found amongst the soiled clothing in the laundry pile."

"That is an excellent plan." She dug into her pocket and brought the locket out. "You might also see if you can open it. There might be a portrait or an inscription inside that will make our job much easier."

He took the locket and put it in his pocket before standing up. "I'm beginning to think this mystery will remain unsolvable."

"Perhaps that would be for the best."

"It's not like you to walk away from injustice, Miss Harrington."

Lucy drew her shawl tighter around her shoulders. "Sometimes it feels that the price one has to pay to uphold the truth is too high."

"As a soldier who has gone into battle to right wrongs, I completely understand your reasoning." He picked up his hat and paused. "Shall we leave things alone, then?"

She looked up at him. "Let's follow through on what we agreed and then decide."

"As you wish."

Lucy stood, as well. "You aren't going to argue with me, Major Kurland?"

"Not this time." He bowed and turned to the door. "I have no desire to drag you into danger again."

"*Drag* me?" Lucy followed him out into the hallway. "I was the one who came up with the plan to capture our last murderer."

"That's hardly the point—"

"Good day, Major Kurland." Marching ahead of him, she opened the front door and stepped back to allow him to go past her. The glare he shot her as he left was almost comforting. She much preferred him being a tyrant than a proper gentleman.

Chapter 7

As Dorothea still refused to leave her bed, it fell to Lucy to help Penelope sort out the rest of her mother's possessions and start on the arduous task of notifying all her family and correspondents of her death. Not that Lucy minded helping. It gave her the perfect opportunity to quiz Penelope about Mrs. Chingford's relationships. As it was less than two weeks before the funeral, the letters would need to be sent out soon so that mourners could arrive in time for the service.

While Penelope wrote a list of her mother's jewelry, noting which pieces would have to be returned to the Chingford family and which were her own property, Lucy began to tidy the desk.

"Your mother was a great letter writer."

"She liked to keep abreast of all the gossip."

"I can make a start on informing her friends about the funeral, if you wish."

Penelope shrugged. "Most of them won't come. They used her as much as she did them."

"Luckily, some of the Stanford family are still here and are aware of the upcoming funeral." Lucy paused. "Was there anyone else at the wedding who you think your mother knew well?

I noticed her speaking to Mrs. Fairfax on several occasions."

"My mother thought that she and Mrs. Fairfax had shared the same nurse for their children."

"That's quite a coincidence."

Penelope held up a pair of diamond earrings to the light to inspect them. "Mrs. Fairfax insisted it wasn't possible, but my mother wasn't deterred. She was quite convinced that our old nurse had taken a position at the Fairfaxes."

"And Mrs. Fairfax denied it."

"She did. My mother might have been lying. She liked to keep people on edge by claiming she knew things about them that weren't proven."

"Like Mr. Stanford having hastened his wife's end."

Penelope's mouth twisted. "She was quite proud of that little controversy. Upsetting the bride, the groom, *and* the groom's sister at a wedding was quite an achievement for her."

There was a knock at the door, and Betty came in.

"Miss Harrington, Mr. Fairfax is in the parlor. He has a message for you from Major Kurland."

"Then I will be down directly." She glanced over at Penelope, who was staring into space. "Do you want me to fetch Anna to help you when she returns? I believe she went driving with Mr. Jenkins."

"She likes him, doesn't she?"

"I'm not sure. They've known each other for years. Nicholas has always had a *tendre* for her."

"Then he probably wouldn't be interested in me."

Lucy stopped walking. "I'm sure you wouldn't think of throwing yourself at a man who is obviously in love with someone else." She hoped Penelope heeded the warning in her voice. "Anna might seem disinterested in Nicholas, and they do have a tendency to squabble, but—"

"That seems to be a family characteristic." Penelope picked up her pen again. "You and Major Kurland quarrel like an old married couple."

"We do not."

Penelope gave her a skeptical look, and Lucy chose not to speak and left the room. She reached the parlor, where Mr. Fairfax was speaking to her father. He bowed as she approached.

"Good morning, Miss Harrington. I trust you are well? Major Kurland was hoping to obtain your advice on a particular matter and asked if you might accompany me back to the manor."

Her father patted her shoulder. "You run along with Mr. Fairfax and help Major Kurland, my dear. We'll somehow manage without you." He turned back to Mr. Fairfax. "And please tell the major that all the details for the service are well in hand, and we can proceed as necessary."

"I'll do that, Mr. Harrington."

Lucy went to find her bonnet and pelisse and joined Mr. Fairfax at the front door. Just as they were about to leave, Dorothea Chingford came down the stairs. Her fair hair was hanging down her back, and her black gown was wrongly fastened at the neck. The vacant expression on her face had Lucy starting toward her.

"Dorothea?"

Mr. Fairfax bowed. "Miss Dorothea."

She stumbled down the last step and came to a stop in front of him.

"Is she still at Kurland Hall?"

"I'm not sure who you are referring to—"

"Mrs. Fairfax."

Mr. Fairfax shot a bewildered look at Lucy over the top of Dorothea's head. "Yes, she is still in residence. Do you wish to speak to her?"

Dorothea shrank back. "No. She probably wouldn't wish to see me again."

"I know she was disappointed when you weren't present when we visited. She wanted to offer you her condolences in person, Miss Dorothea." He paused. "Are you feeling quite well? You *are* very pale."

Dorothea turned to Lucy. "Mrs. Fairfax came here? Why didn't you *tell* me?"

Lucy moved between Dorothea and Mr. Fairfax. "I believe you were asleep at the time. Your sister did speak to Mrs. Fairfax on your family's behalf."

"Yes. That's correct," Mr. Fairfax agreed.

"Mrs. Fairfax should leave Kurland St. Mary."

There was a rising note of hysteria in Dorothea's voice, which made Lucy cup her elbow. "Please don't distress yourself. I'm sure Mrs. Fairfax will be returning home right after your mother's funeral."

Dorothea wrenched her arm free. "She should leave now!" Turning, she ran back up the stairs and slammed her bedroom door.

Lucy winced. "I do beg your pardon, Mr. Fairfax. Dorothea has been behaving rather strangely since her mother's death."

"It is of no matter. She is very young and is obviously distraught by what has happened."

"That is very forgiving of you, sir."

He offered her his arm, and they set off down the drive together. It was a dreary gray day, but at least there was no rain, which was a blessing.

"How is Miss Penelope Chingford this morning?" Mr. Fairfax asked.

"She is busy sorting through her mother's possessions and deciding who to invite to the funeral. Mrs. Chingford had a wide circle of acquaintances." Lucy gave him a sideways glance. "In fact, Mr. Fairfax, we wondered if Mrs. Fairfax could tell us the name of their mutual friend so that we could inform her of the funeral."

"Mutual friend?" Mr. Fairfax continued to

walk, his expression puzzled. "I wasn't aware that my father's wife and Mrs. Chingford knew each other well enough to *have* a mutual acquaintance."

"There was some suggestion of them sharing a nursemaid."

"I suppose it's possible, but I can't say Mrs. Fairfax mentioned anything specifically to me."

They turned out of the rectory drive and headed for the gate leading to Kurland Hall.

"One thing I did notice . . ." He stopped speaking and turned to Lucy. "It probably isn't worth mentioning now that the poor lady has died, but if you remember after the wedding, when I escorted Mrs. Fairfax upstairs . . ."

"Yes?" Lucy said encouragingly.

"Well, Mrs. Fairfax was extremely angry about something Mrs. Chingford had said to her." He sighed. "I don't know exactly what it was, but I've never seen her in such a rage."

"I find it hard to imagine Mrs. Fairfax becoming agitated, but Mrs. Chingford did seem to have that effect on the mildest mannered of people."

"Yes. She attempted to sympathize with me about my bastard state," Mr. Fairfax said dryly. "And how difficult it must be for me to be a social pariah."

"Oh dear," Lucy murmured. "I dread to think what she said to Major Kurland."

"I was close enough to hear the end of that exchange. She commiserated with him for being a reclusive cripple whom no woman in her right mind would ever choose to marry."

"Did he give her a terrible set down?"

"No. He smiled and changed the subject."

Lucy shook her head as they approached one of the side doors to the hall.

"Do you know why Major Kurland doesn't ride, Miss Harrington?"

Lucy paused to look up into Mr. Fairfax's face. "You should probably ask him that question."

"You are right. I should. I did wonder if his injuries meant that he could never ride again." He hesitated. "It's just that I've noticed he doesn't like to go anywhere near a horse if he can help it."

"Riding would certainly still be very difficult for him, Mr. Fairfax," Lucy said carefully. "His whole left leg was crushed under the weight of his horse at Waterloo, and he was very lucky to keep the limb. It is perhaps understandable that he is reluctant to even attempt to ride again."

"So I should imagine." Mr. Fairfax bowed. "He is a brave man and more than deserved his elevation into the peerage."

"He blames me for that."

Mr. Fairfax grinned. "So he told me. It is a shame that you cannot take on the duties of secretary for the major, Miss Harrington. I believe we would make a formidable team."

She smiled back at him. "Then you have decided to stay here and not follow Mrs. Fairfax back to your old home?"

He glanced around the deserted corridor and lowered his voice. "I am not convinced Mrs. Fairfax has recovered sufficiently from her grief to make good decisions about the estate. I suspect if I returned, she would constantly undermine my authority or use me as a scapegoat if things went wrong."

"Then you should definitely stay here," Lucy said firmly. "Major Kurland may be many things, but he would never lie to you or be underhand."

"I appreciate that, Miss Harrington." He cleared his throat. "After years of dealing with Mrs. Fairfax's suspicious nature and being denied the opportunity to get to know my young half brother, I—" He stopped speaking. "I do beg your pardon. There is something about you, Miss Harrington, that makes it all too easy for a man to confide in you."

Lucy tried not to blush. "Mrs. Fairfax does seem to be driven by her emotions."

"You have no idea, Miss Harrington. She convinced my father that I was out to steal the estate from my half brother, and nothing I could say to him made any difference." He sighed. "We were estranged at his death, and I could see there was no future for me at my only home."

"Then one wonders why Mrs. Fairfax came after you."

Mr. Fairfax started walking again. "I have wondered about that myself. It is almost as if she has no memory of how badly she treated me before."

"Some people find it impossible to accept that they are in the wrong, and they pretend that nothing happened. A man in our village ran off to London with his wife's best friend. After a week or so, the woman decided she had made a mistake, abandoned her lover, and returned to the village. She even had the nerve to try to take up her old friendship with his abandoned wife." Lucy shook her head. "It didn't take her long to realize that people here have very long memories and her chances of being forgotten or forgiven were relatively small."

Mr. Fairfax chuckled appreciatively. "Ah, the perils and joys of village life." He paused at the door to the dining room. "I believe Major Kurland is in here."

Robert looked up from his seat at the head of the breakfast table to see Thomas and Miss Harrington framed in the doorway. Judging from Miss Harrington's approving smile, they appeared to be having a mutually agreeable conversation. It belatedly occurred to him that they would suit each other very well.

He stood and bowed. "Good morning, Miss Harrington."

"Major Kurland." She curtsied. "Are you still at breakfast? I can wait in your study, if you prefer it."

"Please come and join us." He pulled out the chair to his left. "I'm sure all my guests would appreciate any new information on the welfare of Miss Chingford and her sister."

Miss Stanford almost choked on her toast, and Mrs. Green helpfully patted her on the back. "Yes, how are the two young ladies doing?"

Miss Harrington took the seat Robert offered her, and Thomas sat at the foot of the table, across from Mrs. Fairfax, who was nibbling halfheartedly at a piece of toast.

"Miss Chingford is coping remarkably well. Dorothea is still very upset."

Mrs. Green nodded. "She seemed to be at odds with her mother before she died. It is always a shock when one realizes it is too late to make amends or apologize."

Robert knew that all too well. He'd lost many friends in battle, men he'd joked with and shared billets with, dead by the end of the same day, never to return. It hadn't made him walk around, telling everyone he *loved* them, but he'd felt their loss all the same.

Miss Harrington accepted a cup of coffee and leaned toward him. "Was there something in particular you wanted to speak to me about, Major?"

"Yes. I decided it would be a good idea if you were present when Foley mentioned the locket to my guests. You are far better at reading faces than I will ever be."

"I developed that ability when dealing with my younger siblings." Miss Harrington sipped her coffee. "Dorothea Chingford accosted poor Mr. Fairfax at the rectory and insisted that Mrs. Fairfax should leave Kurland St. Mary immediately."

"Why would she do that?"

"I think she knows more about this matter than she has admitted so far. I intend to question her closely when I return home."

"Perhaps Mrs. Fairfax saw Dorothea push her mother down the stairs."

"It's possible." Miss Harrington sighed. "I suppose the locket could be Dorothea's. Mayhap she has a secret lover who gave it to her as a gift. Although, according to her mother, she was in love with Mr. Stanford."

"What is it about Andrew that attracts such feminine adoration?"

She raised an eyebrow. "It's quite simple. He is a pleasant, well-mannered, and charming gentleman."

"Unlike me, you mean."

"You have the ability to be all those things, Major, but you don't often choose to do so."

Robert snorted. "When I *attempt* those things, Miss Harrington, you look at me as if I have magically become a toad."

Her color heightened. "Perhaps I have become too used to your . . . uncivil behavior."

"And it is far easier to dislike me and keep me at bay if you continue to provoke me into behaving that way."

"I do *not* dislike you. I—" She met his gaze. "This is an extremely improper conversation to be having at the breakfast table."

"Then perhaps we should pursue it when we are more at liberty to discuss such issues privately." Robert glanced at the door, where Foley had appeared. "I think we are about to be interrupted, anyway."

Foley came over to stand beside Robert's chair and, after a nod from his employer, loudly cleared his throat. "Good morning to you all." He bowed very slowly and held up the locket Robert had given to him. "One of the maids found this in the laundry. Do any of you recognize it?"

No one said anything, and after a long pause, Robert took the locket from Foley. "If any of you realize it is your property, please come and find me, and I will return it to you immediately." He put the locket in his waistcoat pocket. "Now, shall we discuss our plan to visit Saffron Walden this afternoon? I understand the weather is expected to stay sunny."

He turned back to Miss Harrington, who appeared rather troubled. "Will you extend the invitation to the Chingford ladies and your sister?"

"I will do that, Major. Will you make sure Mrs. Fairfax comes?"

"I'll do my best. Do you wish to speak to her? Maybe I should attempt that. She seems rather afraid of you."

"And she will wrap *you* around her little finger."

"One can't help but feel sorry for her being widowed so young and left with all those responsibilities."

Miss Harrington gave a rather inelegant snort. "Thomas says she refused his help with the estate and made him leave."

"*Thomas* said? You are on very familiar terms with my land agent, Miss Harrington."

"You call him Thomas."

"Because I am his employer." Robert rose from his chair and pushed away from the table. "Speaking of Thomas, I need to consult with him about my dairy herd."

"Please don't let me stop you."

He paused to glare at her. "If you're quite certain you don't have need of his services first." She tightened her lips in a way that made him want to shake her. "No? Then I'll be on my way. I do hope to see you this afternoon for our excursion, but if you are too busy, I will take it upon myself to speak to Mrs. Fairfax."

"I'll be there, Major Kurland."

He bowed. "I look forward to it."

Infuriating. The harder he tried to be nice to her, the more she goaded him into returning to his irascible self. It was remarkably frustrating. She behaved completely differently with his land agent. Thomas stood as Robert reached the end of the table.

"Do you wish to discuss the dairy herd now, sir?"

"Indeed I do." Robert gestured for Thomas to precede him out of the door. He'd had quite enough of trying to understand Miss Harrington for one morning. At least with his herd of cows, he was on steady and knowledgeable ground.

Lucy stomped back down the drive of Kurland Hall, muttering to herself about the inconsistencies of men, and of Major Kurland in particular. He'd implied that she was making him behave in an ungentlemanly like manner, which was ridiculous! She had nursed him back to health, suffered through his temper and biting wit, and knew him better than anyone. By attempting to be *pleasant,* he only confused her.

And why was he even attempting it? What did he hope to gain?

If she could just find out whether anything untoward had happened to Mrs. Chingford, she would no longer need to be in Major Kurland's company so much. That would probably be for the best.

She reached the rectory and went in through the kitchen, where Mrs. Fielding was actually singing as she went about her work. She even managed to smile at Lucy, which was unheard of. Lucy sighed and trudged up the back stairs. It would've been far easier if the cook had simply bashed Mrs. Chingford over the head with one of her cast-iron pans. If someone had wanted Mrs. Chingford dead, they had found a very clever way of achieving it. Even the locket in Mrs. Chingford's fingers could be explained away if the person who pushed her down the stairs had come forward to confess.

Lucy paused on the top step. But no one had come forward, so the opportunity to confess to pushing Mrs. Chingford accidentally had not been taken. Either she'd fallen herself, which was unlikely because of the locket, or someone had deliberately pushed her and didn't want anyone else to know about it.

Betty came clomping up the stairs, and Lucy beckoned to her.

"Yes, miss?"

"Will you please ask Miss Chingford if she wishes to accompany me and some of Major Kurland's guests on an excursion to Saffron Walden?"

"I'll go and ask her right now, miss."

"Betty, wait one second." Lucy lowered her voice. "Has Mrs. Fielding intimated that she is planning on leaving the rectory?"

"Not that I know of, Miss Harrington, although she *was* thinking about accepting that offer from the butcher when Mrs. Chingford—may her soul rest in peace—was alive and was threatening to marry the rector."

"What offer from the butcher?"

Betty giggled. "Marriage, of course. Why do you think we've been getting such lovely pieces of meat?"

Lucy could only nod and wait as Betty knocked softly on Penelope's door. The meat *had* been remarkably good recently. . . . Was it possible that Mrs. Chingford had found out that Mrs. Fielding was carrying on with the butcher, and had threatened to reveal all to her potential bridegroom? It sounded all too likely. Would Mrs. Fielding have fought to retain her place at the rectory and in the rector's bed?

When she next went up to Kurland Hall, she would question the kitchen staff about the whereabouts of Mrs. Fielding during her time in the kitchens on the wedding day. Once the main meal had been served, there would have been an opportunity for the cook to slip away and maybe confront Mrs. Chingford.

A slight sound from one of the guest bedchambers made Lucy look up. Someone was in Mrs. Chingford's bedroom. Holding her breath, Lucy tiptoed along the landing until she was outside the relevant door. It was slightly ajar, so she pushed it with a fingertip until it quietly swung open enough to reveal a figure rifling through the contents of the desk.

A small fire burned in the grate and was rapidly consuming the balled-up paper being thrown at it. Lucy came in and closed the door behind her.

"Dorothea, what are you doing?"

"You frightened me!" Dorothea gasped and spun around, an armful of letters crushed to her chest.

"What are you *doing?*"

Dorothea's face went red. "Nothing that concerns you, Miss Harrington."

"You and your sister are guests in my father's house. I have a perfect right to ask you what you are about." Lucy paused. "Do you wish me to fetch your sister or the rector?"

"Please don't!"

"Then tell me what you are looking for." Lucy advanced on the girl. "Does it have something to do with your mother's death?"

"Of course it does!"

"Are you looking for evidence?"

"Evidence of what?"

Lucy raised her eyebrows. "You tell me. You were the last person to see your mother alive. What *happened*, Dorothea?"

"My mother liked to tell lies and spread untruths."

"So I've been told." Lucy sat on the corner of the bed and tried to look as unthreatening as possible. "She's dead now, so who exactly are you trying to protect?"

"People whose reputations should not be in shatters because of *her*."

"People like Mrs. Fairfax?"

Dorothea looked at Lucy as if she was an idiot. "No!" She shivered. "Although she should leave Kurland St. Mary as fast as she can."

"Why?"

"Because my mother loved to meddle in other people's lives. I'm going to destroy her correspondence so that no one will be able to read her untruths anymore."

Lucy fixed Dorothea with her most quelling stare. "You will not burn another thing. Your sister needs to make sure that all your mother's acquaintances are notified of her death. If you destroy those letters, she will not be able to perform this task."

Dorothea made no effort to put the letters down, and Lucy stood up.

"Don't be ridiculous, Dorothea. There is nothing here that can harm anyone now."

Tears shone in Dorothea's blue eyes as Lucy advanced toward her. "What if I promise to burn everything that your sister doesn't want to keep after the funeral? Would you trust me to do that?" Lucy offered. She didn't want Dorothea destroying anything more.

"I suppose so." Dorothea didn't look convinced, but as Lucy had suspected, she was too young to have acquired the necessary will to disobey an older woman in a position of authority.

Dorothea let go of the now crumpled letters and placed them back on the desk.

"Thank you," Lucy said. "You have made a very wise decision. I will destroy everything as soon as your sister is done with it." She moved past Dorothea and spent a few moments straightening out the papers and returning them to Mrs. Chingford's traveling writing case

"Please don't tell Penelope about this."

"I won't say a word."

Dorothea took out a handkerchief and wiped her eyes before turning to the door.

"Why do you think Mrs. Fairfax should leave before the funeral?" Lucy asked.

"Because she is in danger."

"From whom?"

"Whom do you think?" Dorothea's sneer was

unmistakable as she slammed out of the room, rattling the door on its hinges.

"I don't know. I do wish I understood what was going on." Lucy spoke to the empty room. Was Dorothea worried that her dead mother had stirred up trouble for Mrs. Fairfax? Or was it far simpler, and Dorothea wanted the widow out of the way for her own reasons? Had Mrs. Fairfax witnessed the argument between mother and daughter and perhaps seen the fateful push? That would make the most sense.

Lucy glanced at the clock and then sat down at the desk to go through Mrs. Chingford's remaining correspondence more carefully. She had at least half an hour before she was due to leave on her outing with Major Kurland and his guests. She would certainly make the most of it.

Chapter 8

Were you looking for something earlier, sir?"

Robert looked up as his valet, Silas Smith, appeared in the doorway with a jug of hot water and placed it beside the shaving stand.

"Like what?"

"I'm not sure." Silas put a warm folded towel beside the basin. "Everything on your dressing table and desk was in a muddle, as if you'd been searching for something."

Robert stopped unbuttoning his waistcoat. "I haven't been up here since before breakfast."

"Then I wonder who it was." Silas frowned. "I suppose it could've been Mr. Foley or one of the new maids, but you'd think they'd come and ask me first."

"You would indeed."

Robert felt inside his waistcoat pocket and produced the broken locket Miss Harrington had given him. He weighed it in his palm. Had someone been after the locket? On a normal day he would probably change into riding dress after breakfast in preparation for going out to manage the estate. This morning he had been closeted with Thomas and then dealt with his farm manager and balanced his accounting books.

There had been no need for him to change, especially as he'd have to do it all over again before the afternoon excursion.

"Silas."

"Yes, Major?"

"Make sure you lock my door if I'm not in here, will you?"

"Do you think we have a thief, sir?"

"I'm not sure. You might care to check and see if anything has been taken."

"I'll do that immediately." Silas hesitated. "Do you want me to inform Mr. Foley?"

"Good God, no. Don't tell him, or else he'll set everyone into a flutter."

He just caught Silas's grin before he smothered it. "As you wish, Major."

After he'd washed and donned buckskin breeches, tall boots, and a wool coat suitable for a typical, cloudy English spring day, Robert picked up his caped driving coat and headed down the stairs. If he were to make a guess, he'd have to assume that someone wanted that locket back.

The trouble was, it could be anyone. His rooms weren't guarded or locked, and there were numerous staircases and passages for someone to traverse to avoid detection by him or the household staff. What it did suggest was that the locket was important. He'd tucked it back in his waistcoat pocket for safety. If it came down to it, he was quite prepared to use it to lure the owner out of hiding.

He looked down from the top of the stairs to ascertain who awaited him in the hall below. Mrs. Fairfax was present with Thomas, as were Mrs. Green and Miss Stanford. Most of his other guests had declined his invitation or were getting ready to leave Kurland Hall. Mrs. Chingford's funeral was less than two weeks away, and then all opportunities to discover if she had been deliberately killed would be at an end.

Robert pulled on his gloves and came carefully down the stairs, using his cane. If nothing came of Miss Harrington's attempt to speak to Mrs. Fairfax, he would lay his own plans to catch a murderer, using the locket as bait. It was time to resolve this matter and move on. If he could do it without placing Miss Harrington in danger, he would be greatly relieved.

Two carriages arrived on the circular drive in front of the rectory, and Lucy shepherded her charges out of the house. George, the curate, helped Miss Chingford into the second carriage, where Miss Stanford and Mrs. Green were already seated. Lucy found herself sitting with Major Kurland and the Fairfaxes, which suited her purpose admirably.

The widow was swathed in black veils and, despite Lucy's best efforts to engage her in conversation, hardly spoke above a whisper during the journey. Major Kurland and Mr. Fairfax conferred about farming matters involving the expansion of the dairy herd, which was hardly something Lucy could contribute to, so she spent most of the time looking out the window at the tall hedges and patchwork fields.

When they arrived in Saffron Walden, it was market day and the carriages were forced to drop their respective passengers at the Sun Inn, amongst a gaggle of visitors and farmers from the surrounding villages. Major Kurland invited everyone inside to partake of a luncheon in the private parlor he had reserved for the duration of the visit.

Lucy looked up at him as he escorted her through the door. "What an excellent plan to reserve a parlor."

"It was Thomas's idea. He is very efficient."

"Thank goodness for that." Lucy entered the warm low-beamed room and untied the ribbons of her bonnet. "I have discovered more information from Mrs. Chingford's correspondence."

"About what?"

"The woman she wrote to is definitely called Madge." She hesitated. "The only thing is that there appear to be three Madges she wrote to regularly." She handed him a scrap of paper on which she'd copied the names and addresses.

The major snorted as he folded it up and put

it in his waistcoat pocket. "Typical. What do you propose to do about them?"

"I intend to write to all three, but two of them live within twenty or so miles of Kurland St. Mary. It might be worth paying them a visit to inform them of Mrs. Chingford's demise."

"That's an excellent idea. We can discuss it when we return to Kurland Hall."

The rest of the party came into the parlor, and Lucy excused herself from the major. Mrs. Fairfax lifted her veil and sank into a chair by the fire. Lucy immediately went over to her and took the seat opposite.

"May I fetch you some refreshment, ma'am?"

The widow jumped as if Lucy had stabbed her. "Oh! No thank you, Miss Harrington. I couldn't eat a thing."

"A warm drink, then, perhaps? You must attempt to keep your strength up, Mrs. Fairfax. Think of your little boy and the stresses of your journey home."

Mrs. Fairfax shuddered as Lucy continued speaking. "Have you heard how your son is faring in your absence? He is probably missing you terribly. Having a good nurse must make all the difference when you leave a child at home." She paused. "I understand that the nurse you employ used to be with Mrs. Chingford. What an interesting coincidence."

"Who told you that?" Mrs. Fairfax whispered. "It isn't true."

"I believe Mrs. Chingford mentioned it." Lucy pretended to frown. "But perhaps I was mistaken."

"*She* was mistaken."

"If you say so, ma'am." Lucy rose to her feet. "I assumed that's what you and Mrs. Chingford were arguing about at the wedding. She could be remarkably persistent when she wanted to make her point."

"We were not arguing! I barely spoke to the woman." The widow's voice rose on each word and became tinged with hysteria. "The only people I remember *arguing* with Mrs. Chingford were Miss Stanford and her own daughter Dorothea, who was most upset about her impending marriage to your father."

"Miss Harrington?"

Lucy turned around to find Major Kurland and Mr. Fairfax at her side. The major was frowning, and Mr. Fairfax looked rather bemused. She accepted the major's hand to rise and brushed down her pelisse.

"I was just asking Mrs. Fairfax if she wanted some refreshment. You did say that you had ordered a luncheon for us, didn't you, Major?"

"Indeed I did."

He took her elbow in a firm grip, and she was

steered away from Mrs. Fairfax to the other side of the room.

"What were you thinking, Miss Harrington?" Major Kurland demanded. "It looked as if you were bullying the poor woman. I thought you intended to be discreet."

"I asked her only if she shared a nurse with Mrs. Chingford. Her overwrought reaction to my question was hardly to be expected."

"She is a recent widow!" He sighed. "I *told* you to let me deal with her."

"Because you are so good with the delicate sensibilities of widows?"

"I am apparently better at it than you are. At least I've never made her cry."

Lucy glanced over her shoulder, where Mrs. Fairfax was ostentatiously dabbing at her eyes with a black lace handkerchief.

"She cries at everything. I didn't get the opportunity to ask her if she'd seen Dorothea near her mother, although I suppose she intimated that was the case by suggesting Miss Stanford and Dorothea had pursued Mrs. Chingford and were continuing their arguments with her. Although, how could she know that if she wasn't there herself?" Lucy looked up at Major Kurland. "Perhaps I should let you talk to her."

"Perhaps you should." He turned to the spread of food on the table and loaded a plate with a few small, tempting morsels. "I'll try to coax her out of her sullens."

Lucy surveyed the food, and her stomach grumbled. She helped herself to a large slice of mutton pie and some pickled eggs and retired to sit beside Miss Stanford, who was hardly eating anything at all.

"Miss Harrington."

"Yes, Miss Stanford?"

"I overheard your conversation with Mrs. Fairfax."

Inwardly Lucy winced. "I suspect everyone did."

"She did see me."

Lucy stopped eating to stare at her companion. "I beg your pardon?"

"At the wedding. I went up the main staircase to help Sophia, and then I doubled back to see if I could find Mrs. Chingford." She swallowed hard. "I'm not proud of that, but I was so consumed with anger over her cavalier attitude to my brother's future career that I could hardly think."

"I understand that Mrs. Chingford also suggested that your fiancé was not all that he seemed."

"That's correct. She had designs on him herself and resented me horribly for winning his heart. Unfortunately, her fury at our engagement led her to start questioning his reputation."

"I believe she suggested he was a confirmed gambler." Lucy paused. "That must have been very difficult for you."

"He . . . he has changed. I know that every woman says that about the man she loves, but he truly has grown up and has learned to face his responsibilities. I fear that if his reputation is called into question again, he might stop trying." Miss Stanford drew an unsteady breath. "I couldn't bear to see him lose hope again."

Mrs. Green came to sit on the other side of Miss Stanford, and Lucy left them to talk as she considered what she had learned from her conversations. Mrs. Fairfax was impossible to speak with, and Miss Stanford continued to suggest that her emotions had led her toward making a fatal mistake. But would she ever confess? She was so consumed with protecting her brother's and her fiancé's reputations that it was highly unlikely that she would want to mire her own.

Lucy withdrew her shopping list from her reticule and consulted it. She had a horrible suspicion that Mrs. Fairfax wouldn't seek her company for the remainder of the day, which at least left her free to pursue her own ne .

Miss Stanford, Mrs. Green, and Penelope were more than willing to accompany her around the shops and the market in the square. George offered to guide them through St. Mary's Church which, he proudly proclaimed, was the largest church in the county of Essex.

Mr. Fairfax looked over at Major Kurland, his smile resigned. "I think Mrs. Fairfax would prefer to stroll quietly down by the river. We will meet you in the church or back here at the inn, ready for our return journey." He hesitated. "If that is acceptable to you, sir?"

The major inclined his head. "Indeed. I am more than happy to escort the rest of the ladies through town." Lucy raised an eyebrow at that, but he ignored her. "Perhaps we should agree to meet back here at three for the trip home."

"Yes, Major."

Lucy put her plate back on the table and strolled over to Major Kurland with a sympathetic smile.

"What, Miss Harrington?"

"It seems that neither of us will get the opportunity to converse with the widow."

He sighed. "She was remarkably resistant to my charms. I learned nothing except that she can cry quite beautifully without ruining her complexion."

"Then she is very lucky, indeed. As you know, it is a skill I do not possess." Lucy gathered up her possessions, put her bonnet back on, and produced her list. "The first place I simply must visit is Prynne's Haberdashery."

Major Kurland groaned and offered her his arm. "I can't wait."

With the addition of all the shopping, the carriage was packed to the gunnels for the return journey. Lucy's feet rested on numerous bulky packages, and several more were stashed under the seat. Major Kurland seemed resigned to being squashed into his corner, and Mr. Fairfax and the widow were separated by a large basket containing more precious foodstuffs on the seat between them.

Lucy hid a yawn behind her gloved hand as she watched the sun set over the green fields. They might not have learned much about Mrs. Chingford's death, but it had been a most satisfying day in other ways. She noticed Major Kurland was surreptitiously rubbing his left knee, and she had a moment of compunction for dragging him around every single shop in Saffron Walden.

She slid the largest brown paper parcel toward him with the side of her foot. "Rest your heel on this, Major. It is just skeins of darning wool, so you cannot damage anything."

"Thank you."

The fact that he didn't argue made her realize he must truly be in pain. She knew better than to mention it. At least the drive was almost over. Her eyes half closed, and she found herself leaning toward the comfort of the major's broad shoulder. Mrs. Fairfax also appeared to be sleeping. With a resigned shrug, Mr. Fairfax moved the basket out of the way and allowed the widow to curl up against his side.

Lucy wished that Major Kurland would do the same for her. . . . She'd already experienced the felicity of being pressed against his chest once before, and she hadn't disliked it at all. Lucy sat bolt upright, her hands twisted in her lap.

"Miss Harrington?" Major Kurland murmured. "Are you quite well?"

As she turned to answer, several things happened at once, and she was thrown toward him while the carriage appeared to lurch and tip and finally fall onto one side. For the second time in her life, Lucy found herself in physical contact with Major Kurland. He'd wrapped his arms around her and protected her from the fall. Her face was buried in the curve of his neck, and she breathed in his particular comforting scent.

"Are you all right, Miss Harrington?"

His voice was close to her ear. She struggled to right herself until he stopped her.

"Wait. Your skirts are tangled with my legs."

He sounded far too calm for her liking. Outside she could hear shouting and the sounds of distressed horses. The major's back was now against the door of the carriage, and she was sprawled most inelegantly on top of him. Where were Mr. Fairfax and his companion?

"What happened?" she managed to ask.

139

"I'm not sure. The carriage is on its side. We are currently underneath all the parcels and Mr. Fairfax, who is attempting to open the door."

She tried to see past the wicker basket and caught sight of a booted foot wedged against the seat and the drab black of the widow's pelisse dangling over her head.

"I have it open now, sir. I'll get Mrs. Fairfax out and come back for you." Mr. Fairfax sounded almost as calm as the major.

Lucy tried to adjust her position, but there was nowhere for her to move. The major's breath hissed out as her knee connected with something.

"Good Lord, Miss Harrington. Be *careful*."

Having brothers, she blushed scarlet as she realized exactly what she had done. "I was just trying to move away from your wounded leg."

"Then stop it." He spoke through his teeth. "Thomas will be back in a moment, and he will get us both out of here."

"I've got you, Miss Harrington." A pair of strong hands locked around her waist, and she was manhandled upward and out into the fresh air.

"Thank you," she gasped to the coachman, who had aided her escape. "Be very careful with the major. Watch his left leg."

"I will, Miss Harrington. Don't you worry."

Lucy sank down onto the grass verge on the side of the road. There was no sign of the other carriage, which had been ahead of them. Mr. Fairfax was kneeling by the widow, patting her hand and calling her name. The carriage was indeed on its side, and the horses were still attached to it and fighting the tangled reins.

She staggered to her feet and went toward the lead horse.

"Don't go anywhere near that animal, Miss Harrington!"

Major Kurland's shout came from just behind her. He was now standing next to his coachman, his face a mask of pain, his intense gaze fixed on the out-of-control horse.

"Someone has to calm them down, or they will injure themselves." Lucy held out her hand and took another step toward the horse, who snapped his teeth at her. His eyes were rolling back in his head, and flecks of foam were gathering on his muzzle. "It's all right. Let me help you."

"Devil take it, woman! Wait for the coachman!"

"He is attending to the other horse." She tried to keep her tone reasonable, even as the horse kicked out at her.

"Oh, God . . . ," she heard Major Kurland mutter, and then he was limping toward her, his gaze fixed on the horse. "Let me do this."

"But—"

"Get out of the way." He glared down at her. "I cannot stand back like a coward and watch you being trampled to death."

141

"I won't—"

He shouldered past her and in one quick motion had his hand locked on the horse's bridle, turned its head away from the other panicked horse, and whispered in its ear.

"I'll cut the traces, sir, if you can just hold Jupiter still," the coachman called out.

"I can do that."

The horse calmed down as Major Kurland continued to talk to it, his voice soft, his hands running over the horse, checking for injuries and reassuring the beast at the same time.

"I've got him, sir." The coachman took hold of the horse and attached a lead rein. "I'll walk them to make sure they aren't badly injured, and then I'll tie them up under that tree."

"Thank you, Coleman."

Major Kurland let go of the horse with a final pat and then turned away. His face was ashen, and he stumbled to the side of the road.

"Major Kurland—"

"Not now, Miss Harrington."

Before she could even frame a reply, he doubled over, turned to the ditch, that ran alongside the road and was violently sick.

Lucy walked away to give him some privacy. She could only imagine what confronting a terrified, rearing horse had done to him. But he hadn't faltered. He'd conquered his fears to protect the horse from further injury. And to keep her safe . . . Perhaps that was a little far-fetched, but he'd certainly not wanted her to be in danger.

She glanced over at Mrs. Fairfax, who was now sitting up and being supported by Mr. Fairfax.

"Is everything all right, Miss Harrington?" he called out to her. "I apologize for not being more helpful, but . . ." He looked down at the widow, who was clinging to him like bindweed.

"All is well, Mr. Fairfax."

She turned back toward where she'd left the major, and then had to sit down, as her legs were shaking so badly. She wrapped her arms around her knees in a most unladylike manner as her teeth started to chatter. For some reason, she suddenly had an inexplicable desire to weep.

Coleman, the coachman, came over to her. "Major Kurland said to tell you to sit tight. I'm going to ride to the next village and get some help. It's not far. We'll have you home before midnight."

"Is he all right?" Lucy asked.

"The major?" Coleman smiled. "He's feeling a lot better now that he's cast up his accounts."

She met his gaze, realizing that he knew more about Major Kurland's aversion to horses than perhaps his employer suspected.

"He'll be fine, miss." He winked at her. "And back on a horse soon, I should think."

"I hope so."

She waited for a few more minutes, until the

143

wave of dizziness passed and she felt more the thing, and then marched back toward the wreck of the carriage.

"Miss Harrington, what are you doing?"

Major Kurland sat on the ground, his back against the tree where the horses were tethered, his legs stretched out in front of him. She knew from the set of his jaw that he was in considerable pain.

"I'm just going to retrieve our belongings from the carriage, sir. There is no need for you to get up."

His mouth twisted up at one corner. "I don't think I could even if I wanted to." He hesitated. "Be careful."

"I will, Major."

She had managed to retrieve his walking stick and most of her parcels before Coleman arrived back with another carriage. Mr. Fairfax carried Mrs. Fairfax into the carriage. Lucy went next, determined not to fuss Major Kurland, who needed Coleman's help to ascend. She also succeeded in not lecturing him about what he should do to ease his leg when he got home, which, considering the state of her nerves, was extremely forbearing of her.

Nobody spoke for the remainder of the journey, and for once Lucy was glad for the silence and reluctant to fill it. When they reached the rectory, she stepped down and went inside with a thankful heart, to be met with a chorus of questions about the lateness of her arrival.

By the time she had reassured them that no one had been injured, she was so tired she could barely climb the stairs to her bedchamber. As she undressed, she noticed the beginnings of a myriad of bruises and lacerations on her skin. If Major Kurland hadn't held on to her, she suspected she would look much worse. She could only hope that his leg hadn't been damaged when she'd collapsed on top of him. . . . She was certainly no featherweight. It was her last coherent thought as sleep finally claimed her.

Chapter 9

M ajor Kurland!"

Robert opened one eye and then closed it again. It was far too early for him to get out of bed—if he could get out. The pain in his left leg had been excruciating the evening before, and he'd almost given in to Foley's urging to take some laudanum. He had substituted three large glasses of brandy and now had a headache to accompany the nagging pain in his thigh.

"Major *Kurland!*"

"What the devil is it?" he demanded, aware that Silas and Foley were both beside his bed and that sunlight streamed in through the opened curtains. He managed to sit up and glare properly at them. "What in God's name demands my attention at this hour of the morning?"

Foley wrung his hands together. "It's Mrs. Fairfax, sir." He hesitated. "She's dead."

"What?"

"Ruth took her in some morning tea and discovered her lying fully dressed on top of the bedcovers. Cold and dead, sir. *Dead!*"

Robert forced himself to get out of bed, his breath hitching as his feet hit the wooden floorboards. Silas helped him into his banyan and offered him his cane.

"Who else knows about this?"

"Ruth came straight to me, Major, and I told her to remain in the butler's pantry until I returned." Foley proffered a key. "I also locked Mrs. Fairfax's door."

"Good work, Foley." Robert looked at Silas. "I'll have to get fully dressed. I can't be seen going into a widow's bedchamber in my night-shirt and banyan."

"Yes, sir." Silas was already turning toward his clothes chest. "I'll be as quick as I can."

Within a quarter of an hour, Robert was limping down the corridor toward Mrs. Fairfax's bedroom. All was quiet within the house, and he was grateful that no one would either witness his shambling gait or wonder where he was going. He let himself into the bedchamber and leaned back against the door to catch his breath and survey the room. As Foley had reported, Mrs. Fairfax was fully dressed, her black veil drawn down over her face, her hands twisted together on her chest. Robert was reminded of one of the medieval effigies on his ancestors' tombs in Kurland St. Mary Church.

Holding his cane firmly in one hand, he took three halting steps to the side of the bed and looked more closely. He'd seen more than his fair share of dead bodies in his military career, and he sensed no life left in Mrs. Fairfax. She looked as if she was sleeping. Reaching out a gentle finger, he raised her veil and touched her cheek. She was quite cold, and her body was already rigid.

By the side of the bed was a large black bottle. Robert picked it up and sniffed the contents, recoiling from the sickly scent of laudanum. He was just about to put the bottle down when he noticed there was a folded sheet of paper propped up against a worn copy of the Bible. It was addressed to Thomas.

With unsteady fingers, he picked up the letter before uttering a quiet oath. He needed to speak to Thomas and the occupants of the rectory immediately. He left the room and returned to his bedchamber, where Foley and Silas awaited him.

"Do you know where Mr. Fairfax is, Foley?"

"He breakfasted early, and I believe he said he intended to look in on the home farm before going down to the rectory to see how Miss Harrington was faring after the accident."

"How long ago did he leave?"

"About two hours ago, sir."

Robert nodded. "Silas, I want you to go down to the rectory and fetch Mr. Fairfax for me."

"What shall I tell him, sir?"

"That I need him to return immediately." Robert hesitated. "If Miss Harrington is available, ask her to accompany Mr. Fairfax."

"Yes, sir."

"Foley, I want you to send someone to fetch Dr. Fletcher."

"Not Dr. Baker, sir?"

"No. I don't want the whole village knowing what's going on." Robert sat down on the side of the bed, as his left knee threatened to give out. "I'll be in my study."

Foley paused on his way to the door. "Do you want me to get James to give you a hand down the stairs, Major?"

Robert sighed. "Yes, devil take it. Send him up."

Lucy followed Mr. Fairfax in through the kitchen door, up the stairs, and into the corridor that ran to the front of Kurland Hall. He was walking rather quickly, and it was hard to keep up with him. She couldn't blame him for his haste. Major Kurland's abrupt summons had surprised them both and necessitated the borrowing of her father's gig to get them back to Kurland Hall with all speed.

"I hope Major Kurland is all right," Mr. Fairfax murmured as he finally paused to open a door for her. "He did take rather a beating in the coach yesterday."

Aware that she was the one who had landed squarely on top of the major, Lucy quashed a horrible feeling of guilt.

She opted for a positive tone. "If Major Kurland is well enough to issue orders, he's probably not in any real danger. It is when he

149

stops complaining that one really has to worry."

Mr. Fairfax had the beginnings of a black eye where, he'd explained, Mrs. Fairfax had inadvertently kicked him as she climbed out of the carriage. Lucy was bruised and battered and could hardly bear to think how much worse Major Kurland must be feeling.

They reached the main hall just as Foley admitted Dr. Fletcher, who paused to take off his hat and bow to Lucy.

"Good morning, Miss Harrington, Mr. Fairfax. What bee has gotten into the major's head now?"

Lucy lowered her voice. "He was in considerable pain after the carriage accident yesterday. In truth, the fact that he has called you here is significant in itself. He hates dealing with physicians, but he is obviously in need of your help."

"I know exactly how stubborn he is." Dr. Fletcher smiled. "You should have seen him in battle. I'll take it as a compliment that he called for me."

They followed Mr. Fairfax and Foley to Major Kurland's study and went in to find their host sitting behind his desk. He looked rather grim, and Lucy took an involuntary step back, bumping against Mr. Fairfax. The major didn't rise to greet her, but for once she didn't feel inclined to comment on his lack of manners.

"Good morning, Miss Harrington, Dr. Fletcher." Major Kurland inclined his head. "Thomas, I have some bad news for you."

Mr. Fairfax's face paled. "Is it my half brother? Don't tell me he is ill. Should I arrange to get Mrs. Fairfax home or—"

"It isn't your half brother." Major Kurland spoke gently, but in a firm, no-nonsense manner, which Lucy couldn't help but admire. "It's Mrs. Fairfax. I'm sorry to tell you that she is dead."

If it was possible, Mr. Fairfax went even whiter. "How . . . how can this be? She wasn't badly hurt yesterday! True, she swooned, but—"

"I don't think the carriage accident was a factor in her death, although Dr. Fletcher might have an opinion on the effect a blow to the head can have on a person."

"Did someone break in and murder her?" Mr. Fairfax came toward Major Kurland. "What in God's name *happened?*"

Major Kurland sighed. "There was an empty bottle of laudanum by her bedside and this note." Lucy pressed a hand to her mouth as the major drew out a letter and handed it to Mr. Fairfax. "It is addressed to you. I haven't read it."

Mr. Fairfax took the letter and broke the wax seal.

"To whom it may concern. I confess to pushing Mrs. Chingford down the stairs. It was an accident. I swear it. Please forgive me and pray

151

for my soul. I commend my son into Mr. Thomas Fairfax's care. Emily Fairfax."

Silence fell over the study as Mr. Fairfax shook his head, as if unwilling or unable to believe what he had just read.

"Is this Mrs. Fairfax's handwriting?" Major Kurland asked.

"Yes." Mr. Fairfax swallowed hard. "I didn't like her very much, but I never wished for this to happen." He crumpled the letter in his hand, and it fell to the floor.

"None of us thought you did." Major Kurland heaved himself to his feet. "I'd appreciate it if you could accompany us upstairs to view the body, Dr. Fletcher."

"You should stay here." Dr. Fletcher ran a critical eye over Major Kurland. "You are obviously in pain."

"And yet I am still coming with you. I have the only key." Major Kurland gestured at the door. "Shall we?"

Lucy took a moment to pick up the discarded letter. She smoothed it between her fingers, then read the confession silently to herself before folding up the paper and putting it in her pocket. She went up the stairs and allowed Mr. Fairfax and Dr. Fletcher to precede her into Mrs. Fairfax's bedchamber, where the widow lay in state on the bed. It took Major Kurland quite a while to join them. James, who steered him into a chair and then went to stand outside in the hallway, accompanied him.

Lucy took a slow circuit of the room, noting where everything was, and checked the interconnecting door that led into a former dressing room, which was locked. Mrs. Fairfax's possessions were neatly laid out, as if she had been about to pack them away. Had she considered leaving Kurland Hall, and had she eventually decided to kill herself instead? Lucy approached the bed and stared down at the pale features of the widow.

Dr. Fletcher sighed as he straightened up. "It looks like laudanum poisoning to me. She has a bump on her head, which might have given her such a bad headache that she mistook the dosage she needed, or forgot that she had imbibed the laudanum and took more." He turned to Mr. Fairfax, who was standing beside him, his expression grief-stricken. "I'm sorry, Mr. Fairfax. The only good thing is that she was probably unaware of what she'd done, and died peacefully in her sleep."

"But she left that note," Mr. Fairfax said hesitantly. "She made it sound as if she did this *deliberately*."

"I cannot speak as to that, but if she was dazed from the carriage accident, she might even have been confused enough to confess to something she didn't do."

153

Major Kurland spoke up from his position by the door. "Mr. Fairfax, would you prefer it if we kept the note between ourselves? This confession doesn't change the fact that two women have died, and from what Dr. Fletcher is suggesting, it might have been made in error."

Lucy turned to look at the major, who was watching Mr. Fairfax carefully. He continued speaking.

"We could say that Mrs. Fairfax died due to unexpected complications from the carriage accident. It would be better for her son if her legacy was untainted by other matters."

Mr. Fairfax drew in a long shuddering breath. "That is true. But what of the Chingfords? Aren't they entitled to the truth? It sounds as if Mrs. Fairfax inadvertently killed their mother."

"I ask you again, what good will it do to tell them?" Major Kurland shrugged. "Mrs. Chingford is still dead, and for all intents and purposes, her death was seen as a tragic accident. It still *is* a tragic accident. I'm sure even if Mrs. Fairfax was guilty of pushing her down the stairs, she never intended to kill her."

Silence fell in the bedchamber, and Lucy moved to stand next to Major Kurland's chair.

"I suppose you are right, Major. There's nothing I can do to fix this, is there?" Mr. Fairfax made a hopeless gesture. "The only thing we can do is save what we can for my half brother and leave the Chingford ladies to mourn in peace."

Lucy cleared her throat. "I will tell the Chingfords and my father what has happened to Mrs. Fairfax. There is no need for you to be involved, Mr. Fairfax."

"Thank you, Miss Harrington." He bowed to her. "And thank you, Major Kurland and Dr. Fletcher, for your Christian charity in this matter."

"I'll arrange with Foley for the body to be sent to my house, and I'll speak to the undertaker." Dr. Fletcher moved toward the door. "I assume you will take her back home to be buried?"

"I suppose I should. There is a family plot." Mr. Fairfax shoved a hand through his hair. "I'll contact her man of business and send a message through to Fairfax Park."

"Do what you need to do and don't worry about your work here," Major Kurland said. "I understand that your circumstances have changed considerably and that you might need to return home to manage your half brother's estate."

"That rather depends on what Mrs. Fairfax put in her will. I'm not convinced she would appoint me as a guardian. The best thing I can do is write to her solicitor in London. Perhaps, if you permit it, sir, he might come to Kurland Hall to discuss what will happen with the estate." Mr. Fairfax hesitated. "I would appreciate your help with this. I admit to feeling rather overwhelmed."

"That's understandable. Please invite the solicitor here. I would be more than happy to stand your friend in this matter."

"Thank you, sir."

Major Kurland nodded. "Then may I suggest you make a start on those letters? Tell Coleman to send them out posthaste."

Mr. Fairfax started for the door and paused beside the major's chair. "I can't adequately express my gratitude to you, Major Kurland, but—"

Major Kurland waved him onward. "Get along with you. Come and report back to me when the letters have gone out."

The room fell quiet as Mr. Fairfax and the doctor left. Lucy remained, with one hand on the back of the major's chair.

"Well, what is it now, Miss Harrington? I can almost hear you thinking."

"I find it difficult to believe that you are willing to let this matter go—to prevent the Chingfords from ever really knowing what happened to their mother." She studied his set features. "It isn't like you."

"To accept that I can't change anything?" He snorted. "Death is rarely expected or comfortable, Miss Harrington. I learned that during the war. When I had to write letters of condolence to the families of my men who died, I didn't mention *how* they died, because it was rarely heroically

156

or bravely. Sometimes they died of disease or were killed by their own incompetence or by our allies. They were still dead, and all their relatives needed to know was that they died bravely on the field of battle for their King and country."

He looked up at Lucy, his blue gaze clear. "What good would it do to tell Miss Chingford who was responsible for pushing her mother down the stairs? Mrs. Chingford is still dead."

Lucy nodded. "I suppose that is the end of it, then. We know what happened to Mrs. Chingford, and we know that Mrs. Fairfax took her own life." She looked over at the bed. "She looks so perfect in death, doesn't she?"

"Almost as if someone had come in and laid her out like that."

"Exactly."

They both contemplated the body for another moment.

"The thing is . . . ," Lucy said tentatively.

"What now?"

"We still don't know what Mrs. Chingford said to anger Mrs. Fairfax enough to push her down the stairs and kill her."

"Does it matter?"

"I suppose not." Lucy heaved another sigh. "I just hate these loose ends." She tentatively patted Major Kurland's shoulder. "You will ask Dr. Fletcher to take a look at your leg before he leaves, won't you?"

"I damn well will not." He shrugged off her hand and slowly and painfully stood up. "I am perfectly fine."

"You are not if you need James to help you up and down the stairs."

He raised an eyebrow. "If you wanted the opportunity to continue to nag me, Miss Harrington, you should've accepted my offer to become my wife. As it is, my condition is no longer any of your concern."

She raised her chin at him. "And now I know that you really *are* in pain. Your language and your behavior toward me always become intolerably rude." She swept him a grand curtsy. "Good morning, Major. I am going back to the rectory to share the news of Mrs. Fairfax's death. I promise you I will not utter another *word* on the subject of your obviously damaged leg!"

She opened the door and beckoned to James, who was standing against the wall. "Major Kurland is ready to be helped downstairs now."

"Yes, Miss Harrington."

She cast one last dark look over her shoulder and was given a scowl in return. "Good day, Major Kurland."

She went down the staircase and had a quick word with the doctor before taking charge of the horse and trap and driving back to the rectory. As she maneuvered down the drive, she considered what she would say to the Chingfords. Luckily, as the daughter of the rector, she was skilled in delivering bad news. She agreed with Major Kurland that throwing blame around for Mrs. Chingford's death was not beneficial to anyone, but she still didn't like to lie, even by omission.

And, if she was honest with herself, she desperately wanted to know *why* Mrs. Fairfax has pushed Mrs. Chingford down the stairs. She pulled the gig up to the rear of the rectory and handed the reins over to the stable hand. There was another carriage parked on the drive, which she didn't recognize. Brushing the dust off her skirts, she walked through the house to the back parlor and found her father sitting with Miss Stanford, Miss Chingford, and an unknown man with black hair and a somewhat strained appearance.

Her father turned to her, his expression cold. "Lucy, Miss Stanford brought her fiancé to pay his respects to Miss Chingford. I'm sure you will make him welcome." He bowed. "Please excuse me. I have a sermon to write."

Lucy gazed inquiringly at Miss Stanford, who placed her hand on the unknown gentleman's sleeve. "Miss Harrington, may I introduce Mr. Reading?"

"Enchanted, Miss Harrington." Mr. Reading bowed. "I wish my visit was being made under happier circumstances, but I am pleased to make your acquaintance." He glanced around the room.

"I haven't been in Kurland St. Mary for many years. I seem to remember the rectory as a far older building."

"My father rebuilt the house about ten years ago." Lucy gestured at him to take a seat. "Did you spend much time in the village, sir?"

"Not much." Mr. Reading smiled. "I am sad to be here in such circumstances, but I wished to support my dear Miss Stanford and hastened to her side when she wrote to tell me of the tragedy."

Miss Chingford snorted, and Lucy turned to look at her. "Is there something wrong, Miss Chingford?"

"No, not at all. I am just surprised to see Mr. Reading here. He once offered to marry my mother, when he thought she was wealthier than she actually was."

Miss Stanford straightened in her seat. "That isn't true. Paul explained it all to me. I do not wish to speak ill of the dead, but it was your mother who was doing all the pursuing."

Lucy moved between the two women. "Did my father ring for some tea? Perhaps I should—"

"I do beg your pardon if I have offended you, Miss Chingford, but I understood that your mother had become engaged to the rector here." Mr. Reading looked bewildered. "Is that not true?"

"She did it to make you jealous." Miss

160

Chingford glared at Mr. Reading. "Much good it would've done her. It was obvious to everyone that you were committed to Miss Stanford."

"Thank you for your understanding, Miss Chingford." Mr. Reading inclined his head.

"But only because she is far wealthier than my mother," Miss Chingford added.

Miss Stanford shot to her feet. "Paul came to offer you his condolences! How can you treat him so abominably?"

"I'm just being truthful." Penelope raised her chin.

"Like your mother was? Why do you think she ended up dead?" Miss Stanford gasped and covered her mouth with her hand. "Do forgive me. That was an unpardonable thing to say."

Mr. Reading put his hand on her shoulder. "Perhaps we should go. Thank you for your hospitality, Miss Harrington. I apologize for any distress I might have caused. Please believe me that it was unintentional."

Lucy could only watch helplessly as Mr. Reading escorted a white-faced Miss Stanford out the front door of the rectory. She assumed they would return to Kurland Hall, where Major Kurland could share the news of Mrs. Fairfax's untimely death. It was her duty to tell the Chingford sisters and her father.

She returned from seeing the couple out to

find Penelope sitting in the back parlor, helping herself to a cup of tea.

"You were remarkably rude to Miss Stanford and Mr. Reading," Lucy said.

"I'm allowed to be rude. I'm in mourning, and Miss Stanford is a fool if she thinks that man is truly in love with her. He is a scoundrel and a rake."

"He might well be, but surely that is for Miss Stanford to discover for herself."

Penelope's shoulders slumped. "I suppose you are right. She is in love with him and cannot see his faults. That's why you should never be in love with the man you intend to marry. It clouds your judgment."

Unwilling to become involved in a discussion about matrimony with Major Kurland's ex-fiancée, Lucy focused on her own agenda. "Is Dorothea awake? I have some news from Kurland Hall."

"I will go and fetch her if it is important." Penelope stood up.

"I would appreciate that. I will tell my father and then will come back to you." Lucy turned and went down the corridor to her father's study. Just as she reached the door, George came out with a pile of papers clutched to his chest.

"Good morning, Miss Harrington!" He smiled brightly and pushed the door open wide to allow her to get past him. "Is Miss Chingford in the parlor?"

"She is, George, but—"

He departed with some alacrity.

She turned to her father, who sat behind his desk. "Is George enamored of Miss Chingford, Father? He seems remarkably keen to speak to her."

"I have no idea." Her father wasn't smiling. "Is there something you want, Lucy? I am rather busy today."

"I have some bad news from Kurland Hall. Mrs. Fairfax died last night."

"Mrs. *Fairfax?* The young widow?" He frowned. "I had no idea she was ill."

"She wasn't. It seems as if she inadvertently took too much laudanum. Dr. Fletcher believes she might have injured her head more badly than we realized in the carriage accident yesterday."

"Dear God, what a tragedy." He shook his head. "Should I send George to the manor to say a prayer over the body?"

"I don't think that is necessary. I believe she is being laid out in Dr. Fletcher's house and will be transported back to her home for burial in the family plot."

"Well, thank goodness for that." He sat back in his chair. "I was dreading having to perform another funeral."

"Father."

"I didn't mean it like that, Lucy, although it would be rather inconvenient for me to have to devote more hours away from my horses. I *meant* that it would be difficult to bury another young woman who reminded me of your mother."

Lucy briefly closed her eyes. "I'm sorry, Father. It must be a very difficult time for you, especially as you intended to marry Mrs. Chingford."

"And find myself conducting a burial service rather than a wedding." He grimaced. "That man who came here today . . ."

"Mr. Reading?"

"Yes. Mrs. Chingford mentioned him to me on the day of the Stanford wedding. She was annoyed with me for announcing our engagement without consulting her." He met Lucy's gaze. "I gained the impression that she wished to use *my* marriage proposal as a threat to inspire Mr. Reading to abandon Miss Stanford and marry her instead."

"She told you that herself?"

"I don't think she truly wished to marry me, after all, Lucy." His smile was rueful. "I can't help but feel a somewhat unchristian sense of relief that she died so tragically before I had to honor my promise."

"Under the circumstances, that is perfectly understandable, Father," Lucy said firmly. "She didn't deserve you. Now I have to go and inform the Chingford sisters about Mrs. Fairfax's death, so I shall leave you in peace."

She was already at the door when he spoke again.

"Thank you, Lucy."

"For what, sir?"

"For not telling me what a fool I've been."

She left the room and headed for the parlor, her mind whirling as the implications of the morning's events turned in her head. Two tragedies had occurred that, in her opinion, could and should have been avoided. How likely was it for two perfectly healthy women to die within days of each other in the same small village? There had to be more to it than blind bad luck.

Lucy entered the parlor to find Dorothea sitting beside Penelope on the couch. She still looked disheveled, but at least she wasn't weeping.

"Did George find you, Penelope?" Lucy asked.

"He did. I offered to read over his Sunday sermon for him." Penelope smiled complacently. "He appreciates my insights."

"It is very kind of you to help him. He is still rather self-conscious about speaking in public and finds giving a sermon quite impossible." Lucy sat down and took a deep breath. "I regret to tell you that I have more bad news to share. Mrs. Fairfax died last night."

Dorothea gave a gasp. "Oh, no. That's not

possible. She—" With a shudder, she got to her feet and ran for the door, her skirts clutched in one hand.

"Oh, good gracious, that girl!" Penelope half rose. "What is wrong with her *now?*" The front door slammed, and they both flinched. "I suppose she'll come back when she's finished crying." Penelope rearranged her skirts and turned her attention back to Lucy. "What exactly happened to Mrs. Fairfax?"

"Dr. Fletcher thinks she might have been more affected by the carriage accident than we realized, and suffered from such a severe headache that she took too much laudanum to stop the pain and accidently killed herself."

"How terrible. She had a young son, didn't she?"

"Yes. I should imagine Mr. Fairfax will have to leave Kurland Hall now and deal with his family's affairs. Major Kurland will miss him if he chooses not to return."

"And what about you? Will you miss him?"

"Mr. Fairfax?"

"I've seen how he looks at you."

"I like him. He is intelligent, hardworking, and makes dealing with Major Kurland look easy. But that is the extent of my interest in him."

"Because you are still waiting for Major Kurland to notice you himself."

Lucy scowled at Penelope. "For goodness'

sake, will you let that particular bone go? Major Kurland is not for me."

"My mother told me he proposed to you and you turned him down. Is that true?"

"Your mother, God rest her soul, was an extremely indiscreet woman." Lucy rose and started putting teacups and saucers back on the tray. "I must take this back to the kitchen."

Penelope stood, too, a small smile playing on her lips. "He *did* propose, didn't he? Why on earth didn't you accept him?"

Lucy picked up the tray. "That is my business, Miss Chingford. Not yours."

"Take care, Miss Harrington. If you keep turning away husbands you might find yourself in my position one day, desperate to marry anyone."

"I hope I never feel that desperate."

"Because you feel safe here?" Penelope gestured at the cozy sitting room. "Your father obviously wants to get married again if he considered marrying my mother. You will be replaced. Don't ever doubt it."

"Then I hope one of my siblings will invite me to live with them."

"So you can become a favorite aunt?" Penelope snorted. "You will have no power. You are far too managing to stand for that."

Turning her back on her companion, Lucy marched away to the safety of the kitchen. She had enough questions to answer without complicating matters by worrying about her potential future. She wouldn't allow herself to believe what Penelope was predicting. Whether her father chose to marry again or not, she would *never* put herself in a position where she had no choice but to accept a proposal of marriage. She would rather be an old maid than end up under the thumb of a man she couldn't love and respect.

Drawing a deep breath, Lucy started up the stairs. She had a decision to make—either she let the unanswered questions about the two deaths go or she embraced her fate and sought justice.

Chapter 10

D orothea hasn't come back."

Lucy looked up from counting the sheets to find Penelope blocking the doorway of the laundry room.

"Do you want me to send one of the maids to search for her in the village?"

"I intend to go out with Mr. Culpepper and look for her myself, but any additional assistance would be most welcome. It is already clouding over, and I fear it will turn into rain."

"I do hope Dorothea is all right." Lucy placed the last folded sheet in the basket. "Perhaps I should come with you, or maybe go up to Kurland Hall and ask them to watch out for her, as well. There aren't many places for her to find shelter around here."

She followed Penelope out into the kitchen and spied Betty sitting at the table, peeling apples.

"Betty? Would you mind helping Miss Chingford?"

"Of course not, miss."

"Don't you leave those apples unfinished, girl. It's my afternoon off, and I want everything done before I leave." Mrs. Fielding's sunny mood had obviously dispersed. "I need those apples for a pie. The rector loves a nice piece of apple pie."

"Then come and find Miss Chingford when you have finished your task for Mrs. Fielding, Betty," Lucy said, amending her request. "Miss Dorothea is missing. We fear she has lost her way in the village somewhere." She turned back to Penelope, who was putting on her bonnet. "Do you want me to go up to Kurland Hall?"

"I'd rather you stayed here, in case Dorothea returns. Otherwise there will be no one to greet her and make sure that she is all right. The rector is out, Mrs. Fielding is leaving, and it is the kitchen maid's afternoon off."

"I'll send Bran, the stable boy, up to the manor to inquire about Dorothea instead, then."

By the time Lucy located Bran and sent him on his way, thick clouds were massing overhead, making the skies dark and threatening, even though it was only two o'clock. The slight drizzle turned to rain, and it was definitely getting chilly. When she returned to the kitchen, it was deserted, apart from the lingering fragrance of apples and cinnamon. There was a note in the cook's handwriting, telling Betty to take the pie out of the oven in an hour and that there was a cold collation of meats and pork pies in the larder to serve for dinner.

Lucy made note of the time. If Betty didn't return, she didn't want to incur Mrs. Fielding's wrath by leaving her apple pie to burn in the oven. The rectory was unusually quiet around her.

She missed the racket of her twin siblings and her brother Anthony clattering around the place. Even well-behaved Anna had contributed to the noise when she squabbled with her brothers. . . .

Lucy took a deep breath. Sometimes it felt as if everyone had moved on without her. The brief few moments when she had realized she would have to relinquish her responsibilities to Mrs. Chingford had reminded her that her tenure at the rectory wasn't permanent. Her father did deserve a loving companion, and so did she. It was unfortunate that London was the only place where she would find a husband.

After checking the pie in the oven, she lit a solitary candle, kicked off her boots that were muddy from the stables, and made her way upstairs. The creak of a floorboard made her go still.

Had Dorothea already sneaked back into the house and gone to sleep in her own bed? Lucy started toward Dorothea's bedchamber and saw a crack of light shining underneath the door of Mrs. Chingford's old room. She frowned. Perhaps Dorothea was back to destroying her mother's correspondence. It was a good thing that Lucy had already retrieved the names she required and had them hidden securely in her reticule.

Not that she needed the names anymore if she obeyed Major Kurland and let go of the mystery surrounding the deaths . . . Grasping the latch,

171

she slowly raised it and went into the room. A man spun around, with a pistol aimed at her. She gasped and almost dropped her candlestick.

"Miss Harrington!"

"Mr. . . . *Reading?*"

"I do apologize." He placed the pistol carefully back on the table. "I thought that everyone was out, and that it would be all right if I just came up here and . . ." He spread his hands wide, his smile engaging.

"And what, Mr. Reading?" Lucy placed the candle down on the bedside table and maintained the distance between them. "What on earth could you possibly want that merited you sneaking around in the dark?"

He sighed. "I suppose this looks rather incriminating, doesn't it?"

Lucy didn't say anything, and eventually, he sat down at the desk, where Mrs. Chingford's correspondence was now on view.

"I will have to throw myself on your mercy, Miss Harrington." He gave her a rueful smile. "Miss Stanford suggested that Mrs. Chingford had written . . . certain things about me that might prove detrimental to my current financial and social position." He picked up one of the letters. "I was attempting to read her correspondence in the hopes of removing all references to myself."

"*Did* you write to Mrs. Chingford?" Lucy asked.

He licked his lips. "I fear I might have said things that *could* be misconstrued if taken out of context."

"Like an offer of marriage?"

He smiled again, a quick flash that reminded her of someone she couldn't quite place. "You are obviously a very intelligent young lady, Miss Harrington. I would not go so far as to suggest *marriage* in a letter, but my romantic soul sometimes leads me toward the sin of exaggeration."

"But Mrs. Chingford is dead. What harm can she do you now?"

"That's an excellent question. But I do not think her daughters are predisposed to like me. If Miss Chingford finds evidence that her mother made *assumptions* as to our mutual future happiness, then she might chose to exploit them for her own personal gain and sue me for breach of promise."

"Surely that is up to her."

"I can't accept that, Miss Harrington. I cannot allow another person to control my destiny."

There was an implacable note in his voice, which made Lucy wary.

"And what of Miss Stanford? Do you not owe her an explanation as to your conduct?"

He shrugged. "She knows all. Why do you think she asked me to come down here? She knew I would help her."

"Do what?"

His eyebrows rose. "Whatever needed to be done. Make no mistake, Miss Harrington, I have no qualms about saving myself and those I love."

Lucy raised her chin. "Is that a threat, Mr. Reading?"

He laughed. "Of course not, Miss Harrington. Merely a statement of fact. As I have already mentioned, my fate is completely in your hands. I am trying to be a better man for Miss Stanford, and I cannot allow Mrs. Chingford's malicious lies to be spread any further."

"I think you should leave now," Lucy said firmly. "You have no right to be here, and you know it."

He rose slowly from his seat, and she tensed. "May I make a suggestion, Miss Harrington?"

"If you must."

His gaze dropped to the writing case. "Destroy everything Mrs. Chingford ever wrote. Nothing good can come from such a malicious source."

"I'll suggest that to Miss Chingford. It is her decision to make."

"If you say so." His head angled toward the window. "I hear a horse."

"It is my father coming home for his dinner. He is always punctual." She hoped God would forgive her for that lie.

"Luckily for you." He strolled toward her and inclined his head. "Good evening, Miss Harrington. I appreciate your forbearance in this matter. I'm sure you wouldn't wish to upset the Chingford ladies or Miss Stanford by mentioning my slightly ungentlemanly behavior."

"I'll think about it. Are you staying at Kurland Hall until the funeral?"

"At the manor house? I don't think I'd be welcome there. I've been staying in Saffron Walden, but now I'm at the village inn." His blue gaze narrowed. "If you wish to contact me, that's where you will find me. I doubt you will have the need, but if I'm apprehended, I'll know exactly whom to blame."

"Good afternoon, Mr. Reading."

He blew her a kiss and slipped noiselessly down the back stairs, leaving her leaning against the door frame for support. Beneath his superficial charm she sensed he could be a dangerous man to stand against. It was only pure luck that her father had decided to return early for his dinner.

With hands that shook, she picked up the candlestick and brought it over toward the desk. Unlike Dorothea, Mr. Reading had conducted his search in a neat and methodical manner, with one stack of letters already discarded and the rest in another pile. As quickly as she could, before her father finished with his horse in the stables, she went through the rest of the correspondence, pulling out any mentions of Miss Stanford, Mr. Reading, or anything that was written in a different hand.

Mr. Reading had implied that Miss Stanford knew what he was doing. Had she begged him to come to Kurland St. Mary to make sure she was not suspected of any evil intent toward Mrs. Chingford? Was it possible that Mrs. Fairfax had indeed confessed to something she hadn't done? Or had Mr. Reading simply used the excuse of visiting Miss Stanford to make sure he was in the clear and she knew nothing of his plans?

"Lucy? Where are you?" Her father's voice boomed up the stairs, making her jump.

Grabbing the pile of paper, she folded it up and put it in her inside pocket before walking down the stairs to greet her father.

"Major Kurland, we've found Dorothea Chingford."

Robert looked up from his frustrated contemplation of the view from his study window to find Foley at the door.

"Where was she?"

"Coleman found her in the stables, sir. It looks like she was trying to steal a horse and ended up falling and knocking herself out." Foley shook his head.

"She is alive, though?"

"Yes, sir. One of the footmen is bringing her up to a bedchamber where Mrs. Bloomfield will get her settled. I've already sent someone for Dr. Fletcher."

"Thank you, Foley." Robert exhaled. "I felt so damn useless sitting here, doing nothing."

"Dr. Fletcher said that if you rested up for the remainder of the day, you would probably be able to walk much better tomorrow, sir."

"I damn well hope he's right," Robert muttered as he eased his left leg off the footstool. "We should let Miss Chingford know that her sister is safe. It might be worth telling them that Dorothea is sleeping and that they should visit her in the morning." He paused. "Not that anything I say would make a difference to a pack of females who are determined to bring comfort to an invalid."

Foley crossed to the windows and closed the curtains. "It is most unpleasant out there, sir. Perhaps if you told the ladies that Dr. Fletcher would call in on his way home and give them a report as to Miss Dorothea's condition, that might stem the flood of concern?"

"That's an excellent idea." Robert sat down at his desk and wrote a short note, which he addressed to Miss Chingford. There was a knock on the study door, and Dr. Fletcher appeared. He set his bag down on Robert's desk.

"Good evening, Major Kurland. Miss Dorothea is suffering the effects of a severe chill and a blow to the head. Her temperature is elevated, and she is slipping in and out of consciousness. I would not recommend any visitors."

"But she will recover?" Robert asked.

"I don't see any reason why not. She is young and healthy, and I know Mrs. Bloomfield will give her the best of care." He came farther into the room and ran a critical eye over Robert. "You shouldn't be on your feet."

Robert pointed at the chair and footstool by the fire. "I've been sitting there all damned day. Ask Foley, if you don't believe me. I didn't go out searching for Miss Dorothea, either."

"Good." Dr. Fletcher smiled. "You are finally listening to me." He picked up his bag. "I'll call again in the morning. Do you want me to visit the rectory on my way home and let them know how Miss Dorothea is faring?"

"I was just going to ask if you'd mind popping in and reassuring them. I've written Miss Chingford a note, which you can deliver into her own hands," Robert said. "I'd rather not have all the ladies descend on me tonight."

"Then consider it done." Dr. Fletcher took the sealed letter and picked up his hat. "Good night, Major Kurland. Rest that leg."

Foley escorted the doctor to his gig, leaving Robert to tidy his desk and contemplate going to bed. It was still early, but, in truth, he was exhausted. Struggling with pain made everything harder. Using his cane, he managed to lever himself to his feet and turn toward the door. He'd still need James to help him up the stairs, but he could at least manage a few steps on his own.

A scrap of paper tucked into his blotter caught his eye, and he picked it up, recognizing Miss Harrington's clear handwriting. It was the list of women with the name Madge that she had given him when they'd been in Saffron Walden. He started to crumple it into a ball and then frowned. How had it gotten from his waistcoat to his desk?

"Damnation." He breathed the curse as he investigated his waistcoat pocket and realized the locket was gone, as well. Miss Harrington was going to be extremely annoyed with him. He was fairly certain that he'd tucked the paper in on top of the locket. Silas had taken the waistcoat away to be cleaned after the accident and had presumably emptied out the pockets. But what he had done with the contents, Robert had no recollection, owing to the pain of that night.

He grabbed his cane and made his slow way out toward the stairs, where James was patiently waiting for him. He would speak to Silas first, but he suspected the items had been removed from his bedroom during the confusion of the past few days. As Miss Harrington had mentioned, there were still more questions than answers, and now he had another one. If the matter of Mrs. Chingford's death had been satisfactorily cleared up by Mrs. Fairfax's confession, who had stolen the locket and why?

Chapter 11

Lucy allowed Penelope to go up to her sister and sought Major Kurland in his study. He looked up as she tapped on the half-open door and went in.

"Miss Harrington. I was hoping to see you this morning."

She curtsied. "I came with Penelope to see Dorothea. I'm so glad you found her."

"I did nothing. Give your thanks to Thomas and my staff. Dr. Fletcher says Dorothea shouldn't be moved for a few days, until her fever abates. I will make sure Mrs. Bloomfield takes excellent care of her."

"Where exactly did you find her?"

"In the stables, attempting to steal a horse."

Lucy took the seat in front of the major's desk. "I wonder where she thought she was going." She sighed. "I told her and Miss Chingford that Mrs. Fairfax had died. Before I could even explain the circumstances, Dorothea leapt to her feet and was out the front door before either of us could stop her."

"It certainly is strange." Major Kurland folded his hands together on his desk. "At least she is safe here for a while. I'll make sure that she doesn't get the opportunity to run away again."

"But *why* is she running, Major? What does Mrs. Fairfax's death have to do with her?"

"That's an excellent question." He fiddled with some of the items on his desk and then looked up at her. "Would you be willing to come out with me this morning?"

Lucy stared at him. "And do what?"

"Some investigating."

"But I thought we'd decided there was nothing left to investigate."

"I'm not so sure. Dorothea's behavior makes me think that we haven't come close to the truth yet. Why is she still scared, Miss Harrington, and what don't we know?"

Lucy clasped her hands to her chest and beamed at him. "I am so glad you said that, because I have my doubts, as well." She studied his face. Should she mention the strange behavior of Mr. Reading or simply start with her observations about Mrs. Chingford's letters? If she mentioned Mr. Reading, she was fairly certain Major Kurland would want to ring a peal over her head about getting into dangerous situations, and she didn't want to distract him just yet. She decided to start with the evidence in her pocket.

"I wanted you to see these." She came around the side of the desk and brought out the sheets of paper she had extracted from Mrs. Chingford's writing case. "I'm afraid Dorothea had already gotten to the letters before I had a chance to read through them all properly." She pointed at one of the letters. "In this one, her correspondent mentions Miss Stanford's betrothal to a rake of the first order and goes on to comment on several rumors about his fitness to be considered a gentleman."

Major Kurland raised an eyebrow. "What does Miss Stanford have to do with anything? I'm more interested in any correspondence between Mrs. Chingford and Madge."

"I couldn't find anything from her." Lucy grimaced. "I did write to all three Madges and ask them if they knew the nursemaid, but I haven't received any replies."

"Which is why we will take the opportunity to drive over and invite at least two of them to the funeral personally."

"I still don't understand why you are suddenly so certain that this is important. For all we know, Dorothea's current emotional state might have nothing to do with her mother's death and everything to do with her age."

He sat back in his chair until she could see his face. "It's not just that. Last night I dreamed about finding Mrs. Fairfax. She'd been strangled. I could see the vivid marks around her throat. I woke up, and while I attempted to regulate my breathing, I realized something important. If Mrs. Chingford *were* strangled, how would such a petite woman as Mrs. Fairfax manage it?

Her fingers would hardly have the strength to succeed."

"But we don't *know* if Mrs. Chingford was strangled."

"I know, but something else has happened." He took a deep breath. "The locket has disappeared."

"You mean that you've *lost* it?"

"I *mean* that it was taken from me. The last time I saw it was on the night of the carriage accident. My clothes were filthy, so Silas took everything away, including my waistcoat, to get them clean. The locket was in my pocket, along with the list of names you gave me. The list turned up here, but the locket is gone."

"Did you ask Silas what he did with it?"

"He swears he left it on my dressing table." He groaned. "I slept like the dead that night. God, I hate the thought of someone standing over me while I slept. Anyone could've come into my bedchamber and taken the locket."

"Even Mrs. Fairfax." Lucy shook her head. "Did you ever get the locket open?"

"No. Yet another thing I failed to do," he growled. "I am a most incompetent accomplice, Miss Harrington."

"Then finding the right Madge becomes even more important. I will accompany you to meet the two candidates."

"All we can hope is that we have the devil's own luck and one of them is the right woman."

He rose to his feet. "Are you ready to leave right now?"

She raised her eyebrows. "I can't come with you unchaperoned, Major, and I haven't even seen Dorothea yet."

He frowned at her. "Then go and see her, and I'll find a maid to accompany us. I will meet you in the stables in a quarter of an hour."

"Major Kurland, do you have a moment?"

Robert looked up from his contemplation of the state of the paddock fencing to find Coleman, his head coachman, standing in front of him.

"What is it, Coleman?"

"Begging your pardon, sir, but I thought you should know that we've retrieved the wreck of the carriage and that the horses are both doing well."

"Thank you." A vision of how close Miss Harrington had been to the out-of-control lead horse flashed through his head. "Will it be possible to save the carriage?"

"I don't think so, Major, and as to that . . ." Coleman paused. "I went over the wreckage quite thoroughly me self to be sure that I hadn't made a mistake while I was driving you, sir."

"And?"

"Something weren't right. Someone had tampered with the wheels on the right side of the coach. One of them sheered clean off, which has never happened before in my tenure at this stables, sir. We keep your horses and carriages in perfect order."

"Yes, you do." Robert saw Miss Harrington coming down the path toward the stable yard, one of the maids at her heels. "Who knows about this?"

"Only me and young Crawford, sir, and he can keep his mouth shut." Coleman hesitated. "I did wonder if someone at the Saffron Walden inn meddled with the carriage while we were all eating our dinner, sir. It's the only time the carriage was left unattended."

"Can you keep this to yourself, Coleman? I don't want to worry my guests or the rest of the staff."

"Aye, Major. And I'll set a lad to sit up for a few nights to make sure nothing funny is going on around here. You can't be too careful." The gig appeared, driven by Reg, and Coleman looked it up and down. "Nothing to worry about with this one, sir. I checked it over me self this morning."

"Thank you. I wouldn't want Miss Harrington to take another spill."

Coleman chuckled. "She's a right brave young lady, isn't she? Came to help with the horses without a moment's thought for her own safety."

"Yes, she's definitely impulsive." He eyed his companion as she arrived at his side, her cheeks flushed with color. "Sometimes I wish she was a little more careful."

"Are you ready, Major Kurland?" Miss Harrington turned to smile at his coachman. "And how are you, Mr. Coleman? Has your daughter recovered from the mumps yet?"

"She's doing much better, miss. Thanks for asking." He touched his hat and stepped back. "Mr. Fairfax was inquiring about your whereabouts earlier, Major. He said that if I saw you to tell you he had business in Kurland St. Anne's and would be back by nightfall."

"He did mention it to me yesterday. I'm glad that he was feeling well enough to go."

"He seemed fine, sir—apart from that shiner he got in the accident yesterday." Coleman shook his head. "You'd better be getting along before the rain comes back, Major. You don't want Miss Harrington getting soaked now, do you?"

Robert helped Miss Harrington up into the gig and followed her up. Coleman seated the maid beside Reg, and they were ready to leave.

"If it rains, I have my umbrella, Major," Miss Harrington said as she retied the ribbons of her very practical bonnet. "We will not get wet. How far away is the first Madge's house?"

Less than two hours later they arrived at the village of Great Dunmow, where Robert paused at the Saracens Head to ask for directions to

Goose Green Cottage. It seemed as if the address in question was very close, so Robert elected to leave the gig with Reg at the inn and test his leg by walking the rest of the way.

With the maid following along behind, he offered Miss Harrington his arm and walked slowly across the market square and out onto a smaller less traveled road. It felt good to stretch his legs. The cottage stood within a large thriving garden and was red bricked and thatched. A line of washing blew in the breeze, and from within the house came the sound of barking as they approached.

Robert unlatched the front gate and ushered Miss Harrington into the garden.

"I assume you still have your umbrella," he murmured as two dogs tore down the path to greet them. "Let's hope these beasts are friendly."

A woman appeared in the doorway and waved at them. "Don't worry about the dogs. They won't hurt you."

"Thank you, ma'am," Miss Harrington called out. "Are you Mrs. Madge Troughton?"

"Aye, and who might you be?"

"I'm Miss Harrington, from the rectory at Kurland St. Mary, and this is Major Sir Robert Kurland. May we come in for a moment? We have some news to share with you."

Mrs. Troughton twisted her hands in her apron. "Oh yes, miss. Come in, come in." She stepped back and opened the first door on the right. "Sit yourselves down, and I'll make some tea."

"That would be most kind of you, Mrs. Troughton." Miss Harrington smiled.

Robert sighed as he took the chair opposite Miss Harrington. "Why do we have to drink tea? Why can't we just ask our questions and leave?"

Miss Harrington smoothed down her skirts. "Because we are being *polite,* Major Kurland, and we wish to engage her goodwill. Behaving like reasonable members of society will help her to trust us."

Robert said nothing more but waited meekly for his hostess to return with three strong cups of tea and a plate of biscuits. He was unwise enough to take one and almost cracked a tooth. While he surreptitiously left the rest of the biscuit on the side of his plate, he listened to Miss Harrington exchanging innumerable pleasantries. After a few minutes he caught her eye and gestured to the clock.

"Mrs. Troughton, we came to deliver some sad news to you," Miss Harrington said gently. "A mutual acquaintance of ours, a Mrs. Maria Chingford, is dead. I did write to you with this news, but as we were in the area today, we thought it best to contact you directly in case you wished to attend the funeral in Kurland St. Mary."

"Mrs. Chingford?"

"Yes. She was visiting Kurland St. Mary for a wedding with two of her daughters when she suffered an unfortunate accident and fell down the stairs."

Mrs. Troughton sat down abruptly. "She's dead?"

"Yes. I'm so sorry."

"Good riddance," Mrs. Troughton snapped. "She was a terrible employer. She cast me off without a reference after she found out that Mr. Chingford had spoken well of me." She snorted. "As if I would've allowed that old man any liberties."

"In what capacity did you work for her?" Robert asked.

"I was her dresser, her lady's maid, and she treated me like dirt." Mrs. Troughton folded her arms across her chest. "When my husband came courting, I was more than willing to leave that house for good."

"You weren't involved in the nursery, then?" Miss Harrington said.

"No, but I did meet her daughters. In truth, I felt sorry for them."

"Please excuse the question, but if you parted on bad terms, may I ask why you continued to correspond with Mrs. Chingford?" Robert intervened again.

Mrs. Troughton sighed. "Because my cousin Rachel still worked for her. It was the only way

Mrs. Chingford would allow me to write to her."

Robert frowned. "I don't understand."

"Mrs. Chingford insisted on reading all our letters before she passed them on, so I addressed them to her, and she gave them to Rachel."

Miss Harrington leaned forward to pat one of the dogs on the head. "Then our errand was probably unnecessary, and I apologize for disturbing you. I doubt you would wish to attend Mrs. Chingford's funeral in person."

"That's all right, miss. I'd rather know." Mrs. Troughton hesitated. "What will happen to the household now that both the master and mistress have gone?"

"I believe Miss Chingford and her sisters will be going to live with relatives and the house will be closed up," Miss Harrington said.

"Then my cousin will have to look for a new position."

"Unless a Chingford family member takes on the house and decides to retain the staff."

"It's unlikely, miss. At least Rachel knows that she always has a home here. I wonder what everyone else will do with themselves."

"Did Mrs. Chingford retain a nurse for her younger daughter—the one who is currently at school?"

"No. Madge Summers left about the same time that I did."

"Another Madge?" Miss Harrington smiled. "That must have been confusing."

"Oh, no, miss. We kept to our own parts of the house and barely saw each other."

"Did she take up another position as a nurse, or did she leave for good?"

"I'm not sure, miss. She didn't say."

"A good nurse is always in demand." Miss Harrington finally rose to her feet, and Robert followed suit. "Thank you so much for the tea, Mrs. Troughton, and apologies for disturbing your day."

"It's no bother, Miss Harrington, sir." Mrs. Troughton bobbed a curtsy. "I'll write to Rachel today and hope she will come for a long stay."

"Well, I'm glad some good came of our visit." Miss Harrington smiled. "Good-bye, Mrs. Troughton."

"Bye, miss." She opened the front door and stood back to let them both go past her. "Bye, sir."

Robert waited until they were well clear of the cottage before he voiced his thoughts. "We didn't learn much, did we?"

"Well, she certainly wasn't the Madge we were looking for, but she did confirm that the *other* Madge was Mrs. Chingford's nurse. We now know which of the remaining two candidates is the woman we need to speak to."

"I suppose that is true—although this Madge

did have something of a grudge against Mrs. Chingford. If she found out from Rachel that her former much-disliked employer was going to be in Kurland St. Mary, would she take a trip over there to maybe cause some mischief?"

"And you say I make ridiculous suggestions." Miss Harrington looked up at him. "That is a rather far-fetched theory, isn't it, Major?"

"I suppose it is," he sighed as the village came into view. "Does Madge Summers live near here, or are we out of luck?"

Miss Harrington consulted her list and turned to him with an optimistic smile. "She lives in Thaxted, which is only another hour from here."

"Then let us make haste and visit her before the light disappears, and we are forced to drive back in the dark, and I have to explain myself again to your father."

By the time they reached Thaxted, the clouds had gathered overhead and the sun had disappeared, making Lucy glad that she had worn her stoutest boots and thickest coat. As they approached the Swan coaching inn, they met the breeze head-on and she began to cough.

"Either the chimneys of the inn need sweeping or there has been a fire somewhere," Major Kurland observed. He swallowed hard. Having listened to many of his nightmares involving the horrors of war, Lucy wondered exactly what he was remembering.

Major Kurland instructed Reg to pull into the stable yard of the Swan and then slowly alighted to help Lucy and the maid down. A stable boy came out to hold the horses, and the major called out to him.

"What's on fire?"

"A house down the street, sir," the boy answered. "But there's nothing to worry about. The fire is out."

"Thank God for that," Major Kurland said. "Can you tell me where Field Lane is please?"

"It's just behind the inn, sir. Go out of the front door and turn left and then turn left again at the corner."

"Thank you. Are you ready, Miss Harrington, or do you need to . . . use the facilities of the inn?"

"Maybe before we leave." She gestured at Alice, the maid, who was shivering. "Alice should stay here with Reg."

"All right then. I doubt we'll bump into anyone we know who might wonder what we are doing out together, unchaperoned."

"It certainly is unlikely, sir." She put her hand on his sleeve, and they walked through the inn to the front door and out the other side. "Madge Summers lives in the eighth house."

As they walked along the muddy street, the

smoke grew thicker and Lucy pressed her handkerchief to her mouth.

"Good Lord." Major Kurland stopped, and they both surveyed the smoking remnants of Number Eight Field Lane. "There's nothing left of it."

Chapter 12

W"e can't leave," Lucy protested as Major Kurland took her arm in a firm grip and started to march her back along the lane.

"We have no choice. The house is burned to the ground. There is no one there to talk to. If I was a suspicious man, I would say that someone didn't want us to visit Madge Summers."

"All the more reason why we should stay and question her neighbors. Just because the house is destroyed doesn't mean that she is dead. She might have taken shelter and . . ."

He stopped and faced her. "Miss Harrington, I am not going to allow you to question the whole village."

"I don't believe I was seeking your permission, sir."

"If you were my wife, I wouldn't even have to ask. I'd *assume* you would do as you were told."

"Well, thank goodness we aren't married."

They were glaring at each other now, oblivious to the people moving around them.

"You refused my offer of marriage purely because you didn't want to obey me?"

"That wasn't the only reason, and you didn't really want to marry me. You should be glad that I didn't say yes, because even if we *were* married, I would still be defying you about this!"

"Indeed." He raised one chilling eyebrow.

"Yes, because you are wrong. If we don't act now, we might never find out whether Madge survived."

For a long moment they glared at each other. "As you wish. We will go and inquire as to Madge's current whereabouts from her immediate neighbors, and then if she isn't here, we will leave. Agreed?"

"I suppose so."

"Good." He did another about-face and walked back to the house next to the burning ruin. He rapped on the door with his cane until an elderly man came to answer his call.

"Yes, sir?"

"The woman who lived in the house next door. Where is she?" Major Kurland demanded.

The old man's gaze slid away from Major Kurland to the smoldering ruins. "Who's asking?"

"I'm Major Robert Kurland. I'm looking for Madge Summers."

"I don't know anything, sir. I wasn't here when the fire started."

"Do you even know if the woman is alive?" Major Kurland said.

"Try Mr. and Mrs. Collins at number seven

sir. They might know." The man closed the door firmly in Major Kurland's face.

He turned back to Lucy, and she had to bite her tongue as he stomped down the path and headed for the house on the other side of the burned-out shell.

"Would you let me—"

"I'll handle this, Miss Harrington."

"But—"

He marched up the path and knocked on the blue painted door. Lucy saw the curtains in the front parlor twitch, but no one answered the major's imperious summons.

Major Kurland knocked again. "Perhaps there isn't anyone there."

"I think there is. Maybe they are too scared to answer the door because you are banging on it so loudly," Lucy suggested.

He turned slowly to stare at her and then stepped back. "You try, then."

"Thank you." Lucy moved past him and knocked more gently. Eventually, a small child, who stared at them as if they were ghosts, opened the door.

"Is your mother home, dear?" Lucy inquired gently.

The little girl shook her head.

"Your father, then?"

This resulted in another shake.

Lucy crouched down so that her face was on

level with the child's. "Will you be in trouble for opening the door? We won't tell anyone." She produced a lump of barley sugar from her pocket and held it out. "Did you see the fire today?"

A nod this time, and a hesitant hand reached toward the proffered sweet.

"Was the lady who lived in the house all right?"

"Yes."

Lucy handed over the barley sugar. "Do you know where she went?"

"No."

"Are you quite sure?"

A nod this time as the child sucked vigorously on the sweet.

Behind her, Lucy sensed Major Kurland moving restlessly about. After rising to her feet, she turned to him. "As you can see, she doesn't know much. I think we'll have to come back and speak to her parents."

"And I think we should return to the inn, regroup, and decide what to do after we return to Kurland St. Mary."

There was an implacable note in his voice, which she recognized all too well from her previous dealings with him.

"If you insist."

"I do, Miss Harrington. Has it occurred to you that the person who set fire to the house could still be here in Thaxted? If this tragedy is connected to the deaths in Kurland St. Mary, then our appearance here could cause further complications and even endanger our lives."

"Then we should definitely return home. We can talk on the way." Lucy smiled at the little girl. "Close the door now, and don't let anyone else in, will you?"

She solemnly shook her head and shut the door.

Lucy walked back to the Swan in silence, aware that her clothes now held the stink of the water-drenched wood from the fire. When she reached home, she would have to wash the smell of the smoke out of her hair, as well. What if Major Kurland was right and someone from Kurland St. Mary had seen them in Thaxted? Were they now both in danger?

They found Reg and Alice at the inn, enjoying a bowl of soup and a mug of ale, and joined them. While Reg went off to get the horses harnessed to the gig and Alice visited the necessary again, Lucy finished her soup.

"I wish I'd brought the closed carriage," Major Kurland muttered. "From the look of the sky, it's going to be devilishly cold on the way back."

"Your closed carriage was damaged the other night."

"That's correct." Major Kurland lowered his voice. "Coleman thinks it was tampered with."

Lucy choked on a crust of bread. "I beg your pardon?"

"It wasn't an accident." The major's voice was

grim. "Now, who in God's name would do that? We could've all been killed."

"Maybe it was an attempt to silence Mrs. Fairfax."

"Which failed or frightened her badly enough to make her take her own life?"

"I can't think of any other reason . . . unless . . ." She hesitated. "Mr. Reading was staying in Saffron Walden."

"Who is Mr. Reading?"

"Miss Stanford's betrothed. Apparently, she wrote and asked him to come down to Kurland St. Mary for the funeral. He came to pay his respects to Miss Chingford at the rectory, and things didn't go very well. Miss Chingford claimed that he once offered marriage to her mother but changed his mind when he realized she wasn't very wealthy."

"He sounds like a cad."

"I believe he is." Lucy took a deep breath. "I don't think he came to Kurland St. Mary to support Miss Stanford, but to make sure he hadn't left any incriminating evidence in his correspondence with Mrs. Chingford."

"You sound remarkably informed about a gentleman you met only for a few minutes in the rectory parlor."

"He came back when everyone was out searching for Dorothea. I found him in Mrs. Chingford's bedchamber, going through her letters."

Silence followed her admission, and she kept her gaze on her bowl of soup for as long as she could manage it.

"And I assume you confronted him." The major sounded far too calm for her liking.

"I didn't really have a choice."

"Of course you didn't. No *sensible* woman would decide to run and get help."

She winced. "Once he lowered his pistol, I didn't feel as if he would—"

"He had his *pistol* aimed at you?"

"Only until he realized who I was, and then he was most apologetic and quite charming in his way."

More silence. This time she risked a glance upward and encountered a furious blue gaze.

"You have no idea how much I yearn to pick you out of that seat, Miss Harrington, and shake you until your teeth rattle." The major's tone was almost conversational, but not reassuring at all.

"I know what you are thinking, Major," Lucy said hastily. "But I wasn't expecting him to be there and was caught somewhat by surprise. What I was trying to say was that maybe Mr. Reading had something to do with the carriage accident, because he was in Saffron Walden that day." When he didn't answer her, she carried on speaking. "Is it possible that Miss Stanford has more to do with this matter than we realized? Maybe she asked Mr. Reading to help her cover up *her* crime. Remember, she was defending the reputations of her brother *and* her betrothed. She could have pushed Mrs. Chingford down the stairs and made sure Mrs. Fairfax didn't survive."

Major Kurland slowly rose to his feet. "We need to get back. I'll meet you in the stable yard."

Lucy stared after him, her thoughts in confusion as he limped out of the room and disappeared, leaving her alone. She took a deep breath and realized she was shaking. His lack of reaction to her confession was surprising. She'd expected him to rip up at her and tell her she was stupid, not walk away as if she didn't exist. . . .

She retied the ribbons on her bonnet and started after him. He would be trapped in the gig with her for at least two hours even on the more direct route home. There was plenty of time for him to chastise her in a more private setting than the inn provided. Then she would be able to defend herself, he would see reason, and everything would be all right again.

At least she hoped it would.

Robert stared straight ahead as the gig moved swiftly down the country road toward Kurland St. Mary. It was dark now, but he could see the distant lights of the village and the manor house outlined against the purple-tinged sky. He loved his home, but even the sight of its unpretentious beauty couldn't calm his temper tonight.

"Major Kurland . . ."

He set his jaw and realized it actually hurt from restraining himself from shouting at Miss Harrington.

"I know you are angry with me, but please consider the situation from my point of view."

He wrapped his gloved hand around his cane and squeezed hard. Part of him still wanted to reach across the carriage, grab Miss Harrington by the shoulders, and shake her. Even though that picture gave him some satisfaction, he suspected that after he'd shaken her, he would have to gather her into his arms and hold her, beg her not to be so stupid, to not put herself in danger, to allow him . . .

"Major *Kurland*."

He cleared his throat and shouted at Reg. "Let Miss Harrington out at the rectory, will you?"

"Yes, sir."

The gig slowed and took the turn into the drive of the rectory, which circled around to the front of the house. Robert got out and walked around the carriage to help Miss Harrington descend.

When she reached the ground, her gloved hand tightened on his arm and she didn't move away. "I'd much rather you shouted at me than ignored me. How are we going to continue our investigations if we are at odds?"

He finally met her gaze. "We are not going to investigate anything together ever again."

Hurt and shock flashed across her hazel eyes. "Why not?"

"Because . . ." *Because I cannot bear for you to be hurt or threatened. I cannot bear to see how brave you are, when I cringe in fear like a coward.* "This investigation is over."

"But it isn't. We—"

"We are not going to do anything," Robert said fiercely. "As far as the world is concerned, Mrs. Chingford fell down the stairs, and Mrs. Fairfax accidentally took too much laudanum after suffering a head injury."

Miss Harrington raised her chin and stared him right in the eye. "You have no authority over me." Her voice was shaking as hard as his hand was gripping her arm. "If you don't choose to be involved, then that is up to you. I cannot—"

"You damn well can." He caught her wrist. "If you think I will allow you to place yourself in danger, then you are sadly mistaken. I will tell your father what you are doing and will ask for his help in keeping you at home."

"In my rightful place?" She shook free of his hand. "I never realized how much alike you and my father were until this moment. How *dare* you treat me like some kind of chattel!" She turned on her heel and walked away from him, then entered the rectory slamming the door behind her.

Robert winced at the sound and let out his breath. Better she thought him an arrogant male than an overanxious one who cared too much for her well-being. He turned back to the waiting gig and hauled himself up into his seat.

"Let's go home, Reg."

Reg turned and gave him a sympathetic look. "Yes, sir."

At Kurland Hall all was quiet. Miss Stanford and Mrs. Green had retired early for the night, and Dr. Fletcher had called to see Dorothea and had left a message with Foley that her condition remained the same. Robert took himself into his study, sat behind the desk, and stared out over the gardens toward the village church. He still stank of smoke from the fire in Thaxted and wasn't sure if he had the energy required to go upstairs and order a bath.

A light tap on the door made him raise his head and look up to see Thomas coming in with an unknown gentleman. Robert forced his tired body to rise, gripping the desk to stop himself from swaying with weariness.

"Major Kurland, I apologize for disturbing you so late in the evening." Thomas bowed. "Mr. Tompkins has very little time to spare from his duties and wishes to travel back to London on the morrow."

Thomas wore unrelieved black and had shadows under his eyes. He looked as if he hadn't slept for days.

"Good evening, Mr. Tompkins." Robert bowed. "I assume you are the solicitor who represents Mrs. Fairfax and her estate."

"Indeed, Major Kurland, I am." Mr. Tompkins bowed. "Mrs. Fairfax actually came to see me before she continued her journey to Kurland St. Mary. To say that I was surprised that she had died is something of an understatement."

"It was a shock to us all, Mr. Tompkins." Robert sat down, as did the other men. "My physician suspects that Mrs. Fairfax sustained a blow to the head after a carriage accident that caused her considerable pain and resulted in her taking too much laudanum."

"So I understand." Mr. Tompkins began taking documents out of his bag. "After receiving Mr. Fairfax's letter, I collected together all the information I could find about the estate and Mrs. Fairfax's new will."

"She made a new will?"

"Yes. I had been urging her to do so since her husband's demise. It is somewhat fortuitous that she heeded my request and set her affairs in order before her untimely death. It will make things so much easier for her heir."

"Indeed." Robert pressed two fingers to his brow, where his head had started to throb. "With Mr. Fairfax's agreement, might I inquire as to the provisions of the new will?"

"Certainly, Major. I have it right here. The

part that concerns Mr. Fairfax most directly is this." He cleared his throat, unrolled the document, and began to read. "In the event of my death, I appoint Mr. Thomas Edward Fairfax as guardian to my son Robin Edward Fairfax and give him control of the Fairfax estate until Robin reaches his majority." He looked over the top of his spectacles at Thomas and Robert. "In the previous will, guardianship was left to the partners at Tompkins, Bailey, and Dibbs."

"Did she mention why she made this change?" Robert asked, as Thomas appeared incapable of speech. "I understood that relations between her and her husband's son were never very cordial."

"Perhaps she decided that a blood relative, no matter how . . . indirect, would be more involved in her son's future and would manage the estate in a more sensitive manner. Not that we wouldn't have done our utmost to provide young Robin with the best advice possible, but we aren't his family."

"I understand, Mr. Tompkins." Robert held out his hand. "Do you have a copy of the will? I'm sure Mr. Fairfax will want to read it through at his leisure. He can then write to you with his concerns and questions."

"I do have a copy, sir." Mr. Tompkins placed the document on Robert's desk. "I am more than willing to answer any questions that Mr. Fairfax might have in the future weeks, as he takes on his new responsibilities."

"What time do you intend to leave in the morning?"

"Quite early, Major. I've never been one to lie abed when there is so much to be done." Mr. Tompkins stood up. "Thank you for your hospitality. Your butler has allocated me a bedchamber, and I have dined very well."

Robert stood, too, and shook the solicitor's hand. "Thank you for coming out of your way to see Mr. Fairfax."

"It was a pleasure, sir. I do hope Mr. Fairfax intends to keep the estate business with us."

"Yes, of course." Thomas jumped as if someone had poked him. "Thank you for everything, Mr. Tompkins."

Robert rang the bell, and Foley appeared with such alacrity that Robert guessed he had been loitering outside the door.

"Ah, Foley, please take Mr. Tompkins up to his room and make sure he is woken in a timely manner in the morning."

"Yes, Major Kurland." Foley bowed. "If you would like to come this way, sir?"

Thomas remained standing, his gaze unfocused, as Robert resumed his seat. He swung around, his fists clenched at his sides. "I . . . can't believe she did that. I thought—" He paused and then resumed speaking. "I was convinced she would bar me from the estate and from ever contacting my brother again." He took an agitated turn around the room. "Why didn't she *tell* me? She came here, and she said nothing, except that she wanted me back to run the estate as an employee."

"Perhaps she didn't think you needed to know about her will, because she wasn't anticipating dying."

"Oh, God, I suppose that's true. She probably hoped it would never happen, but still." He swallowed hard. "I feel so unworthy. She forced a wedge between me and my father and made me feel unwelcome in my own home, and yet she did this." A tear slid down his cheek, and he hastily rubbed it away. "If only I'd known, I would've tried so much harder, treated her offer to return with more respect . . ."

"Hindsight is a wonderful thing, Thomas," Robert said gently. "You did your best. And in the end, she realized that her son would be safe with you, and there is no finer compliment than that, is there?"

Thomas nodded and cleared his throat. "Thank you, Major Kurland."

"Go to bed. If it is all right with you, I will read through the will before I retire. I need something stultifying to peruse before I can sleep."

"Of course, sir. I will see you in the morning. There are a few other matters of business that I need to discuss with you before I—"

"Leave for Fairfax Park?" Robert inclined his

head. "I understand that you must go, but I admit that I will miss your competence."

"And I will miss everyone here," Thomas replied. "Good night, sir."

"Good night, Thomas."

Robert stared unseeingly at the will. At this rate he would soon be alone again in his house, with just Foley to minister to his needs. Thomas was leaving for better things, and Miss Harrington . . . After his earlier dictatorial behavior she would probably never speak to him again. But he had to keep her safe. He had a sense that if they kept on poking their noses into such matters, sooner or later one of them would regret it. Miss Harrington had almost died once due to his inability to help her, and he was never going to allow that to happen again.

With a sigh, he put on his spectacles and concentrated his attention on the will.

"Are you all right, Miss Harrington? Lucy?"

Lucy looked up with a start to find Penelope watching her from the top of the stairs. She blinked rapidly to clear the sudden and unexpected descent of tears.

"I appear to have something in my eye," Lucy said as she searched for her handkerchief, only to have Penelope offer her one. "Thank you."

She walked across the landing to her bedchamber, and Penelope followed her in.

"How is Dorothea?" Lucy asked as she discreetly mopped her face. "Did you return to see her this afternoon?"

"She is still asleep, and I was told not to wake her. Dr. Fletcher seems to think she will make a complete recovery." Penelope leaned against the door, her gaze fixed on Lucy. "Where did you and Major Kurland go?"

"The major just brought me home."

"That's not an answer." Penelope crossed her arms. "You appeared to be arguing."

Lucy took off her bonnet and mud-splattered pelisse. "As you have mentioned more than once, we seem destined to argue all the time."

"About what?"

"Everything." Lucy summoned a smile. "I have to get changed before dinner. Would you mind sending Betty up to help me?"

"I've never seen you cry before."

"I am not crying. We went past a burning building, and I got smoke in my eyes."

"*We?*"

Lucy bent to unbutton her boots. "I do wish you would stop asking me all these ridiculous questions and go away."

"If I don't ask them, who will? It's not as if either of us has a mother to look out for us, and your father is far too immersed in the running of his stables to notice much."

"Unless it affects his comfort or is drawn to

his attention," Lucy muttered. How could Major Kurland threaten her like that? She'd thought they were friends. . . .

There was a knock on the door, and Betty appeared with a jug of hot water. "There you are, miss." She made a face as she picked up Lucy's discarded pelisse. "I'll take this away and sponge off the mud." She pressed her nose to the cloth. "It smells of smoke."

Lucy handed over her bonnet, as well. "Do you think I have time for a bath?"

"Cook won't like me using the stove to boil water right before dinner, miss, but I'll do my best."

"Thank you, Betty." Lucy glanced pointedly at Penelope, who had remained by the door. "I'm sure you don't wish to stay and watch me bathe."

Her companion shuddered. "No thank you." She still lingered, though, one hand on the door frame. "May I say something?"

"It appears that you are intent on saying it, anyway, so why not go ahead?"

"Major Kurland . . ."

Lucy turned her back on Penelope and pretended to warm her hands at the fire. "What about him?"

"Don't let him bully you."

"I don't intend to." Lucy took a deep breath. "In truth, I don't intend to have anything more to do with him ever again."

Chapter 13

So, Mr. Fairfax, when do you intend to return to your father's estate?" Lucy asked as she handed the land agent a cup of tea. He'd ventured down from the manor house in the rain to inform the ladies that Dorothea still had the remains of a fever and was too weak for visitors. Dr. Fletcher had also promised to call later and give them a full report on his patient's condition.

"I'm intending to leave in the week after Mrs. Chingford's funeral. I haven't yet settled on a day. It depends when I finish my work for Major Kurland." Mr. Fairfax hesitated. "If I might be so bold, Miss Harrington, but have you and the major fallen out? I haven't seen you at the manor all week, and my employer is extremely short-tempered."

Lucy sat back in her seat. They were alone in the parlor of the rectory. "Perhaps the major's leg is bothering him. I have noticed that he becomes less easy to deal with when he is in pain."

"Maybe that's the case, but I suspect there is more to it than that." Mr. Fairfax held her gaze. "Has he offended you in some way?"

"When has he not?" Lucy said and winced. "I do apologize. My petty squabbles with Major Kurland are not worthy of public discussion."

"You forget, I work closely with the major, and I know he can be difficult at times. Without meaning to cause you embarrassment, Miss Harrington, I truly believe that he misses your company."

"I doubt that," Lucy said tartly. "He has made it very clear that I am not worthy of sharing his confidences and should stay at home and mind my father's family."

"Then he is a fool. I have yet to meet another woman with your strength of character and intelligence, Miss Harrington." He sat forward. "In truth, if it wasn't for the fact that most people consider you and the major as destined to wed, I would have made my admiration for you much clearer."

Lucy belatedly remembered what Penelope had said about Mr. Fairfax being interested in her. "You have been misinformed. There is nothing between Major Kurland and myself. We are just old friends who still tend to behave like children."

"Nevertheless, Major Kurland does have a rather proprietary attitude in regard to you."

"Which is more due to his arrogance than any acquiescence on my part."

"That is well worth knowing." Mr. Fairfax smiled at her. "May I have some more tea?"

Lucy refilled his cup. "Do you intend to hold a funeral service for Mrs. Fairfax when you return home?"

His smile disappeared. "There is a chapel attached to Fairfax Park, where we can hold a ceremony, and there is also a burial ground for the family. I have written to the local vicar to apprise him of the situation and to ask him to preside over the service." He sighed. "I cannot believe she is dead. I just wish there was something I could've done to save her."

"It is not your fault, Mr. Fairfax. The carriage accident obviously affected her far more than we realized."

"But . . ." He lowered his voice. "Do you really think she pushed Mrs. Chingford down the stairs?"

Lucy shrugged. "I cannot understand why she would wish to do such a thing. I know that Mrs. Chingford was insisting they had shared a nurse for their children, but that hardly seems a reason to become angry enough to deliberately push someone down the stairs."

"I agree." He paused. "I wish she'd confided in me, but I suspect I wasn't the most patient of companions. And to be fair, we didn't know each other very well. There were years of mistrust between us. Just getting her to admit that she wanted me to come back and run the estate took several days of persuasion."

"She struck me as a rather timid woman."

"She was." He sighed. "I suppose we will never know exactly what happened, will we?"

"I suppose not."

He put down his cup. "I hope you don't mind me speaking to you about these matters, Miss Harrington, but you are the only person, apart from Major Kurland, who knows the full circumstances of her death."

"And I promise you that I will never reveal that information to another soul."

"I appreciate that. My half brother will have a difficult enough life bereft of his parents without his mother being branded a murderer."

"But he will have you to guide him. How could he not be successful?"

Mr. Fairfax took her hand and squeezed it hard. "Thank you, Miss Harrington. Your confidence in my abilities means a lot to me."

Betty knocked on the door, making Lucy pull her hand out of Thomas's warm grip. "Miss Stanford and Mr. Reading to see you, Miss Harrington."

Mr. Fairfax stood up. "I'd better go."

"Would you mind waiting a few minutes more, Mr. Fairfax? I'd appreciate your opinion of Mr. Reading."

"Of course, Miss Harrington."

He remained standing as the engaged couple came in, and introduced himself to Mr. Reading, who was all smiles today. Lucy couldn't quite believe Mr. Reading had the audacity to enter the rectory again. His gaze met hers with an insolent challenge, which made her bristle.

She realized Mr. Fairfax was speaking. "Have we met before, Mr. Reading? You look quite familiar."

"I've spent most of my adult life in India and in London, Mr. Fairfax. Is it possible that we met in Town?"

"I doubt it, sir. I have spent very little time there myself, and I'm certain we don't move in quite the same circles."

Miss Stanford accepted a cup of tea from Lucy, and Mr. Reading took the seat beside her. After a glance at Lucy, Mr. Fairfax bowed.

"I do apologize, Miss Harrington, but I have to get back to my duties at the manor. Dr. Fletcher will come down at six to discuss Miss Dorothea's condition and continuing care."

"The poor girl," Miss Stanford murmured. "She has had quite a high fever."

"What on earth was she doing in the stables of Kurland Hall?" Mr. Reading asked as he crossed one elegant booted leg over the other.

"We're not sure, sir," Mr. Fairfax said. "She has been in great distress since her mother died."

"Perhaps there is a good reason for that," Mr. Reading said.

"What do you mean?" Lucy said.

He shrugged. "A young girl, a tyrannical mother . . . Maybe her emotional state is due to guilt."

"Are you suggesting *Dorothea* had something to do with her mother's fall?" Lucy asked.

"It's possible."

Lucy raised an eyebrow in her best imitation of Major Kurland. "I don't believe you were present at the wedding, Mr. Reading. One wonders how you came to believe you alone have the solution to what was surely a terrible accident."

He smiled. "I agree that I was not present, but Miss Stanford told me what occurred."

"I did not suggest that Dorothea was involved in her mother's unfortunate fall, Mr. Reading," Miss Stanford said hurriedly. "I merely said that I saw her in the same corridor as Mrs. Chingford just before the accident occurred."

"And if you saw Dorothea, Miss Stanford, then you yourself were within sight of Mrs. Chingford just before she fell," Lucy said. "Perhaps Dorothea saw *you* and drew her own conclusions." She rose from her seat. "I will just see Mr. Fairfax on his way. I'll return in a moment."

Mr. Fairfax followed Lucy to the front door, his expression distracted. He turned to look down at her.

"Do you think it possible that Dorothea saw Mrs. Fairfax with Mrs. Chingford?" he asked.

"I'm not sure. It seems strange that Miss Stanford makes no mention of meeting Mrs. Fairfax on the landing herself. Perhaps both of them mistook Mrs. Fairfax for the other."

"That seems unlikely. Mrs. Fairfax was the only woman dressed completely in black at the wedding."

"It was rather dark up there," Lucy admitted. "But I agree that it seems unlikely. Perhaps Mrs. Fairfax really didn't push Mrs. Chingford down the stairs, after all. . . ."

Mr. Fairfax sighed. "I hope you are right, for her son's sake. I am sorry that I have to leave, but as I mentioned earlier, Major Kurland is in a rather demanding mood today."

"It was kind of you to stay and meet Mr. Reading."

"I can't say I like the man, and I'm still fairly certain that I've seen him before. I just can't place where."

"If you remember, do let me know. I don't care for him myself."

Mr. Fairfax took her hand and brought it to his lips. "Thank you for everything, Miss Harrington. You are an excellent confidante. I will miss your calm good sense when I leave for Fairfax Park."

"I will miss you, too, sir. You have brought order to Kurland Hall and, more importantly, have managed Major Kurland."

"A difficult task, as you well know." He winked before releasing her hand. "Good morning, Miss Harrington."

Lucy retraced her steps to the parlor, slowing as she approached the door and heard raised voices.

"Are you quite certain you saw Dorothea Chingford?"

"Yes."

"And what if Miss Harrington is correct, and Dorothea saw you and believes you had something to do with her mother's death? What happens when she recovers from her illness and blurts out all her suspicions to our remarkably nosy hostess? Your impulsive behavior has put me in a very difficult position, Melissa. A very difficult position indeed."

"But, Paul, my *dear*—"

Lucy tiptoed back toward the kitchen and opened the door, surprising Betty, who was just bringing a fresh pot of tea.

"Take it through, Betty. I'll be there in a moment." Lucy remained by the kitchen door and considered everything she had heard that morning. Major Kurland might have decreed that their investigation into the mysterious deaths was over, but she was of a different mind. If he didn't wish to help her, she would solve the matter for her own satisfaction.

When Dr. Fletcher called, she would ask him if it would be possible to move Dorothea down to the rectory, where she could be nursed by her sister and herself. With Miss Stanford still a guest at the manor house, the opportunity to attempt to silence the young girl might prove too tempting. . . . Lucy frowned. Was it possible that Mr. Reading knew exactly what Miss Stanford had done, and had come down to salvage his marriage prospects?

One might assume that if Miss Stanford had confessed her crime, that as a gentleman, he would immediately wish to distance himself from her. But perhaps his social standing couldn't survive the loss of a well-dowered fiancée from a prominent family. Perhaps he preferred to help Miss Stanford and buy her silence for life. He was no gentleman. Lucy already had proof of that.

Betty returned without the teapot and studied Lucy curiously. "Are you all right, miss?"

"Betty, does your cousin Alf still work as an ostler at the Queen's Head?"

"Yes, he does, miss. Do you want to speak to him?"

"Not right at this moment. Has anyone alerted Miss Chingford to the appearance of visitors?"

"If you like, once I've taken the seedcake and Madeira in, I'll go and inquire if she wishes to come down."

"Thank you, Betty. You really are a treasure."

Lucy returned to the parlor and resumed her seat by the fire. Miss Stanford still looked rather upset, but Mr. Reading was charm personified. Not that Lucy allowed herself to be charmed in the slightest.

"The lady who recently died was a Mrs. Fairfax, you said, Miss Harrington? Is she being buried in Kurland St. Mary, as well?" Mr. Reading asked.

"No. She will be taken back to her home in Cheshire and buried there in the Fairfax family plot." Lucy studied him carefully. "Were you acquainted with Mrs. Fairfax, sir?"

"I might have been." He shrugged. "It is quite a common name."

Miss Stanford hurriedly started speaking. "I don't think you knew this Mrs. Fairfax, Paul. She told me that even when her husband was alive, she rarely visited London. He preferred the comforts of his own home and was quite set in his ways."

"That's what happens when you marry a man old enough to be your father." Lucy started and turned her head as Penelope spoke from the doorway. "One has to wonder how she managed to persuade a gentleman to marry her, when it was obvious that she wasn't quite a lady."

Lucy turned to Penelope. "On what basis do you make that rather judgmental assumption, Miss Chingford?"

Penelope took the seat next to Lucy. "I spoke to her on several occasions. She hardly uttered a word, because she was terrified of sounding common." She turned to Miss Stanford. "You talked to her. What did you think?"

"I . . . I hardly remember."

Penelope raised an eyebrow. "How very diplomatic of you. Mrs. Fairfax told me that she was hoping to persuade Mr. Fairfax to return to the estate and run it for her. Is he going to leave Kurland St. Mary, Miss Harrington?"

"I believe so." Lucy sighed. "He can hardly do anything less."

Penelope snorted. "If I was him, I'd let that family go and hang. They hardly deserve his help."

"That's a decision Mr. Fairfax will have to make for himself," Lucy said. "He seems the sort of man who would honor his commitments to his family."

"Unlike some other families," Mr. Reading muttered.

"Did your family cast you off, Mr. Reading?" Penelope asked sweetly. "One cannot imagine why."

Lucy shot her companion a fierce look. "Does your family have a residence in this area, sir? You did mention that you once lived in Kurland St. Mary."

"Not in the village itself, Miss Harrington." Mr. Reading rose and offered his arm to assist Miss Stanford. "We really must be going. I have to walk Miss Stanford back to the gates of Kurland Hall and then return to the inn to write some letters."

Lucy turned to Miss Stanford, who was looking miserable. "If you wish to stay and keep me and Miss Chingford company, you would be most welcome."

Miss Stanford glanced quickly up at her smiling companion and then back at Lucy. "I'd better be going. I, too, have letters to write."

"Then I will not detain you." Lucy curtsied and summoned Betty to show the couple out. She remembered that Mr. Reading had read through most of Mrs. Chingford's correspondence. Had he, too, found references to Mrs. Fairfax? The first letter *she* had found had been about Miss Stanford *and* Mrs. Fairfax.

"What is it, Lucy?"

She turned to see Penelope observing her closely. "I'm just wondering why Miss Stanford chose to become engaged to such an unpleasant man."

"He isn't usually so disagreeable. In truth, he can be both charming and charismatic when it suits him. At the moment he doesn't need anything from us, and he has Miss Stanford completely under his thumb, so he doesn't have to be charming. I find him far more intriguing this way."

"I don't." Lucy repressed a shiver. "I wonder why he was interested in Mrs. Fairfax?"

"Because he's rather like my mother. He collects useful information and sells it or blackmails people for personal gain. I believe that's how they met. They both tried to blackmail the same person. A marriage between them would've been a disaster."

"Or a roaring success, where they stole and cajoled money out of thousands of people and then retired gracefully to their mansion in Italy." Lucy looked over at Penelope. "I think your mother had a lucky escape."

"I'm not so sure. If she'd managed to marry Mr. Reading, she probably wouldn't have died." Penelope sighed. "I also suspect he would be quite capable of killing her if she tried to double-cross him."

"Was she?"

"Threatening him? I should imagine so. No woman likes to be publicly replaced by a younger, wealthier woman." Penelope grimaced. "She liked to hurt those who didn't treat her with the proper respect."

"By releasing unfavorable information about them to the scandal sheets or to the *ton*?"

"Exactly. Some of the people deserved what she said about them. The majority did not." Penelope paused. "If my mother's death wasn't an accident, Mr. Reading is the first person I would suspect of murder."

"He wasn't at the wedding."

"But his little puppet, Miss Stanford, was."

Lucy held her finger to her lips, jumped up to

close the parlor door, and returned to her spot. "What are you suggesting?"

"Just before she died, my mother told me that she had found a way to discredit Mr. Reading."

"How?"

"She said it had something to do with Major Kurland."

Lucy stared at her companion as her thoughts rushed around her head. "Major *Kurland?* This is all terribly confusing. Mrs. Fairfax arrives to speak to her husband's illegitimate son during the Stanford wedding, and Mr. Reading, who wasn't invited but who is acquaintance with Miss Stanford, Mrs. Chingford, Mrs. Fairfax, *and* Kurland St. Mary, turns up soon afterward. Do you think he came here to protect his betrothed or his own interests?"

"Well, Miss Stanford's interests *are* his. If he marries her, he will gain complete control of her fortune, which, I am told, is considerable."

"Then perhaps he hoped Miss Stanford would speak to your mother on his behalf and soften her heart."

"Or perhaps he told Miss Stanford to push her down the stairs."

Lucy met Penelope's gaze. Neither of them spoke. "You . . . don't think your mother's death was an accident?"

"There is no need to sound so surprised. I'm sure you've wondered exactly the same thing. I is all so convenient for him, isn't it? My family is ruined. My sisters and I lose our chance to make a good marriage and are thrown on the mercy of our richer relatives, and Miss Stanford has to offer herself irrevocably to Mr. Reading in return for him covering up her crime."

"You believe Miss Stanford pushed your mother down the stairs?"

"It's possible." Penelope's expression was grave. "Don't you agree?"

"But why haven't you said anything before now?"

"What's the point? She is still dead." Penelope sat up straight. "You might hate me for saying this, but I am somewhat relieved that she is gone."

For a long moment, Lucy could not think of a reply. She had promised not to disclose anything about Mrs. Fairfax's confession, and she would keep her word. "What about Dorothea? Why do you think she reacted so badly to your mother's death?"

"I don't know." Penelope stiffened. "Why? Do you agree with Mr. Reading and think Dorothea killed her?"

Lucy raised her chin. "It is a perfectly reasonable assumption. If Dorothea got into an argument with your mother, she might have pushed her down the stairs and not intended to kill her. And, as you said, it doesn't change things. Your poor mother is still dead."

Penelope glared at her. "But Dorothea is my sister. She might be something of an annoyance at times, but I still care for her."

"I know you do. I have siblings of my own." Lucy held Penelope's gaze. "I don't discount your theory that Miss Stanford and Mr. Reading might be involved in this matter, but I do wish Dorothea would get better and tell us what she knows."

"Don't worry, Miss Harrington. I will speak to her when she wakes up and will *demand* answers. Perhaps in the meantime you could do your utmost to discover what on earth Mr. Reading has to do with Major Kurland." Penelope nodded at Lucy, rose, and swept out of the room, banging the door behind her.

Lucy shook her head. She had no intention of asking Major Kurland anything. Since his abrupt refusal to work alongside her to discover the truth, he hadn't sought her out, which suited her perfectly. With sudden resolve, she went out into the hallway, found her stout boots and umbrella, and walked out into the rain, toward the village.

For once, her walk was undisturbed by others, which gave her the opportunity to think. She didn't trust Mr. Reading. Penelope's opinion about him having Miss Stanford under his thumb rang true to her, as well. But how on earth was Mr. Reading connected to Major Kurland? Lucy stopped walking and stared straight across the village square at the market clock.

Perhaps they'd been looking at this all wrong. Was Major Kurland the real reason that Mr. Reading had come back to Kurland St. Mary? And if so, what exactly were his intentions?

Chapter 14

Robert made his way up the stairs by himself. It took him a while, but it was less humiliating than having to call James to help him. All was quiet within the house. He believed Miss Stanford had gone down to the rectory, Mrs. Green was in the library, and Dorothea was presumably asleep in her bed, watched over by one of the maids.

Even as he made his way along the corridor toward the guests' bedchambers, Robert wasn't quite sure what he was doing. Despite his words to Miss Harrington about the matter being closed, it continued to trouble his conscience. He glanced over his shoulder to make certain that he wasn't being observed, unlocked the door to Mrs. Fairfax's old room, and let himself inside.

Everything had been left in place for Thomas to go through. He'd been so busy with the Kurland estate that he'd hardly had time to make any arrangements for his father's deceased wife Robert assumed he would pack Mrs. Fairfax' things away once he'd assessed them and decided what to bring back to Fairfax Park. If he wa careful, Thomas would never know that Rober had felt this peculiar urge to search through th widow's belongings before it was too late.

He crossed to the window and opened the curtains. The bed had been stripped of its covers, and piles of Mrs. Fairfax's neatly folded black clothes sat on a chair beside the walnut-fronted tallboy. Using as much finesse as he could, Robert went through all the garments, checking pockets and shawls and the insides of reticules, and found nothing but a silver sixpence, which he hastily put back. He opened all the drawers of the tallboy and of the clothes chest set under the window, but both had been emptied. There was a cupboard built into the wall under a spiral staircase, but it contained only one bonnet and a black cloak.

Turning to the dressing table, Robert sat on the stool to rest his leg and eyed the contents of Mrs. Fairfax's cosmetics box. He had no idea what most of the lotions and potions did, but he doubted anything could be concealed within the glass pots and jars. A faint trace of lavender perfume drifted over him, reminding him of Miss Harrington's much-prized lavender soap.

He picked his way through the assortment of beauty aids, checked the handkerchiefs and the drawers of the dressing table, and found nothing unexpected. He stared at the bed in frowning silence before moving toward it. Where would he hide something if this were his room? Bending down, he ran his hand between the feather mattress and the bed frame, disturbing two

231

spiders and stirring up more dust than he had anticipated.

The bed was large, and it took him a few minutes to work his way around to the top again. He climbed onto the mattress and slid his hand down behind the headboard, where his fingers connected with what felt like paper. He tightened his grip and withdrew his hand. As he straightened, his glance alighted on the worn copy of the Bible, and he picked it up.

A slight noise in the corridor outside had him climbing awkwardly off the bed and retreating toward the long sweep of the drawn curtains. He almost dropped the Bible and finally stashed it and the scrap of paper in his coat pocket. To his dismay, he heard the voices of both his housekeeper Mrs. Bloomfield and Miss Stanford outside the door and the rattle of a key.

"This is so kind of you, ma'am. I cannot imagine where I lost my necklace, but I have searched everywhere. . . ."

Robert reached the cupboard and dove inside, pulling the door almost shut behind him. He arranged himself behind the hanging cloak and went still as the door was unlocked and Miss Stanford came inside.

Through the crack in the door he watched as she searched carefully through Mrs. Fairfax' belongings and then stood in the middle of the room, her hands clenched into fists. She looked

232

as if she was about to burst into tears. Robert held his breath as she advanced on his hiding place and then turned suddenly toward the bed, which she examined thoroughly.

When she approached the cupboard, he shut the door and held on grimly to the latch as she attempted to open it. To his relief, she soon abandoned her attempt to force the door open, and moments later he heard her leave the room. He made himself count to a thousand before he opened the door and stepped out into the bedchamber. Nothing appeared to have been taken.

Rather than risk being seen leaving the room, Robert retreated to the servants' stairs and went down to the ground floor, emerging into the great hall by the front door. Foley bowed to him and offered to make him some tea, which Robert declined as he headed for the privacy of his study.

Locking that door behind him, he sat down at his desk and took out the scrap of paper and Mrs. Fairfax's Bible. He smoothed out the crumpled piece of paper and attempted to read the copied Bible verses. The handwriting was badly formed and very childish. Robert wondered if he'd stumbled across a keepsake of Mrs. Fairfax's son's schoolwork. He had no idea how old the boy was, but this was the sort of thing a fond mother might keep with her. Had it fallen out of her Bible and ended up behind the bed? It seemed all too likely.

The writing was so atrocious that he couldn't identify the verses. He imagined that if Miss Harrington were at his side, she would have recognized them in an instant. Not that they helped to clear anything up. Robert leafed his way through the old Bible, noticing the under-lined passages, which all seemed to concern death and destruction, and the pages that had been marked with slips of paper and ends of ribbon.

He'd have to put the book back in its place, or it would be missed. He turned to the once blank front pages and noticed that several different sets of handwriting had added extra prayers and a list of names, presumably of those who had owned the Bible. The last name was Emily Fairfax. Robert peered intently at the word preceding *Fairfax,* which had been scored across. Had the Bible belonged to Emily before she married Mr. Fairfax? It was highly likely that it had.

It was a shame that she had obliterated her previous surname. . . . Still, he retrieved his magnifying glass from his drawer and considered the words again. If he was not mistaken, there were two words. . . . Robert frowned. He supposed it was possible she had deleted her second name, as well as her previous surname on the occasion of her marriage. But for what purpose? Had she been ashamed of her family or her more humble origins? Mrs. Chingford had hinted that Mrs. Fairfax was not quite what she seemed. Had she married out of her class and been desperate not to let anyone know of it?

Robert put away his magnifying glass. He'd never understand the intricacies of a woman's mind. That was why Miss Harrington had proved so useful in interpreting what had occurred in their past investigations. The feminine nature of her thought processes had often reached conclusions that astounded him but that had proven to be correct.

But he could not involve her in this. If he wanted to investigate any further, he'd have to find another way. He considered anew what Miss Stanford had been up to in the deceased woman's bedchamber. She was the sister of his oldest friend. Perhaps she might be able to help him discover exactly what was going on.

Lucy walked under the archway into the stable yard of the local inn, the Queen's Head, and immediately stepped out of the way of a cart and four horses that were attempting to exit. The inn wasn't situated on a main highway, so there wasn't much through traffic for the ostlers and stable hands to deal with. It was still busy with local farmers coming into Kurland St. Mary from the surrounding hamlets and farms to sell their wares or send goods onward to London, which was a mere twenty-five miles away to the south.

The ancient Roman road up to Newmarket, which was just two miles away, had been improved by horse mad King Charles II, and although Lucy had never had much sympathy for the man's profligate ways, she did appreciate the quality of the road, which made traveling in both directions so much easier.

Picking up her skirts to avoid the mud and horse dung, she crossed over the cobblestones to the main stable and caught the eye of one of the boys lingering at the door.

"Is Alf Smith here today, Jamie?"

The boy removed the straw from his mouth and jumped to attention. "Yes, Miss Harrington. Shall I fetch him for you?"

Lucy nodded, and the boy sped away, leaving her to admire a tub full of flowering pinks next to the back door of the inn. She wondered whether the innkeeper's wife had placed it there to dissipate the smell of the stables. When she turned back, Alf was coming through the door, grinning at her. At some point in his life his two front teeth had been knocked out by a horse, leaving him speaking with something of a whistle.

"Afternoon, Miss Harrington."

"Alf." Lucy smiled at his weather-beaten face. "Are you well?"

"Very well, miss. My daughter just gave me a new grandson."

"So I heard. How lovely for you all. I sent Betty home with a basket for her."

"That you did, and we thank you for it." Alf tugged his forelock. "Now, how can I help you today? Do you need some rats caught?"

"Not this time." Lucy repressed a shudder as she remembered the three huge rats Alf and his dog had caught at the rectory the previous year. "There is a Mr. Reading staying at the inn. Did he bring a horse with him, or did he come by coach?"

"Tall gent with black hair and blue eyes? Dresses like a toff?"

"That's him."

"He brought his horse with him, but the poor beast is fit only for the knackers yard. Mrs. Jarvis is worried he's going to try to leave without paying his shot."

Alf's complete lack of curiosity as to why Lucy was asking him such pointed questions was a refreshing change.

"You don't recall seeing him here before, Alf?"

He scratched his head. "Like last week, you mean?"

"I meant when he was younger. He suggested

to me that he had once lived somewhere near the village."

"I don't remember him, miss. I was away fighting with the good major in the army for years. I can't say he wasn't here then." He lowered his voice. "Does Major Kurland want me to keep an eye on the blighter and make sure he doesn't disappear without handing over his blunt?"

"That's *exactly* what I was going to ask you to do, Alf." Lucy smiled. "But the major also said that as I am closer to the inn than he is, you must feel free to come and tell me about Mr. Reading's movements."

"Then that's what I'll do, Miss Harrington."

"Especially if you think he is acting sus-piciously or plans to leave."

"Consider it done."

Pleased with the notion that Alf was already suspicious of Mr. Reading, and not at all ashamed of using Major Kurland's authority for her own purposes, Lucy walked out into the village street. The rain increased and drummed steadily on her umbrella as she started the trek back toward the church and the rectory beside it.

Why wouldn't Mr. Reading introduce himself to Major Kurland? When she'd mentioned his name, had the major failed to admit that he knew the man? Had that been why he'd insisted they not investigate the matter further? She'd assumed he was angry with her, but perhaps that wasn't it at all. But why would Major Kurland not acknowledge the connection?

She avoided a large puddle and walked purposefully onward. If she accepted that Major Kurland truly had no knowledge of Mr. Reading, was it possible that Mr. Reading knew the major? If he'd grown up around Kurland St. Mary, he must have connected with the premier family in the district. . . .

But perhaps it was even simpler than that. Mrs. Chingford might have informed Mr. Reading that Penelope had once been engaged to Major Kurland. If they had been as close as Penelope claimed, surely Mr. Reading would have been told the news. And had Mr. Reading decided to use his old connection with Kurland St. Mary to reacquaint himself with the major?

Lucy increased her pace. Perhaps she should abandon her plans and go straight up to the manor house and tell Major Kurland to be careful. The wind speed increased, and she angled her umbrella forward, but it was too weak to withstand the sudden gusts and blew inside out. As she struggled to right it, she heard a horse coming toward her and then was unceremoniously shoved off the road and partially into the ditch.

She fought to right herself, only to be confronted by a smiling Mr. Reading, who did nothing to help her regain her footing in the slippery mud.

"Miss Harrington? I didn't see you there. I do beg your pardon."

Lucy's gloved fingers curled around the handle of her broken umbrella as she took an unsteady step away from the ditch. Mr. Reading moved his horse again, almost knocking her off balance, and she was suddenly afraid. Pushing her wet hair away from her face, she glared at him.

"What do you want?"

He shrugged the rain dripping off his hat. "Just to apologize for not seeing you on the side of the road." He glanced beyond her to the unsavory ditch beyond, which was rapidly filling up with water. "Wouldn't want you falling in there. You might never resurface."

"I suspect I'll be fine if you would just leave." Lucy fought to control her chattering teeth as the cold and wet seeped through her pelisse. She took another wary step, and he moved his horse to block her way again.

"What do you *want?*" she shouted up at him.

"Stop meddling in matters that do not concern you."

"I have no idea what you are talking about," Lucy countered. "If you do not back away immediately, I will be speaking to Major Kurland."

"Oh, I don't think so. I'm told you and he are at odds. He won't help you."

"Then I'll speak to my father." She looked past him as she heard the sound of an approaching carriage. "Get out of my way, or I'll scream."

He backed up his horse before tipping his hat to her. "Good afternoon, Miss Harrington. Remember what I said."

He cantered away before the oncoming gig reached her. Lucy picked up a handful of her sodden skirts and tried to move onto more solid ground.

"Miss Harrington!" The gig stopped, and Mr. Fairfax jumped down and ran toward her. "What happened? Did you fall?" He took her elbow in a firm grip and set her on the path. "I'll take you back to the rectory immediately."

She allowed him to help her into the carriage and sat quietly as he urged the horse into a trot. They arrived at the rectory within minutes, and he drove through into the stable yard, calling out for aid. As soon as Bran came out to hold the horse's head, Mr. Fairfax opened the carriage door, swept Lucy up into his arms, and carried her in through the kitchen door.

"Which way is Miss Harrington's bedchamber?"

Mrs. Fielding gasped, and Betty jumped up from the table and ran to open the door into the hallway.

"This way, sir."

Lucy suffered herself to be carried up the stairs and was tenderly deposited on her bed by Mr.

Fairfax, who scarcely seemed encumbered by her weight and the wetness of her clothes.

"If you permit, I'll wait downstairs to hear if you are quite recovered, Miss Harrington."

She managed to murmur a thank-you before Betty ushered him out of the bedchamber. Penelope came in, her eyebrows raised at Lucy's pitiful condition.

"Good Lord. Did you fall in the duck pond?"

Lucy struggled to sit up. "No, but I almost ended up in the ditch, courtesy of your Mr. Reading."

"He certainly isn't mine." Penelope made a face as Lucy fought to take off her soaking wet pelisse. "Thank goodness Mr. Fairfax arrived to save you."

Lucy was too cold to muster much of a glare, but she attempted one, anyway. "I was in the process of saving myself. Mr. Fairfax arrived in time to offer me a ride home, for which I am extremely grateful."

"Don't forget to thank your heroic rescuer, will you?" Penelope had the audacity to wink before she turned and left.

Betty helped Lucy remove her clothing down to her shift and corset and sat her in front of the fire, wrapped in a blanket, her feet in a bowl of warm water. It took quite a while for Lucy to stop shivering. She could only hope that she wouldn't get a chill after her drenching. But worrying about her health would have to wait until she'd decided what to do about Mr. Reading.

"Find me something warm to wear and pin up my hair again, Betty. I have to go down to the parlor and assure Mr. Fairfax that I am quite recovered."

When she entered the parlor, a mere half an hour since she'd arrived home, Mr. Fairfax was pacing the rug in front of the fire, his expression worried.

Lucy curtsied. "Thank you so much for bringing me home, Mr. Fairfax. I don't know what I would have done if you hadn't come along."

In truth, she would have struggled back by herself, but it never hurt to acknowledge an act of generosity, especially from a man.

He strode over to her and took her hand. "I'm sure you would have managed to help yourself, Miss Harrington. I'm just glad I happened along at the right time to save you an extremely unpleasant walk home."

"As you can see, I am quite unharmed by the experience. But do not let me detain you any further." Lucy gently eased her hand free from his grasp and took a seat by the fire, waiting until he joined her. "I'm sure you have work to do."

"I was intending to visit you this afternoon, anyway, after speaking to Dr. Fletcher. He has made up some medicines for Miss Dorothea and asked me to bring them to you before his patient's return to the rectory." He glanced out of the window with a frown. "If it continues to rain like this, I cannot in all conscience allow Miss Dorothea to risk a drafty carriage ride. But do not concern yourself too much, Miss Harrington. I will make sure she comes back tomorrow, when the weather clears up."

"Miss Chingford will be very happy to have her sister back in her care."

"I'm sure she will. One cannot rest easy when a member of one's family is unwell or away from home. I don't know quite how you bear the absence of your siblings so well, Miss Harrington. I suspect you miss them greatly."

"I do. I miss them all, even the twins, who are quite a handful. But they will all return soon, and I am grateful for that."

Mr. Fairfax smiled. "I must confess that I am looking forward to seeing my half brother again. He is quite an engaging little chap and bright as a button."

Betty knocked on the door and came in with a tray. "Mrs. Fielding says you are to drink her ginger tea while it's hot, Miss Harrington, and that there's a drop of brandy in there to warm your bones."

Lucy gazed at the steaming brown liquid. "That is . . . very kind of her. Please give her my thanks."

Mr. Fairfax spoke after Betty left. "Are Mrs. Fielding's potions undrinkable?"

"I've never been offered one before. She usually leaves me to fend for myself when I'm unwell." She took a sip. "Ah, that is most refreshing."

Mr. Fairfax stood up. "I should leave you to recuperate. I will bring Miss Dorothea back tonight if the weather cooperates. If not, tell Miss Chingford to expect me in the morning."

Lucy set aside her cup and rose, too. "Thank you again, Mr. Fairfax."

He took her hand. "Thomas." Then he hesitated. "I thought I saw another horse as I approached you earlier."

Lucy crinkled her brow. "I believe there might have been *someone* who passed me by, but I don't think he saw me in the rain."

Mr. Fairfax snorted. "Or he couldn't be bothered to stop."

"I suppose that is possible." Lucy took a breath. "Are you likely to be traveling on estate business to Thaxted in the near future, Mr. Fairfax?"

"Thaxted?" He paused. "Strangely enough, I have to go and meet with one of the Kurland manor corn merchants there tomorrow."

"Would you mind if I came with you? Properly chaperoned, of course," Lucy said quickly. "If you are able to take me, I will not have to bother my father to get the horses out. I have to deliver an invitation to Mrs. Chingford's funeral."

"I would be most happy to oblige you, Miss Harrington." He bowed. "What time would you like to set forth?"

Chapter 15

I'm coming with you."

Lucy tried to ignore Penelope as she put on her bonnet. "What about Dorothea? We cannot leave her here alone."

Despite Mr. Fairfax's dire predictions about the weather, the previous evening had brought Dorothea and Dr. Fletcher to the rectory. The younger Miss Chingford was now in bed, being watched over by one of the kitchen maids.

"She is exhausted from the journey and told me she intends to sleep all day," Penelope said firmly. "The new maid said she would sit with Dorothea and keep her company if she awakens. Even Dr. Fletcher said she was on the mend and didn't need to be coddled."

"There won't be much for you to do in Thaxted," Lucy said.

Penelope's pale blue eyes narrowed. "You said you intend to deliver an invitation to my mother's funeral on Saturday. Surely I should be involved in that."

"I was merely trying to take some of the burden from your shoulders." Lucy forced a smile. "If you wish to accompany me, then please do so. I don't have time to argue with you. Mr. Fairfax will be here at any moment."

Penelope smiled in triumph. "I will fetch my bonnet and cloak."

Lucy spotted Mr. Fairfax approaching in the chaise and went down the stairs to see if Betty was ready to accompany them. In truth, having Penelope with her might distract Mr. Fairfax from inquiring too deeply into her sudden desire to visit Thaxted. It might also reassure the woman she hoped to meet that it was all right to speak freely to her.

Penelope raised her handkerchief to her nose as she stared at the blackened ruins of Number Eight Field Lane.

"What on earth are we doing here?"

"Attempting to locate the owner of the house."

Lucy went up the path next door and knocked sharply. They'd managed to leave Mr. Fairfax at the inn, attending to the horses, and had promised to meet him by two o'clock for the return journey home.

The solemn-faced little girl Lucy had met on her previous visit opened the door.

"Good morning. Is your mother at home?"

With a little nod, the girl pushed the door open wide and skipped off down the narrow hallway, calling her mother's name. Lucy followed, and so did Penelope. They emerged into a small kitchen, where a woman stood stirring something on the range.

"Mrs. Collins?" Lucy inquired. "I'm Miss Harrington from the rectory at Kurland St. Mary. I do apologize for disturbing you, but we were told you might have information on the whereabouts of your neighbor, Mrs. Madge Summers."

"Madge is very popular these days." Mrs. Collins wiped her hands on her apron and gestured at the table for Lucy and Penelope to sit down. "Polly, watch the stew."

Her small daughter obediently climbed onto a chair stationed close to the range and began stirring the pot.

"Apparently, some extremely officious gentleman was after her on the day of the fire, as well."

Lucy chose not to comment on that. "We were hoping to find Mrs. Summers so that we could inform her about a funeral being held at Kurland St. Mary for an acquaintance of hers. Did she remain in Thaxted after the fire?"

"She stayed here with us the first night, after I'd taken her to see the doctor for something to calm her nerves." Mrs. Collins shook her head. "She was right shaken by what happened."

"Did she remember how the fire started?"

"She said not, but she was getting on in years and might have left something on the range or not cleaned out her chimneys since last winter. Anyways, once I'd persuaded her to swallow a dose of the good doctor's sleeping potion, she slept like an angel."

"And where is she now?"

Mrs. Collins leaned forward. "Well, that's the thing. The next morning she was gone."

"You mean she disappeared?"

"Oh no, miss. She packed up her things and left like a good Christian, but I'm not quite sure where she went. Madge used to be a nurse for a lot of upper-class families. Mr. Collins and I wondered if one of those families had come to help her out."

"But she didn't tell you which one it was?"

"I didn't see her leave, miss. I was out working in the garden. By the time I came back in, she was gone."

Lucy frowned. "Did she not leave you a note?"

"She told Polly to say good-bye and sent her thanks for our kindness." Mrs. Collins shook her head. "We also found a gold sovereign on the table, which was a mite generous of her, but maybe the people who came for her left it instead."

"She wasn't a wealthy woman?"

Mrs. Collins considered. "She owned her cottage outright and had several small pensions from her former employers, so I'd say she was comfortable. She had a daughter, as well. I doubt she would ever starve."

"Are you quite sure it wasn't her daughter or another member of her family who came for her? Do they live locally?"

"She's never mentioned any family, apart from her daughter. That one married above her station, if you know what I mean, miss, and didn't visit her mother as often as she should've done."

"So it is possible that Madge's daughter did come for her."

"It's possible but unlikely. They'd fallen out the year before. The only thing Madge was sad about was not seeing her grandchild as often. He was a bonny lad, by all accounts." Mrs. Collins stood up to check the stew, and Polly was set to making a pot of tea.

Penelope tugged at Lucy's sleeve and whispered, "Aren't you going to ask her about my mother or whether she knows Miss Stanford?"

Lucy sent her a quelling look as Mrs. Collins sat down again. "Did Madge's daughter ever live here with her mother?"

"On and off. She married very young, to a soldier from the local barracks, who went off to war and never came back. The next thing I knew, she'd married again and gone away. Madge wasn't very happy about that. She thought Emmy had behaved very badly indeed."

"Madge's daughter's name was Emily?"

"Something like that. The higher she married, the less she liked her mother to call her Emmy." Mrs. Collins made a face. "And the less she visited."

"It certainly is a puzzle," Lucy sighed. "If we

can't locate Madge, our journey has been in vain." She accepted a cup of tea and sipped at it slowly. "I wonder if she will come back and rebuild her cottage."

"Who knows, miss? Perhaps she'd rather settle down in one of those big houses and be waited on hand and foot for the rest of her life. I can't say I'd mind that myself." Mrs. Collins lifted Polly off the chair and sat her down at the table while she inspected the stew.

Lucy slid the plate of biscuits across to the girl, who took one and mumbled a thank-you.

"Do you remember the day Mrs. Summers left, Polly?"

Polly nodded. "She went in a big black carriage."

"Who came to the door to fetch her?"

"Someone dressed all fancy." Polly wrinkled her nose. "Like a soldier, but not quite that."

"Like a servant in livery?" Lucy suggested.

"Maybe, miss."

"And Mrs. Summers seemed happy to be leaving?"

"She was crying, but I think she was happy." Polly shook her head. "She hardly bothered to say good-bye."

"You will probably miss her," Lucy said sympathetically.

"She made gingerbread, and I helped her in the garden. Sometimes she gave me a penny."

"Well, I'm sure you will see her again."

Polly looked glum and slid off the chair. "I have to go and see if the washing is dry."

Lucy turned to Mrs. Collins. "Thank you so much for your help. If Madge does return, would you let her know that Miss Harrington from the rectory at Kurland St. Mary was inquiring after her?"

"I certainly will, and God bless you for trying to find her to share such sad news." Mrs. Collins wiped her hands and went to open the door. "Should I tell her whose funeral it was, miss?"

"A Mrs. Maria Chingford."

"I've heard Madge mention that lady. She was one of her employers." Mrs. Collins glanced at Penelope, who was dressed in unrelieved black. "Was she a relation of yours, miss?"

"She was my mother."

"Then I'm sorry for your loss, Miss Chingford." Mrs. Collins bobbed a curtsy.

"Thank you."

Lucy led the way out of the house and down the front path, latching the gate carefully behind her as Mrs. Collins waved them off.

Penelope started speaking almost immediately. "So it appears that Mrs. Summers *did* know my mother. I can't say I recall her mentioning anyone called Madge in our household, apart from her dresser, but then she rarely discussed the servants with me."

"I doubt she wished to bother you with such mundane details."

"But what does this prove?"

"Nothing in itself, but Madge also knew Mrs. Fairfax rather well, didn't she?"

Penelope frowned. "How on earth did you come to that conclusion?"

"You yourself said that Mrs. Fairfax appeared uncomfortable in society. If she married outside her class, she probably was."

"You think Mrs. Fairfax is Madge Summers's *daughter?*" Penelope stopped walking to face Lucy.

"Of *course* I do. She married up, she had a son, and her name is Emily, or Emmy, which is Mrs. Fairfax's name."

Penelope slowly closed her mouth and shook her head while Lucy continued. "Madge knew your mother *and* Mrs. Fairfax."

"And both of them are dead."

"And Madge has disappeared, which means that someone doesn't wish us to make those connections."

"But who?"

"Mr. Reading also had knowledge of both your mother and Mrs. Fairfax." Lucy frowned. "But what could Madge possibly know that made it imperative to burn her out of her home?"

"She was a nurse to both families. Perhaps she

knows some scandal that Mr. Reading cannot allow to come to light."

Lucy sighed. "I don't know what to think. But I am worried about Madge Summers, although she didn't seem reluctant to leave with the servant who came to collect her."

"But she might have thought the carriage came from her daughter."

"Who we know has already been dead for several days." Lucy started walking again. "I need to think about this. Please don't tell Mr. Fairfax anything other than we delivered the invitation."

"You want me to lie to our gallant companion?"

"I don't want him worrying about his step-mother, or going back and telling tales to Major Kurland."

Penelope gave an inelegant snort. "You're right. He's so proper, he probably would go and reveal all. I doubt Major Kurland would be pleased to hear that you and I have been asking questions about murder."

"And we still don't have any answers." Lucy picked up her pace as the inn came into view. "I'm sure there is something I am missing, but I cannot yet see what it is. Perhaps a period of calm reflection over luncheon will help me refine my thoughts."

Robert spotted Miss Stanford sitting in the drawing room and went over to her. She was

255

staring out of the window, her embroidery lying forgotten on her knee.

"Good morning, Miss Stanford, and how are you today?" Robert said cheerfully. "The weather is decidedly unpleasant. I do hope Andrew and his new bride are having better luck in Cornwall."

She glanced up at him and then looked away. "I'm sure they are."

Robert took the seat opposite her and stretched out his legs. "I hope it doesn't rain at the funeral. It makes an already somber occasion even worse somehow." She didn't reply, so he pressed on, wishing Miss Harrington were with him to conduct the conversation in her own inestimable fashion. "It is kind of you and Mrs. Green to stay for the funeral."

"I think Andrew would expect it of me." Miss Stanford directed her attention back to her embroidery.

"It is still good of you to attend the funeral of a woman you probably didn't even know." Robert paused. "Or did you know her? I seem to remember seeing you ladies chatting on more than one occasion."

"I knew *of* her. Everyone in London society did. She was considered something of a malicious gossip."

"I must say that from my own experience, Mrs. Chingford was difficult to like."

"She was impossible! She—" Miss Stanford

stopped speaking and pressed her handkerchief to her lips. "I do beg your pardon. I am rather overwrought this morning."

"Ah, is this because you lost your necklace? Mrs. Bloomfield told me you were in some distress. She also mentioned that you wondered if it had ended up amongst Mrs. Fairfax's belongings."

Miss Stanford swallowed convulsively. "I . . . I helped Mrs. Bloomfield lay out the body. I wondered if my necklace had fallen off then."

Robert looked idly out of the window. "I will speak to Foley about this, if Mrs. Bloomfield hasn't already done so. The piece of jewelry he found recently was an old locket. That wasn't yours, as well, was it?"

"No!" Miss Stanford's voice was shaking now and growing louder. "I have no idea whom that locket belongs to at all."

Robert turned to face her. "Are you quite sure?"

"Why are you asking me these questions, Major Kurland?"

He held her stare. "Why haven't you introduced me to your fiancée, who, I understand, is staying in my village?"

"He has nothing to do with any of this. He wasn't even present during the wedding, so you cannot blame him for anything."

"I wasn't aware that I was." Robert paused. 'Why doesn't he want to come up to the hall and be introduced to the best friend of his fiancée's brother?"

"He has his reasons."

"Dashed impolite ones, if you ask me," Robert said. "Perhaps I should go and make his acquaintance myself."

"There is no need, sir," Miss Stanford said quickly. "As I said, he has nothing to do with the matter of my lost jewelry, or anything that happened at the wedding. He merely came to support me through the funeral and doesn't feel it necessary to involve himself with the local gentry."

"But he will be at the service?" Robert asked. "Then I will certainly attempt to make myself known to him. While Andrew is away, Miss Stanford, I feel as if I should act as he would wish me to. Has he met your betrothed?"

"I believe so." She dropped her gaze. "Our engagement happened only recently. My mother has been informed and gave her consent to the match, and that is all I require."

"It is always a relief when one's family approves of a marriage," Robert said diplomatically. "When do you expect the happy event to take place, Miss Stanford?"

"Within the next year. We didn't wish to intrude upon Andrew's happiness."

"How thoughtful of you both." Robert stood and looked down at Miss Stanford's bowed head

"I do hope you find your necklace. Can you describe it so that I can give Foley an accurate description of what to look for?"

"It is nothing. Merely a piece with sentimental value and not worth making a fuss over."

Robert accepted the dismissal in her words and walked away, none the wiser than he had been before the conversation. He wasn't sure how Miss Harrington managed to extract information from people so easily, and wished he had the skill. In truth, he wished she were by his side, asking the questions. Having deliberately avoided her for a few days, he missed her far more than he'd anticipated.

Had he been too hasty in dismissing her help? Back in the sanctuary of his own house and familiar surroundings, his desire to protect her from some unknown threat seemed somewhat ridiculous. But something was definitely going on. He couldn't decide how Miss Stanford's odd conduct related to the two deaths, but he was certain there was a connection. She was behaving quite strangely.

He also suspected that her entire reason for being in Mrs. Fairfax's bedroom had nothing to do with the loss of her mythical necklace and all to do with something she was searching for, but what? He'd known her for several years, and her conduct seemed uncharacteristic. In the past, she'd treated him almost like a brother, and now he apparently was the enemy. He couldn't forget the antipathy in her stare.

What had changed? Robert continued down the stairs to his study. It appeared that her suitor, the unknown Mr. Reading, had a lot to answer for. Mrs. Chingford's funeral was almost upon them. He would certainly make a point of seeking out Mr. Reading and seeing what kind of a man Miss Stanford had decided to marry. He had a suspicion that he wouldn't like what he found at all.

"But—"

Lucy carried on up the stairs, ignoring Penelope's raised voice.

"Slow *down,* Lucy. I still don't understand."

Lucy finally turned around and put her finger to her lips. "If you must discuss this, come into my bedchamber and be *quiet!*"

With an aggrieved sigh, Penelope followed Lucy into her bedroom and shut the door behind them.

"Why do you think Mrs. Fairfax is related to Madge Summers?"

Lucy sat down to remove her half boots and set them on the hearth to dry. "I'm fairly certain that I am correct. What worries me more is, who sent that carriage the next morning? I doubt any of Madge's employers live within a stone's throw of Thaxted. She worked for the aristocracy and the gentry with houses in London and great country estates. How did someone know to come and help her?"

Penelope took the seat opposite her. "If one was of a suspicious nature, one would assume it was the person who set the fire in the first place."

"Which means that Madge might have been taken away and killed."

"But Polly said she went willingly."

"She might not have known exactly who was taking her. She might have assumed it was her daughter."

"Who is already dead."

Lucy let out her breath. "I'm not sure what to do next. Madge has disappeared, and we have no other clues to follow. I do wish Major Kurland hadn't lost that locket."

Penelope yawned. "At least we got away from the village for a while. I'd better go and see how Dorothea is feeling."

"Do you think she will be well enough to attend the funeral?"

"Dr. Fletcher said she should be fine by then." Penelope hesitated. "In truth, I hope she is. Now that I know Mr. Reading is going to be there, I would appreciate her support."

"Don't forget to ask her about what happened the day your mother died."

Penelope looked back over her shoulder as she opened the door. "Oh, I'll ask her, and this time I won't allow her to give me anything but the truth."

Chapter 16

Robert surreptitiously glanced at his pocket watch as the rector continued to speak from the pulpit, his cultured if disinterested voice echoing around the stone pillars and soaring Norman archways. Even with the presence of most of the staff from Kurland Hall and the rectory, the church was half empty. He knew Miss Chingford had invited many of her mother's supposed friends, but no one apart from the family solicitor and a couple of older ladies had come down from London to offer their support.

It made him wonder how many people would show up to *his* funeral.

Miss Harrington sat in the front pew, with the Chingford sisters on either side of her. She wore a veil, so he hadn't seen her face in the brief moment when she'd walked past him to take her seat. He wasn't even sure if he wanted to speak to her. What would he say? He was aware that *something* needed to be said, but feared once he embarked on an explanation of his reasons for denying her his company, he would inadvertently reveal too much or make matters worse.

His gaze moved away from the front of the church to Miss Stanford, who sat with Mrs. Green. There was no sign of Mr. Reading. Had

Miss Stanford warned him off after Robert had declared his intention of confronting the man? It didn't matter. If Mr. Reading was too cowardly to meet him at the funeral, he would have great pleasure in attending him at the one and only inn Kurland St. Mary possessed.

There was a fluttering of movement amongst the congregation as the rector stepped down and concluded the brief service. There was no music, and the sounds of the pallbearers lifting and taking up the strain of the coffin were loud in the hollowness of the church nave. Robert had offered to help but had been assured that his assistance wasn't necessary.

The rector led the sad procession out of the door and took the path behind the church to the graveyard. After Miss Harrington's unpleasant adventures in the churchyard, Robert wondered if she would be relieved that ladies were not expected to attend the graveside. He had offered Kurland Hall as a suitable venue to hold the funeral breakfast but had been politely turned down by Miss Chingford, who preferred to use the rectory.

Out of the corner of his eye, he watched the black-clad women cross the road to walk up the drive to the rectory. Apart from him, Thomas, and the solicitor from the Chingford estate, there were only the pallbearers and some of Robert's staff left to pay their respects. The grave had already been dug and awaited them at the end of a long row shaded by an ancient elm tree. Within the high stone walls of the cemetery, there was the same sense of peace Robert had noticed in every graveyard he had ever visited, even the ones in war-torn France. It was as if the dead held their collective breath and time stood still.

He buttoned his coat to his throat as the breeze picked up. Having seen many a man die in mid-sentence, with a look of surprise on his face, in the midst of a bloody battle, he understood that sense of timelessness. Despite everything they knew to the contrary, no one ever expected to die, even in warfare.

Rousing himself from his melancholy thoughts and aware that he'd be drowning in nightmares later that night, he lifted his head to study the rest of the graveyard. A movement caught his attention. Half hidden beyond the mourners and the rector, who was intoning another prayer as the coffin was slowly lowered into the grave, there was a man.

Aware that there was nothing he could do about the intruder until the service was finished, Robert listened impatiently to the rector's final words. Would he even want such a ritual at his death? He'd always assumed he would die in battle on foreign soil and be left for the scavengers and crows. After the horrors of war, he wasn't quite sure if he believed in God, but as the local magistrate and the largest landowner in the district, he could hardly avoid a good Christian burial. One had to keep up appearances. . . .

The rector turned away, leaving the grave diggers to continue replacing the soil over the coffin. He glanced up at Robert.

"You will come to the rectory, Major Kurland? Mrs. Fielding has laid on quite a spread."

"Of course, Mr. Harrington." Robert inclined his head. "I appreciate your hospitality on this sad occasion and would be delighted to join you."

To his relief, the rector said no more and went off, accompanied by the Chingford solicitor, toward the house. Robert took a more circuitous route that brought him around the back of the church and up behind the path where he'd spied the unknown gentleman. Who was, of course, no longer there.

"Devil take it," Robert swore quietly. There was still the hint of smoke in the air, and a glance down revealed the remains of a cigarillo stamped into the ground by a booted heel.

The church bell tolled the quarter hour, and Robert headed across the street to the rectory. He needed to pay his respects and offer his condolences to the Miss Chingfords and attempt to speak to Miss Harrington. His thoughts during the funeral had reminded him that life was short, and that he was much happier when he and Miss

Harrington were on good terms. Perhaps if he offered her a sincere apology, she would forgive him without wishing to delve into the various reasons that had driven him to become angry with her in the first place.

As he walked up the drive, he couldn't help but utter a short laugh at his own expense. No woman of his acquaintance had ever accepted an apology without the need to discuss the matter, and Miss Harrington was no exception. The front door of the rectory was adorned with a black bow on the knocker and unlatched, so Robert went through into the hall and left his hat and gloves on the stand.

There was a low murmur of conversation coming from the drawing room and the smell of baking and warm punch, which would be most welcome. As Robert entered the room, Thomas caught his eye and came to stand beside him.

"Would you like me to fetch you some mulled wine, sir? I was just going to get a cup for myself."

"Yes, please," Robert said. "I'll go and pay my respects to Miss Chingford."

He located the two fair-haired sisters on couch beside the fire and made his halting way over to them.

"Major Kurland." Miss Chingford looked up at him. Her eyes were dry, and she appeared her usual composed self. "How kind of you to come

Robert bowed. "I am sorry for your loss, Miss Chingford, Miss Dorothea. I am even more sorry that it happened in my house. If there is anything I can do to help—"

"Apart from marrying me, you mean?" Miss Chingford interrupted him. "It's all right. I have quite given up on that foolish notion."

Robert held her gaze. "I'm glad to hear it, but if there is anything else you need, please do not hesitate to ask."

"Thank you."

He turned away, aware of someone waiting behind him, and found Thomas, who was holding two glasses in his hands.

"Here you are, Major."

Robert took the hot drink and savored the pungent scent of herbs and spices, which reminded him of the exotic woods used in the chest in his bedroom. "That is very welcome."

His gaze traveled around the room and fixed on Miss Harrington, who was conversing with the two old ladies who had arrived from London. Her face was in profile, giving him a moment to admire not only the slight dimple in her left cheek she tried to hide but also the intelligence in her fine hazel eyes. As if realizing she was being observed, she looked across the room and then continued her conversation, as if she'd not seen him. Her dimple disappeared, and her chin was now raised at a challenging angle.

Things were obviously not mended between them, and that was his fault. Perhaps it would be better if he wrote her a letter and apologized. There was less opportunity for him to say the wrong thing. . . .

Good Lord, he was such a coward.

"Major Kurland."

He turned with relief to his land agent. "Yes, Thomas?"

"I was thinking of leaving for Fairfax Park in three or four days."

"Ah, yes. I'd forgotten you were returning home. Will the house still be staffed? If you need to borrow a groom or a couple of the maids from Kurland Hall, I am more than willing to lend them to you."

"That's very kind of you, sir. I believe the house is fully staffed. I haven't been there for quite a while, but I did write and tell them to expect me." He frowned. "I don't think Mrs. Fairfax employed a housekeeper, and I know little about how to manage a house."

"You should ask Miss Harrington for her advice. She is certainly very capable of running a household."

"She is indeed. What an excellent suggestion."

There was a warmth in Thomas's reply, which made Robert look closely at his land agent, whose gaze was currently fixed on Miss Harrington. To Robert's surprise, when she noted Thomas's regard, she smiled at him and blushed. Robert thrust his empty glass into Thomas's hand and went over, trapping her in the corner of the room.

"Major Kurland."

He bowed. "Miss Harrington. I wish to apologize."

She raised her eyebrows, her gaze cool. "Whatever for?"

"For my rudeness at our last meeting. I spoke without proper regard to your feelings." He swallowed hard. "I was . . . worried about you."

She started to say something and then stopped. *"Worried?"*

"Yes. That I would prove incapable of protecting you if the need arose."

She studied him for a long moment. "I appreciate your concern for my well-being, sir, but I am quite capable of taking care of myself."

"I know that, but—"

"You think all women need a strong man with a strong hand to guide them."

"Yes, that's it *exactly*. I—"

"And what if I don't agree with you?" She held his gaze. "You treated me like a misbehaving child, Major Kurland, or a dog that should obey your every command. No woman wishes to be treated like that."

"I didn't intend—"

"I'm sure you didn't, but that is your way, is it not? You are too used to being in command and

269

expect everyone to immediately stand to attention and obey you."

He realized he was glaring at her again. "You are deliberately misunderstanding me. Why do women make the simplest things so complicated?"

"Pray tell me how I am doing that, Major Kurland."

"By refusing to understand that I worry about you because, devil take it, I *care* about you."

Shock flashed in her hazel eyes, and she opened her mouth to reply.

"Major Kurland?" The rector's loud voice right behind Robert's left ear made him wince. "Mr. Fairfax says he is leaving for his deceased father's estates later this week. How are you going to manage without him?"

Reluctantly, Robert turned and faced the rector. "I have no idea. He will be much missed." When he managed to extricate himself from the conversation, he discovered that Miss Harrington was nowhere in sight.

Lucy ran up the stairs, her hand pressed tightly to her heated cheek. She still wasn't certain if she wished to scream at her father for his interruption or thank him profoundly. And why was she so flummoxed, after all? Major Kurland had only intimated that he cared about her. . . .

She slowed to a stop on the landing, aware

that her heart was thudding in her chest and that she had a strange desire to go back down the stairs and slap Major Kurland's handsome face. Perhaps he did care for her—in the way he cared for Mr. Stanford's children and his horses. What else could he possibly have meant?

"Miss Harrington, are you all right?"

She half turned to see Dorothea coming toward her. "I am sorry. I stopped to remember something and didn't realize I was blocking your path." She forced herself to calm down and took a closer look at Dorothea. She wore unrelieved black, and her face was the color of parchment. "You look rather pale. Are you feeling quite the thing?"

"I just want all of this to be over." Dorothea burst out. "I want to go home, but where will that be now we have been dispossessed?"

"Please don't worry." Lucy took the girl's trembling hand. "You and your sister can stay here for as long as you wish. Perhaps the Chingford family solicitor, who came for the funeral today, will be able to set matters straight for you."

"Penelope has already told me that we will be penniless and at the mercy of our relatives." Tears shone in Dorothea's eyes. "I never thought this would happen to us. I didn't *think*."

"About what?" Lucy asked. "The consequences of your mother's death? Are you *quite* certain that you don't wish to tell me what happened on that day?"

Dorothea shook her head. "Penelope has already asked me that question. But what does it matter anymore? My mother is still dead. What is to become of *me?*"

She went back down the stairs, leaving Lucy full of exasperation. Young ladies just out of the schoolroom were often exhausting, and Dorothea Chingford was certainly no exception. Her entire world revolved around her needs and feelings. If she *had* pushed her mother down the stairs, she certainly was learning that her actions had consequences.

And what exactly had Dorothea told Penelope? Lucy frowned as she opened the door into her bedchamber and took a clean handkerchief out of her top drawer. Penelope had promised to tell Lucy the results of her conversation with her sister, but so far she had said nothing. After a deep breath, Lucy resolved to return downstairs. She'd run away from Major Kurland, and that would never do. She still had responsibilities as her father's hostess and had yet to speak to all the guests. A subdued Miss Stanford was there with Mrs. Green, but there was no sign of Mr. Reading. One might almost think he was avoiding being seen.

Once the funeral was over, there would be no further reason for Miss Stanford and her fiancé to remain in Kurland St. Mary, and all opportunities to discover exactly what Mr. Reading was up to would disappear along with the couple. Perhaps, despite everything, Major Kurland was right, and it was better to let things lie.

"Miss Harrington?"

She looked down to see Mr. Fairfax awaiting her at the bottom of the stairs and summoned a smile.

"Mr. Fairfax."

He held out his hand. "I wonder if I might have a word with you in private."

Robert excused himself and walked out into the rectory garden. Because the house was barely ten years old, the space was rather bare, boasting a variety of saplings, trees, and plants that needed time to grow. Luckily for the rector, there was one fine old copse of beech trees grouped toward the rear of the garden, which offered both shade and a softening of the hard boundaries of the newly erected stone and brick walls.

He followed the path toward the trees and paused to light a cigarillo. He'd managed to upset Miss Harrington again and failed to spot Miss Stanford's errant betrothed. All he needed now was for Miss Chingford to inform everyone that he'd agreed to marry her, and his day would be complete.

"Major Kurland?"

He turned to see Dorothea Chingford behind him, her ungloved hands clasped together at her waist and her expression anxious.

"Miss Dorothea?"

She took a step toward him. "I . . . found something at Kurland Hall. I think you should have it."

She held out her hand, and he instinctively opened his palm to receive the all too familiar weight of the battered gold locket.

"Where did you find this?" he asked gently.

She bit her lip. "I don't remember. In one of the upstairs hallways, I think."

He didn't believe that but was reluctant to cross-question her on the day of her mother's funeral. "Why are you giving it to me and not to its rightful owner?"

"You were the one asking about it, sir. I thought you should have it."

"May I ask why you imagined you might . . . need it?"

"I thought it might prove useful, sir."

"For what purpose?"

"As evidence."

Robert studied her carefully. "Of a crime?"

"I'm not sure. I just thought it was better to be safe than sorry." She took a step away from him. "But it doesn't matter now, does it?"

"Do you have an idea who it might belong to?"

"Give it to Mr. Fairfax." She turned away. "Mrs. Fairfax should have it, don't you think?"

"Wait," Robert said. "I'm not exactly sure what you are trying to say."

She looked over her shoulder at him. "Mrs. Fairfax should take the locket to her grave."

"Did you see her wearing it?"

To his annoyance, she set off without answering the question, leaving him staring down at the locket in his hand. Miss Dorothea was as bad as Miss Harrington for making things more complicated than they needed to be—perhaps worse. He really had to take the cursed thing to the blacksmith or a jeweler, who could open it for him.

Even as he had that thought, he became aware that he was no longer alone in the garden. Someone was moving through the beech trees toward him. Robert's hand instinctively went for his sword, which no longer swung at his hip.

"Good afternoon, Bobby."

Robert straightened, put the locket in his pocket, and faced the gentleman dressed in black.

"Paul? What in God's name are you doing here? I thought you were still in India."

His second cousin shrugged. "I wrote to tell you of my imminent arrival on these shores over a year ago. My letter was returned unopened." Paul's gaze swept over Robert and lingered on his cane. "I heard you were a cripple."

"I suffered a broken leg and hip at Waterloo."

"Of course you did. What a hero." Paul's laugh was meant to offend. "You were always such a good little soldier, Bobby, and now I hear that you have been granted a title."

"No one calls me Bobby anymore. I'm rather too old for such a childish name. Why are you here?"

"Not to bother you, dear cousin. Never think it." His gaze moved beyond Robert to the back of the rectory. "Please excuse me. I really must be getting along."

He attempted to move past Robert, who blocked his path. "By the terms of the agreement you signed with my father, you are not allowed to set foot in Kurland St. Mary."

Paul patted his hand. "No, I am not allowed to set foot on Kurland *property*. I don't believe the rectory counts. Now, move out of my way, please, there's a good fellow. I don't want to have to embarrass a war hero."

Robert stepped back. "And I cannot allow you to embarrass yourself as an unwanted guest at a funeral."

"Unwanted?" Paul raised an eyebrow. "I was invited by Miss Chingford, who, I understand, had the good sense to break off her engagement to you." He started walking, and Robert followed him. "I do hope you aren't going to make a scene, old chap. This is hardly the place to air ancient family quarrels, is it?"

"I agree. Why don't we take this discussion back to my study in Kurland Hall?"

Paul reached the door into the house and held it open. "Perhaps after I've had a chance to pay my respects to the Chingford ladies." He raised his voice until it seemed everyone in the room was looking at them. "As delightful as it is to catch up with you, Bobby, my first duty is to my betrothed and to those who mourn." He held out his hand to Miss Stanford, who had risen to her feet, her expression anxious.

"My dear Miss Stanford. I do apologize for my tardiness. Have you met my second cousin, Major Sir Robert Kurland?"

Lucy, who had just returned from speaking to Mr. Fairfax and was still attempting to decide what to do about what he had suggested, stared at Mr. Reading as he made his announcement. Seeing the two men side by side, she could detect the family resemblance, which had previously eluded her. Both he and Major Kurland were dark haired, with blue eyes, and were about the same height. Despite the lines that pain had etched on the major's face, she judged Mr. Reading to be slightly the older of the two.

Miss Chingford walked over to the two men.

"Major Kurland is your cousin, Mr. Reading? Why didn't you mention that interesting fact before? You've been practically living in his village for the past week."

Mr. Reading bowed. "Alas, Miss Chingford, my branch of the family is not considered worthy enough to be granted access to the delights of Kurland Hall."

"That's not quite true," Major Kurland said abruptly. "I am very fond of your mother and sister, Paul. They are welcome to visit me at any time and have done so frequently since you left to 'better' yourself in India." He sounded remarkably calm to Lucy's ears. "I'm more interested in hearing why you felt it necessary to use a false name."

"Hardly *false*." Mr. Reading gave an airy laugh. "As if I would use a surname that I no longer consider my own. I would've thought you would prefer me to use my mother's name."

"I have no objection to it in principle. I just wonder why you chose to deceive those around you."

"I don't believe I have deceived anyone. Miss Stanford knows the truth, as does her mother." Mr. Reading bowed to Miss Chingford and took her hand. "If I might direct this conversation back into rather more conventional channels? I came to pay my respects to your mother, my dear, and to wish you and your sisters well in the years ahead."

"Thank you." Miss Chingford swiftly disengaged her hand from his. "I can't say it has been a pleasure knowing you, but I appreciate the fact that you came to the funeral."

Mr. Reading bowed again and turned toward Miss Stanford, who began whispering urgently in his ear. Major Kurland placed Penelope's hand on his sleeve and brought her back across the room to where Lucy was standing.

"Miss Harrington, I saw Miss Dorothea out in the garden without her shawl. Should I send one of the maids to coax her back inside?"

Lucy managed not to look directly at him as she fussed around Penelope. "Yes, Major. That would be very kind of you."

There was a sharp tug on her elbow, and she obediently sank down onto the seat beside Penelope.

"Why didn't Mr. Reading tell us he was Major Kurland's cousin?" Penelope whispered.

"He didn't even tell you?" Lucy raised her eyebrows. "What about your mother?"

"She might have known, but she certainly never mentioned anything to me about the matter, even when I was engaged to the major."

"How odd," Lucy commented as she watched Miss Stanford and her beau make their way around the guests, presumably making their adieus. "Perhaps he didn't want Major Kurland to know he was here."

"Which brings us back to whether he was involved in planning my mother's death."

Lucy sighed. "Even if he was, what can we do about it? He wasn't at the wedding. We have no evidence against him, Miss Stanford is going to marry him, your mother is dead, and we have no idea where Madge Summers is."

"But Mr. Reading is the key! He knew everyone and has been pretending to be something he is not."

Lucy shook her head. "I can't believe I didn't make the connection sooner. While I was acting as Major Kurland's secretary, I saw at least two letters from a Mr. Paul Kurland, which I was instructed to return unopened."

"I wonder what he wants?"

They both stared at the oblivious Mr. Reading.

"He is officially Major Kurland's heir," Lucy noted.

"Unless the major marries and has children of his own." Penelope gripped Lucy's arm so hard, she jumped. "What if Mr. Reading got to know my mother only because he knew I was engaged to be married to Major Kurland?"

"With what end in view?"

"To prevent the marriage?"

Lucy thought about this. "I suppose that could be true, but your mother must have informed Mr. Reading that the engagement was over, so why is he here now?"

"Because my mother said she knew something that connected him to Major Kurland. She threatened him!"

"But now that we all know about the connection, what harm can he do?"

"Nothing, which is why he has finally chosen to acknowledge it." Penelope sat back with the air of a prosecutor who had finished his speech.

"You are suggesting that having got rid of your mother, he had nothing more to fear?"

"It is possible."

"But what does that have to do with Madge Summers and Mrs. Fairfax?"

Penelope sighed. "I don't know."

"Perhaps the two things aren't connected, after all," Lucy said doubtfully. "Although—" She stopped talking as her father looked for her. "Yes, Father?"

He beckoned her over, and she went to join him.

"Ah, Lucy, Mr. Brewerton, the Chingford family solicitor, would like to speak to the ladies. Do you think you could show him into my study and arrange for a pot of tea while George and I stay here and mingle with the guests?"

"Certainly, Father." She curtsied to the solicitor, who gave her a sharp nod. "Mr. Brewerton, would you like to come with me?"

Chapter 17

G ood morning, Bobby."
Robert raised an eyebrow. It was the day after the funeral, and he'd summoned Paul to the manor house. He'd made certain his cousin would turn up by threatening to come down to the inn and fetch him out of bed himself.

"If you continue to call me that, I'll reciprocate with your childhood nickname of Roly-Poly." He indicated the chair in front of his desk. "Please take a seat."

Paul sat down and crossed one leg over the other. "Good Lord, Robert, did you lose your sense of humor on the battlefields of Europe, along with your health? You really should learn to take a joke."

Robert folded his hands on his desk and focused his attention on his cousin. It was odd seeing that fleeting likeness to himself, which concealed glaring differences that still surprised him. "What exactly do you want, Paul?"

"See, there you go again, forgetting the pleasantries and issuing orders like some kind of drill sergeant."

Fleetingly, Robert thought of Miss Harrington suggesting the same thing about his dictatorial manners and continued to stare until Paul started to fidget.

"I just came to pay my respects to an old friend who had died. I didn't realize my presence would be so unwelcome."

"Balderdash. You knew my father banished you from his sight."

Paul sighed. "But you aren't your father. Perhaps I thought you might be more forgiving."

"*Forgiving?* Paul, you lied and cheated and stole from my family. A family that took you and your mother in after your father died, and tried to give you a decent upbringing."

"Hardly decent. I was never allowed to forget who would be inheriting Kurland Hall."

"Because you constantly pretended it would be you!" Robert shook his head. "The debts you ran up in my name, the loans . . . You could have bankrupted us."

"Don't be ridiculous. This particular branch of the Kurland family is as rich as Croesus."

"But not your branch. You ran through your father's bequest and your mother's and sister's portions. You left them with nothing."

Paul sat up straight. "There's no need to bring up the past, Robert. I am well aware of what happened, and there is no need to revisit it. I've paid the price, and I'm more than willing to move on."

"I'm sure you are." Robert paused. "You do

283

realize that in all conscience I cannot allow you to marry Miss Stanford without her brother being fully aware of exactly who you are and what you have done in your life?"

Paul waved a negligent hand. "There is no need for you to interfere. Miss Stanford's mother has already given her consent to the match."

"Without knowing your true identity?"

Paul shrugged. "She liked me. You've always hated that about me, haven't you, Robert? That people like me more than you."

"I can't say I've ever really thought about it much. I don't crave approval like you do."

"Of course you don't. You are rich. Everyone likes a rich man, especially one who excels in the military." Paul's dismissive blue gaze swept over Robert. "Although from what I understand, a crippled war hero with an extremely volatile disposition appears to put most ladies of the *ton* off the thought of marriage entirely."

"Which means that in the fulfillment of time, you might inherit everything, anyway."

"Exactly!" Paul held up a finger. "Which brings me to the point of my visit. Surely, as your heir I should be entitled to some portion of the profits from the estate."

Robert laughed out loud. "You are jesting, of course. You *had* an allowance from my father. He also paid for your clothing, schooling, horses and travel. In return for his generosity, you took up life as a rake, amassed thousands of guineas of debts, and had to flee the country after a rather nasty duel with the enraged husband of your mistress."

Paul looked pained. "That was ten years ago, Robert. As you very well know, I ended up in India, where I behaved myself perfectly well."

Robert held up a sheaf of papers. "No you did not. My father wasn't stupid, Paul. He received regular reports on your behavior, which were sent to me after his death. You haven't changed a bit." He sat back in his chair. "In fact, I have to assume that the only reason you came back to England was that you had done something outrageous enough to be kicked out of India. No doubt there will be a report on the matter soon."

"I came back to England to offer you my sympathies on your injuries, and to offer to help you out with the estate," Paul said haughtily. "I was told that you were unlikely to walk again and would be bedridden."

"And thus unlikely to reproduce." Robert glared at his cousin. "Well, I'm sorry to disappoint you, but I'm quite well enough to manage both my estates and to contemplate a long and happy marriage with the woman of my choice."

Paul's eyes narrowed. "You have a new candidate in mind?"

"That is none of your business."

"As your legal heir, I believe it is."

"If and when I intend to marry, you can read the announcement in the newspapers like everyone else."

"So you just expect me to disappear again and not bother you?"

"Exactly." Robert rose to his feet. "I'm not paying you an allowance. I'm going to write to Andrew and tell him about your unsavory history. And now I am going to have Foley escort you to my front door and tell you never to darken it again. Are we quite clear?"

Paul remained seated and looked up at Robert. "I'll be staying at the inn for the foreseeable future."

"You'll get bored fairly quickly. There isn't much to do here." Robert walked over to the door and held it open. "I'm not going to change my mind."

"Then get used to having a poor relation haunting your every footstep."

Robert looked over at his cousin. "If you can't pay your bills, don't come running to me for help. If you find yourself in debt, as the local magistrate, I'll make sure you are prosecuted to the full extent of the law."

Paul stood with a lazy grace and sauntered over to the door. "For goodness' sake, Robert. Where's your Christian charity, old man? We're *kin*."

"More's the pity," Robert muttered. "Get out and leave Miss Stanford alone."

"She won't abandon me." Paul hesitated, his gaze locked on Robert's. "She is the only person in the world who believes in me."

"Then she is a fool, and the quicker I can return her to the care of her brother, the better."

"I'm not leaving Kurland St. Mary, Robert."

"Good *day,* cousin, and get out."

"May I at least speak to Miss Stanford before I go?"

Holding his cousin's gaze, Robert shouted, "Foley?"

"Yes, sir?"

"Find James and escort Mr. Reading to the front door. Make sure he speaks to no one on his way out."

"Yes, Major. Now come on, Mr. Paul. You know you aren't welcome here."

The look Paul shot over his shoulder at Robert was full of malice, but he followed Foley meekly enough down the corridor. Robert realized he would have to ask Mrs. Green to keep a close eye on Miss Stanford. He knew the ladies had originally intended to travel back to London together, but he thought it might be safer for Miss Stanford to remain at Kurland Hall until Andrew returned from his honeymoon.

If Miss Stanford was free to see Paul, there was no knowing what his scandalous cousin might do to ensure he gained a wife and a fortune. With a soft curse, Robert went back to his desk and finished the letter he'd been writing to Andrew and explained his intention of keeping Miss Stanford safely at Kurland Hall. Once Paul realized he couldn't gain access to his supposed fiancée, Robert could only hope he'd move on to pastures new.

He sealed the letter with wax and the imprint of his signet ring and, deciding he was too agitated to remain at his desk, took the letter with him to the main hall. He placed it on the table where Foley would see it and then hesitated.

"Major Kurland!"

He looked up at the minstrels' gallery to see Andrew's daughter waving at him through the bannisters.

"Good morning, Miss Charlotte. Have you escaped your nurse again?"

"Not exactly . . ." She had the grace to look a little conscience stricken, which made him want to smile. "Are you going into the village?"

"I thought I might walk down there, yes."

She skipped down the steps, her curls bobbing with every jump. "Can I come with you? Please say yes. I'll be ever so good and . . ."

"Where is Terence?"

"He's out riding with Mr. Fairfax."

He held out his hand. "Then I suppose you should have a treat, as well."

She gave a tiny squeal and leapt down the remaining steps. "Thank you, thank you. I'll b very good, and I won't pester you about anything or expect sweets or—"

He drew her toward the kitchens and asked James to tell the nurse where her errant charge had gone. Charlotte's bonnet and pelisse were in the kitchen, being dried out from the previous day's rain, so she had only to fetch her boots and they were ready to go.

She glanced over at him as they left the house.

"Can you walk that far with your bad leg?"

He appreciated the way she just asked the obvious question. It was so refreshing after dealing with the barbs and subtleties of adult society. "I'll certainly do my best. I've been practicing every day."

She scowled. "Like I have to do on the piano-forte. I hate it."

"Then perhaps you should tell your new mama, and she can help you choose another instrument to play."

She gave an extra skip. "That's a good idea. You are so clever, Major."

They progressed down the driveway and turned out onto the main road that led into the village. The old church loomed up on their right, and on the left was the open gate that led up the drive to the new rectory.

"Miss Harrington is very nice."

"She is indeed." He sighed. "Although she can

be quite intimidating when she puts her mind to it, believe me."

"She is the best friend of my father's new wife."

"That is true."

"Which means that she will come and visit us in London and at Greenbridge House, doesn't it?"

"I should imagine so." It had occurred to him that unless she married, he would be bumping into Miss Harrington at the Stanfords' and at home for the rest of his life. Which made it even more imperative that he mended things between them as quickly as possible.

Charlotte tugged on his sleeve. "Can I run a little bit? I promise I'll be careful."

They were approaching the High Street, and there were some flagstones laid in front of the local shops.

"Go ahead. Stay on this side of the road. I'll watch you."

He checked his pockets and heard the reassuring jangle of coins. He'd stop in the village store and buy Charlotte something sweet or a new ribbon for her hair. When Andrew had asked if he might leave his children at Kurland Hall until his return, Robert had worried whether he would be able to stand the noise and inconvenience children always seemed to bring with them. But the Stanford children had proven remarkably pleasant.

It wasn't quite enough to make him contemplate setting up his own nursery, but he was more open to the idea of fathering an heir in the future.

"Major Kurland!"

Charlotte was running back toward him, her expression determined, her booted feet thumping down on the flagstones. He took a step toward her and then was impeded by a figure that came out of the village shop. It was too late to call out a warning as Charlotte cannoned into the lady, and Robert attempted to catch them both as they fell backward into his open arms.

For a horrible moment he was almost suffocated by petticoats and the press of the two bodies on top of him. Eventually, order was restored, as Miss Chingford lifted Charlotte off Miss Harrington, and Robert was able to offer her a hand to assist her upright.

"Good Lord!" Miss Harrington gasped. "Are you all right, Charlotte?"

"I'm fine, Miss Harrington." Charlotte gave an experimental skip and then beamed up at her rescuer. "You caught me like a ball."

Robert managed to stand up using the window ledge of the store and looked for his hat, which had been knocked clean off his head.

"Do you need help, Major Kurland?" Miss Chingford came toward him, her hand outstretched.

"No. I'm perfectly fine." Robert found his hat

and dusted it down before placing it on his head. "I'm more concerned about the ladies."

Miss Harrington was bent over young Charlotte, checking her for injuries. "We are both quite recovered, sir."

Charlotte grinned at Robert. "You caught us both!" Her smile faded, and she ran over to him. "Is your bad leg hurting?"

"Not at all."

She put her hand on his sleeve. "Are you sure?"

Miss Chingford came up and patted Charlotte on the head. "Major Kurland is a very capable gentleman, Charlotte. Perhaps we should take him back to the rectory for tea and thank him properly. There is something I wish to speak to him about."

Charlotte looked up at him, and Robert found himself agreeing to the suggestion, despite the lack of an invitation from Miss Harrington. Charlotte took his free hand, leaving the other two ladies to walk ahead of them, which suited his slower pace admirably. By the time they reached the rectory, Miss Harrington had already taken off her cloak and bonnet and was issuing instructions to Betty about tea and buttered muffins.

She glanced at him as he ushered Charlotte into the parlor.

"Major Kurland, you are limping quite badly Please sit by the fire."

He did as she asked without comment. Charlotte came to lean on the arm of his chair, one hand patting his bad knee.

"It was quite funny to see you being bowled over, Major, but I'm sorry that you hurt your leg."

He smiled to reassure her as Miss Harrington disappeared in the direction of the kitchen. "It's all right. I'm sure I will be perfectly fine for the walk home."

Betty came in with a tea tray, followed by Miss Chingford and Miss Harrington, who paused by his chair to lay a hot cloth on his knee. She didn't fuss over him or issue any instructions, which was surprisingly comforting.

"Tea, Major?"

"Yes, please." He glanced across at Miss Chingford, who had taken the seat opposite him. "How is Miss Dorothea?"

"She is feeling much better, sir."

"I'm glad to hear it." He hesitated. "Have you decided on your plans for the future yet?"

"Our solicitor, Mr. Brewerton, says that we shall have a small annuity from my mother and that we have been offered a home with my father's oldest sister, who lives in Northumberland."

"Ah." Robert tried to think of something positive to say. "I've heard it is a beautiful part of the country."

"Indeed. I'm not quite certain it would agree

with me, sir, so I am continuing to investigate other possibilities." Miss Chingford flashed a rare smile at Miss Harrington. "The rector has offered us a home for as long as we need it."

"How . . . kind of him."

"Miss Harrington persuaded him."

Robert had nothing to say to that. He accepted some more tea and waited for the ache in his leg to subside, which it did more quickly with the addition of the heated cloth.

"I understand that Mr. Fairfax is leaving in a few days," Miss Chingford said.

"That's correct. He hasn't specified exactly which day yet, but I suspect he'll tell me that soon."

Miss Chingford raised her eyebrows. "But I thought it was all agreed that he was leaving on Wednesday. Isn't that the day he said he would come and collect us, Lucy?"

Robert very slowly put his cup down on its saucer. "I beg your pardon?"

"I believe that's what he said, Penelope." Miss Harrington darted a look at Robert and then raised her chin. "Mr. Fairfax asked me if I would do him the honor of accompanying him to meet his household."

"For what purpose?"

Miss Harrington looked at him as if he were an idiot. "He said that it was your idea, Major. Tha you recommended my housekeeping abilities and thought I might be able to help him make sense of what is required at his new home."

"I don't remember—"

"Be that as it may, Major," Miss Chingford interrupted him with a sweet smile. "Isn't it kind of dear Mr. Fairfax to take such an interest in our Lucy? One might wonder at his motives." She flicked a knowing glance at Miss Harrington. "Perhaps he wishes to see if *you* will make him a good housekeeper, Lucy."

Robert stared at Miss Harrington, who was blushing. Was it possible that Thomas was considering her as a potential wife? That wasn't what he'd meant to happen at all when he'd recommended her housekeeping.

Patting Charlotte's hand, Robert stood up, the cloth falling from his knee to the floor. "It sounds as if Thomas has arranged things to his satisfaction. Now, I really must take Miss Charlotte home before her nurse thinks I've lost her for good." He bowed. "A pleasure, as always, ladies. Please remember me to Miss Dorothea and the rector."

Charlotte obediently followed him to the front door and put on her outdoor things before joining him in the walk back up the long drive to Kurland Hall. Luckily, she seemed tired from her adventures and was more than willing to let Robert contemplate in solitary silence a future without Thomas and Miss Harrington in Kurland St. Mary.

He arrived at the manor house, deep in thought, only to encounter Charlotte's brother Terence and Thomas in the kitchens. While the children were taken up to the nursery wing to be bathed and to have supper, Robert invited Thomas to join him for dinner.

As they sat drinking a glass of port at the end of the meal, Robert said, "I hear you are intending to leave on Wednesday."

"That's correct. Did Foley tell you?"

"It was Miss Chingford. She said that she and Miss Harrington were going with you to assess the state of the house and the staff."

"When you suggested I ask Miss Harrington for her advice, I couldn't believe I hadn't thought of it myself. She was more than willing to come and look over the house with me." Thomas hesitated. "I suspect she longs to have a home of her own."

Robert refilled his glass. "And do you think Fairfax Park might suit her?"

"I don't know, sir. I thought if she went and saw it . . . I'd get a better sense as to whether a marriage proposal would also be acceptable."

The clock on the mantelpiece ticked loudly in the silence as Robert considered what to say. "Do you think she will accept your proposal?"

"I'm not sure, sir. What do you think? You know her better than most people."

"She would be a fool to turn you down. I've often thought you two would suit rather well. You both manage me very competently."

Thomas frowned. "But there is the question of my illegitimacy. Miss Harrington is the granddaughter and niece of an *earl*."

"If she cares about you, she won't let that affect her decision. She is a woman of remarkably good sense." Robert reached inside his pocket for one of his cigarillos so that he could avoid looking directly at Thomas's earnest face. "The rector likes you. I'm sure he would prefer to see his daughter married than wasting away her talents at the rectory."

Thomas stood up and placed his napkin on the table. "You . . . wouldn't object if I courted Miss Harrington, then, sir?"

"How could I possibly object?" Robert managed a smile. "It has nothing to do with me."

Thomas blew out a long breath. "Perhaps she doesn't intend to marry at all and prefers to stay and manage the rectory."

"You won't find out unless you ask her, Thomas, will you?" Robert said rather too heartily. "Take her to Fairfax Park and see how you both feel after that."

"Yes, Major Kurland, I will, and thank you."

"For what?"

"For employing me here, for . . . trusting me." Thomas swallowed hard. "I think I will deal with the Fairfax estate far more competently now."

"You certainly need have no qualms as to your abilities, Thomas. They are all your own." Robert forced himself to meet the young man's gaze. "I wish you all the best with your future."

"Thank you."

With a smile, Thomas left the room, closing the door softly behind him. Robert remained at the dining table and helped himself to a large glass of port. He would miss Thomas.

He would miss Lucy Harrington even more. . . .

With a curse, he downed the port and refilled his glass. Had she realized Thomas was determined to make her his wife? Surely she had. No young woman went to view a young man's estate without realizing why he was showing it to her in the first place. Not that the estate was Thomas's, but it might as well be his for the next ten years or so. And Miss Chingford had done her best to drop lots of hints to Robert about the possibility of Miss Harrington being stolen from under his nose. He suspected that was the only reason she had invited him back to the rectory at all.

Raising his head, Robert stared out into the night and caught the faint lights coming from the church and the rectory opposite. He'd asked Miss Harrington to marry him, and she'd refused. He'd told her that he cared for her, and she'd looked at him as if he'd slapped her face.

Perhaps it was time to realize that whatever

he did would never be right and that Miss Harrington was destined to marry another. Thomas was young, healthy, and ambitious. He was also intelligent, personable, and of an even temperament, which Robert secretly envied. All in all, he was a far better candidate for matrimony than an irritable cripple with an uncertain temper and a terror of horses that refused to go away completely.

He should let her go. Glancing down, he saw his hand had curled into a fist. His fellow cavalry officers hadn't called him "Forlorn Hope" Kurland for nothing. He still wasn't certain if he was prepared to lose this particular battle without one last stand.

Chapter 18

Lucy yawned as the carriage made its way along the bumpy road. She hadn't realized quite how far Fairfax Park was from Kurland St. Mary. They would have to stay at the house for at least a week to prepare themselves for the return trip. The coffin bearing Mrs. Fairfax had already started its slow journey home, and the body would rest in the chapel at the park until the vicar held the funeral service later that week.

Mr. Fairfax was on horseback, leaving the ladies to the carriage. Due to Miss Chingford's machinations and the need for a chaperone, they'd ended up taking Miss Stanford and Mrs. Green with them, as well. Lucy had assumed the two ladies would be leaving for London, but apparently, Major Kurland had insisted that Miss Stanford stay at Kurland Hall until her brother returned. The excursion to Fairfax Park was a blatant attempt to separate her from Mr. Reading, who had stayed in the village. Mrs. Green had privately confided to Lucy that Major Kurland had thought it a good idea to get Miss Stanford away from Kurland St. Mary while he dealt with Mr. Reading.

Lucy nudged Penelope, who was sitting beside

her. Miss Stanford and Mrs. Green were both asleep.

"Do you think Dorothea will be all right by herself? I told Betty to stay with her at all times."

"I don't think she has any intention of running away again. She has nowhere to go. Neither of us does."

There was a bleakness to Penelope's tone, which made Lucy feel terrible. "You can stay at the rectory for as long as you wish. My father was very clear about that."

"Which is very kind of him, but I suspect we would soon be fighting, Lucy. We are both rather managing."

"I suppose that is true." Lucy sighed. "Were you able to get Dorothea to tell you exactly what happened the night your mother died?"

"I believe I understand what happened now."

Lucy sat up. "You agreed to tell me what you found out."

"There is nothing to say." Penelope's shrug was unconvincing. "I am quite certain Dorothea did not harm our mother, and that is an end to the matter."

"But did she see anyone else?" Lucy persisted.

Penelope flicked a warning glance over at the other side of the carriage. "Do you really want to discuss this now?"

Lucy subsided into her seat and gave Penelope her best glare. "We will talk about this later."

"Perhaps," Penelope said. "I would imagine you would be too busy deciding whether Fairfax Park will make a suitable home for you."

Lucy felt her cheeks heat. "There is no suggestion of that. Mr. Fairfax merely values my opinion on domestic matters."

"I think we both know it is more than that." Penelope sniffed. "I only wish I'd had the forethought to engage his interest before he thought of you."

"You are more than welcome to try."

"Would you not like to be mistress of Fairfax Park? I am surprised at you, Lucy. Mr. Fairfax would make an unexceptional husband, and you would live very well."

"Until his half brother became of age to take on the estate himself."

"By which time, if Mr. Fairfax has any sense, he will have sufficiently feathered his own nest to provide you with an alternative home and a good income."

"You are terribly mercenary." Lucy shook her head. "I doubt Mr. Fairfax has any such thought in his mind."

The carriage slowed and rocked as the coachman negotiated a turn through a set of iron gates and past a lodge. The figure of the gatekeeper passed in a blur as the sun began to set and the elm trees lining the long drive closed overhead. Eventually, Fairfax Park was revealed as a sturdy stone building of a similar size to Kurland Hall but built in a later era.

A footman opened the door to the carriage and let down the step. Mrs. Green was the first to emerge, followed by a surly-faced Miss Stanford. Lucy waited until last, her gaze fixed on the set of stone steps leading up to the double front door of the house. The structure appeared to be in excellent order, with a covering of ivy that softened the harshness of the gray stone.

"Welcome to Fairfax Park."

Lucy turned to see Mr. Fairfax striding toward her. "Thank you."

He paused beside her, his face lifted to the line of windows above the door, which reflected back a smattering of the reddish sunset.

"It is strange to be back here. I never thought it would happen, and in such tragic circumstances." He swallowed hard. "I will have to attend to my half brother in the nursery. He needs to hear about his mother's unfortunate death."

"Would you like me to accompany you? I am quite used to dealing with small boys."

He took her gloved hand and brought it to his lips. "That is very kind of you, but I think I must do this alone. Please make yourself at home. I will see you and the other ladies at dinner."

Lucy nodded, and he walked with her up the steps and introduced her to the butler, a Mr. Simmons, who appeared to be a very competent man. Simmons passed her over to the chief housemaid, who escorted her up to a very nice bedchamber, which faced over the park at the back of the house.

It was a relief to take off her bonnet and gloves and wash off the dirt of the road. After speaking to the maid assigned to her and Penelope, Lucy lay down on her bed for a short nap. She spared a thought for Major Kurland, who hadn't once spoken to her before she'd left on her journey. He'd said he cared about her. Had he assumed that her acceptance of Mr. Fairfax's invitation to visit Fairfax Park was also an acceptance of a proposal of marriage? Her father had been delighted at Mr. Fairfax's interest in her and had urged her to consider her options very carefully indeed. She couldn't decide whether Major Kurland's unusual silence on the subject was good or bad. She would almost have preferred it if he'd lost his temper with her. At least then she would have known where she stood.

As her eyes closed, she found herself smiling. *Poor Major Kurland.* When he shouted at her, she refused to have anything to do with him. How on earth did she expect him to behave? The idea of becoming mistress of a large estate with a pleasant husband was not one that any woman in her right mind would discount. But she had always hoped for more than a dutiful marriage

Could she grow to love Thomas Fairfax? She certainly liked him very much.

She reminded herself that the visit did not have to culminate in a proposal of marriage, and that she was perfectly capable of avoiding such a situation if the need arose. Perhaps it wasn't too late to steer Mr. Fairfax's affections toward Penelope. She seemed far more accepting of a marriage of convenience than Lucy would ever be. A year ago the idea of *any* marriage had seemed acceptable, so what had changed? Her last thought as sleep overcame her was of Major Kurland winking at her at Sophia's wedding. She might never marry, but her weeks in London and her encounters with the major had certainly made her think differently about what she required in a husband.

It was unlike her to be so unsettled. She would set her mind to inquiring into the state of Fairfax Park and finding out more about Mrs. Fairfax. That should keep her occupied and less disposed to give in to her emotions.

Robert sat at his desk in the lamplight and studied the immaculate records Thomas had left behind him. When he hired a new land agent, the man would have no difficulty in following his predecessor's plans for the farms, fields, and cottages of the Kurland estate. Thomas had done a fine job.

Robert consulted his pocket watch and calculated that Thomas and the ladies should have reached Fairfax Park earlier that afternoon. He'd almost considered going with them, but his pride had stopped him. If Miss Harrington wanted to marry Thomas, he wasn't going to stand in her way. He wanted her to be happy, and if Thomas made her happy, he was content with that.

A knock on the door announced Foley with his dinner on a tray and a bottle of red wine. With no guests left to entertain, he was back to his more slovenly ways.

"Major Kurland, there is a note for you. I have placed it on the tray."

"Thank you, Foley."

His butler lingered, setting out a glass for the wine and taking his time uncorking the bottle while Robert picked up the note and read it.

"Damn the man," he muttered.

"Is Mr. Paul bothering you again, sir?" Foley shook his head. "He always was stubborn, that one."

"Mr. Paul is threatening to travel up to Mr. Fairfax's home to 'rescue' Miss Stanford." Robert balled up the note and threw it in the fire. "I suppose I will have to go down to the Queen's Head and see him."

"Eat your dinner first, Major. From what I hear, the landlord won't let him leave unless he pays some of what he owes."

"Which I doubt he has the means to do." Robert groaned. "He is *infuriating*. If I let him chase after Miss Stanford, Andrew will have my head, but if I let him stay at the inn, I have to put up with his incessant demands. Get the gig ready. I'll go down and see him after I've eaten."

Robert shoveled down his dinner in a most ungentlemanly way, which would have shocked Foley, and drank half the bottle of wine. As he pulled out his handkerchief to wipe his face, the locket fell out of his pocket, and he stared at it in exasperation.

He put on his spectacles, drew his new pocket-knife and investigated the minute crack between the two gold surfaces. He then eased the tip of the knife inward until the locket was forced apart. Inside was a portrait of a dark-haired baby and an inscribed date. Squinting at the lettering, Robert could only assume that the baby was Mrs. Fairfax's son. But why hadn't she claimed the locket that first morning, when he'd asked who it belonged to? Had she feared being incriminated in Mrs. Chingford's death?

Robert considered the locket. Was this what Miss Stanford had been searching for? If it was, why had she wanted it, or had she simply been ordered to find it by Paul, who, despite his physical absence from the wedding, seemed rather too involved in the matter for Robert's liking? His cousin had a genius for creating trouble and, by all accounts, had known Mrs. Chingford rather well.

"Damnation," Robert muttered as he pocketed the locket. "I'm going to have to talk to him."

The gig was already waiting for him at the door, so he set off in the gathering darkness to the inn. There was no sign of Paul in the crowded bar. The landlady, who assured him that his cousin was in his room, directed Robert up the stairs.

Robert knocked hard on the door with the head of his cane, and eventually Paul answered. He had taken off his coat and had his shirtsleeves rolled up. His smile widened as he invited Robert in.

"Cousin, how good of you to call. Perhaps you could prevail on the landlady to bring us a decent bottle of brandy. She refuses to give me any unless I pay for it directly."

"I'm not surprised." Robert took a seat by the fire. "I've already ordered a bottle."

Paul sat opposite him, his relaxed posture at odds with the wariness of his gaze. "Thank you. I assume you got my note."

"I'm not going to allow you to follow Miss Stanford to Fairfax Park. She is quite safe there."

"Safe from me, you mean. For God's sake, Robert, I would've thought you'd be pleased if I went out and found myself an heiress."

"Not this one."

"Then what do you expect me to do? Starve?"

"How about earning your own living?"

"I'm a *gentleman*. Do you expect me to engage in trade?"

"Why not? That's how my grandfather made his fortune. It's the only reason I can still afford to run Kurland Hall."

"Then appoint me as your steward. Let me take over Mr. Fairfax's duties."

Robert sighed. "I don't trust you not to ruin me."

There was a knock at the door, and Paul got up to retrieve the bottle of brandy and two glasses.

When they'd both taken a shot of brandy, Robert looked up at his cousin. "I want you to leave Kurland St. Mary."

"And, as I keep telling you, I have nowhere else to go and no money."

Robert poured them both another measure of brandy. "What if I made it worth your while to leave?"

"It depends. If I can't marry Miss Stanford and claim her dowry, I will need to be compensated very heavily."

"You are not going to marry Miss Stanford."

"Then give me an incentive to leave."

Robert looked down into his glass and gently swirled the remaining brandy around. "What was your connection with Mrs. Chingford?"

"What's that got to do with our present negotiation?"

"Your ability to answer some questions honestly might lead me to offer you more favorable terms."

Paul refilled his brandy glass and sat back. "I met Mrs. Chingford before I left for India, and kept up a correspondence with her for many years."

"I understand that she was a voracious letter writer."

"She also lacked the funds to sustain her lifestyle and had turned to . . . other less reputable revenue streams to remain solvent."

"Such as?"

"Selling information to the scandal sheets. Deliberately starting gossip and innuendo within the *ton* to see what dirt she could stir up, thus fueling more gossip for the papers." He shrugged. "Genteel blackmail."

"A match made in heaven, then."

"We did share some common goals, but there is no need to sneer. We both needed money."

Robert thought back about all the information he and Miss Harrington had gathered between them before he'd put an abrupt end to their investigation.

"Mrs. Chingford knew Mrs. Fairfax, as well?"

"I believe she did."

"Did you know her?"

"I knew of her. Mrs. Chingford said that she thought Mrs. Fairfax was the daughter of her old nurse and that she had risen far above her social station."

"And bearing in mind Mrs. Chingford's propensity for gossip and blackmail, what did she intend to do about that information?" Robert asked.

"I have no idea." Paul shrugged. "You have to remember that Mrs. Chingford was dead when I arrived in Kurland St. Mary."

"But she wrote to you."

"Occasionally."

"And you came close to marrying her, by all accounts." Robert caught his cousin's gaze. "Which is possibly why you stole into her bedchamber at the rectory and went through her correspondence."

"Who told you that?"

"That is irrelevant. What matters is what you wanted to find and destroy."

"There was nothing specific, Robert. I was just being careful."

"And what about when you sent Miss Stanford to search Mrs. Fairfax's room at my house? Were you writing to Mrs. Fairfax, too?"

"From what Mrs. Chingford told me, Mrs. Fairfax could barely read and write. I doubt I would've enjoyed corresponding with her."

Robert frowned. "I've seen her handwriting. It was completely legible."

"Then Mrs. Chingford was just being unkind.

311

Why does it matter, anyway?" Paul sat forward. "I did not correspond with Mrs. Fairfax, and I don't know what Miss Stanford was looking for."

"I don't believe you."

Paul's mouth set in an obstinate line. "I have nothing further to say to you about this matter."

Robert leaned on his cane and started to rise. "Then I have nothing further to say to you. Good evening, Paul."

"Wait. You can't just walk out without giving me my money!"

"I can if you insist on lying to me. I was quite clear. If you won't answer my questions, I won't help you."

"Then sit down again," Paul snapped. "And I'll tell you the little I know."

The food at Fairfax Park was adequate, and the service rather slow. The house itself lacked the neatness Lucy would have expected and bore the hallmark of an establishment that had been neglected either by a mistress who didn't care or a staff who didn't obey their orders. She had yet to determine which it was, but had scheduled an interview with the butler after dinner to discuss the matter in depth.

She'd also been taken up to the nursery to meet Robin Fairfax, who proved to be a delightful boy of around seven or eight. Mr. Fairfax had mentioned that Mrs. Fairfax had been reluctant to send her son away to school, but that he meant to rectify that. Despite missing her own twin brothers, she had to agree that sending the boy to school was for the best. As an only child, he would benefit from the company of other boys of his class.

To her surprise, after taking her down to the butler's pantry, Mr. Fairfax excused himself and returned to the drawing room to entertain the other ladies. Lucy wasn't sure whether to be pleased with his trust in her abilities or worried at the responsibility and what it might imply.

Simmons sat her down in a comfortable chair beside the fire and poured her a cup of tea from an old brown china teapot that rested on the tiled hearth. A clock ticked on the mantelpiece, and the green curtains were drawn against the slight chill of the night.

"It is pleasant to have Mr. Fairfax back at the house, Miss Harrington. He was sorely missed."

"I'm fairly certain that he didn't want to return under such difficult circumstances, but I'm sure he will do his best to keep the estate together for his half brother." Lucy sipped her strong black tea and repressed a shudder. "Mr. Fairfax is considering employing a housekeeper. Do you have anyone on the current staff who might qualify for that position?"

"Alas, no, Miss Harrington. Mrs. Fairfax liked to handle such matters herself." He hesitated.

"I don't wish to speak ill of the dead, but I fear she felt somewhat *intimidated* about having a housekeeper."

"I understand that she came from a slightly different social class," Lucy said diplomatically. "Perhaps she wasn't used to dealing with servants."

Mr. Simmons relaxed his stance. "That is correct, miss. She didn't have the right 'way' of speaking to those of a lower social order. As a result of this, despite my best efforts, some of the staff didn't take her orders very seriously."

Which explained the slightly unkempt appearance of the house.

"Even the nursery staff found her difficult. She liked to have access to her son at all times, which, I understand, disrupted his routine and made things very trying for his nurse."

"I seem to remember Mrs. Fairfax mentioning to me that she found it hard to find a nurse she liked. Did she have difficulty retaining staff?"

"Oh yes, miss, she did."

"How long has the current nurse been employed?"

"Mrs. Williams has been with us for almost a year now. She came after . . ." Mr. Simmons hesitated. "Another lady."

"Would that have been Mrs. Madge Summers?" Lucy inquired. "She was also nurse to an acquaintance of mine's youngest child. I seem to recall my friend mentioning to Mrs. Fairfax that they had shared the same nurse before Mrs. Summers retired."

"There was a Mrs. Madge Summers employed here, miss."

Lucy waited a moment, but from the set of Mr. Simmons's face, she suspected he wouldn't say anything more at this point. It was a pity, but at least she'd established a connection between Fairfax Park and Madge Summers.

"Perhaps you would consider drawing up a list of tasks a housekeeper would be required to perform at Fairfax Park and sharing it with me, Mr. Simmons. I will also speak to Mrs. Williams about her needs and position, as it seems young Robin might be going away to school."

Simmons leaned forward. "If I might be so bold as to say I think it will be for the best. After the young master left and Mr. Fairfax died, Mr. Robin became subject to rather too much maternal influence in my opinion."

Lucy nodded but didn't comment as she finished her tea. "Did Mrs. Fairfax keep her own account books? Mr. Fairfax asked me to have a look at them to gain some sense of the monthly expenditure for the house."

"She did, Miss Harrington. They would be in the yellow parlor at the rear of the house, where she kept her desk and her sewing basket."

"Then perhaps you might show me that room

before you take me up to see Mrs. Williams."

Simmons stood and took the cup from Lucy. "A pleasure, Miss Harrington. It is something of a relief for the staff to find out that Mr. Fairfax intends to stay and manage the estate. We were all rather worried that he would never return."

"I believe he considers it his duty, Mr. Simmons," Lucy said tactfully as he opened the door for her. "Despite everything, loyalty to one's family should come first, don't you agree?"

"I do, Miss Harrington. I said the very same thing to Mr. Fairfax before dinner." He led her through the green baize door into the main house and down another corridor. "The yellow parlor is here, beside the servants' stairs. This particular set leads straight up to the nursery, which is why I think Mrs. Fairfax liked to sit here."

After glancing into the room, Lucy nodded. "Perhaps we can go straight upstairs and save ourselves a walk."

Simmons glanced doubtfully at her. "If you don't mind using the back stairs, Miss Harrington."

In answer, Lucy picked up her skirts and started climbing. It was two floors up to the nursery level, but she managed it perfectly well, unlike Simmons, who was panting for breath. The nursery, as she had discovered earlier, was a well-planned and airy space, with big warm fires and large windows that let in a lot of light.

Mrs. Williams sat beside the fire, darning, and went to stand as Lucy approached her.

"Miss Harrington. Did you wish to see Robin? He is asleep."

Lucy smiled as Simmons withdrew. "I would not want to disturb him. I wished to speak to you."

"Then come and sit down by the fire, miss. Mr. Fairfax said I was to offer you every assistance." She glanced up at Lucy. "He is a fine young man."

"He is indeed." Lucy sat down and smoothed out her skirts. "Mr. Simmons was telling me that you have been employed here for a year or so."

"That's correct. Robin is a nice little boy when he's left alone."

"I understand that Mrs. Fairfax was rather an involved mother."

"She was . . . difficult, miss. She loved her son very much, but sometimes . . ."

"She spoiled him?" Lucy nodded. "Having met Mrs. Fairfax, I gained the impression that the livelihood of her only child was of primary importance to her. Such mothers are to be commended for their devotion to their offspring but, I should imagine, make establishing a schedule for a child quite difficult."

"Exactly, Miss Harrington. She wasn't *familiar* with the way a young gentleman should be brought up. She thought it cruel."

"I suppose that's why she struggled to keep a

nurse for the boy. Is that why your predecessor left?"

Mrs. Williams bit her lip. "I can't say for certain, Miss Harrington, as I wasn't here at the time, but I got the impression that Mrs. Summers's reasons for leaving were more of a personal nature."

"I did hear that Mrs. Summers was a relative of Mrs. Fairfax. Perhaps that's why they fell out," Lucy confided. "However good one's intentions, it can be difficult to employ a member of one's own family."

"I heard there were big ructions, miss, with Mrs. Fairfax shouting at Mrs. Summers and sending her away the same day." Mrs. Williams shook her head. "Not the sort of environment for the boy to thrive in at all."

"I agree." Lucy paused. "Do you know if Mrs. Fairfax ever saw Mrs. Summers again?"

"I don't know, miss. She did say she might be visiting family after her trip to London, but she didn't mention exactly who it might be. She rarely spoke of her family. I don't think anyone was supposed to know that Mrs. Summers was related to her. Of course, when they fell out, the whole staff knew. Her husband was already dead at that point, and she'd gotten rid of young Mr. Fairfax, so I suppose she thought she could bring Mrs. Summers in without anyone being the wiser."

Lucy shook her head. "What a shame. But at least you have restored order to the nursery and to the boy's life."

"And now it seems as if he might be sent away to school." Mrs. Williams sighed. "I know it is for the best, but I will have to consider moving on." Her glance fell to Lucy's waistline. "Unless there will be a new family to raise here soon?"

"You'll have to ask Mr. Fairfax about that." Lucy stood and smiled down at the nurse. "Thank you for speaking to me."

"It was a pleasure, Miss Harrington."

Lucy left the nursery and tried to remember the route back to her bedchamber. She had learned a lot and wished Major Kurland was present to help her make sense of it all. His blunt good sense and ability to cut through to the heart of the matter would be most helpful. It appeared that Mrs. Fairfax, crippled by her own social anxiety, hadn't enjoyed being mistress of Fairfax Park very much at all. She'd obviously loved her son. The thought of him growing up without his mother made Lucy very angry.

The idea of Mrs. Fairfax accidentally pushing Mrs. Chingford down the stairs for daring to expose her common roots did have a strange logic to it. But even though everyone agreed she was highly emotional, would she really have killed herself and left her son alone? Lucy was no longer sure of that. Perhaps it had been an accident, after all. But Mrs. Fairfax had left a note confessing to a crime. . . .

Lucy found her bedchamber door and went inside. The fire had been banked for the night, and her candles were lit. Her nightgown lay on the quilt, facing the warmth of the fire. There was no sign of Penelope, and the light under the connecting door had been extinguished. Lucy decided to put herself to bed. There was much to think about and a whole new day to attempt to understand whether poor Mrs. Fairfax had died accidentally, by her own hand, or had been murdered.

And plenty of time for Lucy to find out if Mr. Fairfax had any ulterior motive for bringing her to Fairfax Park.

Robert arrived back at Kurland Hall and went straight into his library. He lit the candles closest to his desk and searched for the piece of parchment he had retrieved from behind the headboard in Mrs. Fairfax's bedchamber. He put on his spectacles and studied it anew. Was it possible that *Mrs. Fairfax* had written the verses and not her young son? And even if she had, why was it bothering him? It was hardly Mrs Fairfax's fault if she hadn't been to school.

Delving into his pocket, Robert took out the locket and considered what Paul had told him Mrs. Chingford had been convinced that Mrs

Fairfax had lied to her husband about her birth and had concealed the fact that she had been married previously to a soldier who had never returned home. Had that been enough to frighten Mrs. Fairfax into killing Mrs. Chingford? Was it possible that the first husband was still alive and her union with Thomas's father had been a bigamous one, thus making her child illegitimate?

That might be a good enough reason to kill. He shook his head. Now he was becoming as fanciful as Miss Harrington. Robert went back into the hall and shouted for Foley, who appeared after a rather lengthy wait and with a long-suffering expression on his face.

"Yes, Major Kurland? I was just getting into bed."

"I'm going to Fairfax Park tomorrow. Have the gig at the door by six. I'll get Silas to pack a bag. There is no need for anyone to come with me."

"Yes, sir." Foley yawned discreetly behind his hand. "May I go back to bed now?"

Chapter 19

Has he asked you yet?" Penelope said.

"Asked me what?" Lucy was busy scanning the park beyond the house and wondering how big a gardening staff would be needed to keep it in such immaculate condition. It was late afternoon on the day after their arrival, and she was beginning to feel in much better spirits.

"To marry you, silly."

Lucy swung around to look at Penelope. They were strolling down an elegant line of topiary trees that led, so Mr. Fairfax had said, to an excellent vantage point of the whole valley. Mrs. Green had accompanied them, leaving Miss Stanford sulking in her room.

"Mr. Fairfax is far too busy dealing with the estate to have time for such ridiculous questions. I can only commend his diligence and hope to match him when I present my report of his household."

Penelope raised her eyebrows. "Indeed. You are such a paragon, Miss Harrington. How can he fail to be impressed?"

Lucy started walking again. "The funeral fo Mrs. Fairfax is in two days. I think we shoul consider leaving after that."

"Are we not supposed to wait until Majo

Kurland writes to tell us that he has gotten rid of Mr. Reading? That *was* his plan, wasn't it?"

"Who told you that?" Lucy asked.

"Mrs. Green, of course. She is constantly worried that Mr. Reading will appear and attempt to run away with Miss Stanford."

"Do you think he is desperate enough to try it?"

"He has no money and no prospects, beyond his faint hopes of succeeding Major Kurland. I should imagine an heiress like Miss Stanford would be very hard to give up."

"Then perhaps we should keep an eye out for him." Lucy sighed. "What I can't understand is why Miss Stanford is so attached to him. With her family and fortune, she can hardly want for suitors."

"He can be very charming when he wants to be," Penelope observed. "And Miss Stanford is even older than we are. Perhaps she thinks he is her last chance to make it to the altar."

"It is such a shame that we have no other options," Lucy said passionately. "Why *can't* we live independently and manage our own fortunes?"

"And be thought peculiar and not be invited anywhere?" Penelope snorted. "Who would want a life like that? Any husband is better than being a spinster or a drudge."

Lucy turned away to consider the view, which was as pleasant as Mr. Fairfax had promised.

"At least you don't have to worry about being left on the shelf, Lucy. You have the very eligible Mr. Fairfax after you and have already turned down Major Kurland. I would be delighted to be in your shoes."

"Please be my guest."

Penelope sighed loudly. "I don't quite understand how Mr. Fairfax could look at me and *not* want to make me his wife."

Lucy refrained from replying to that. "Shall we turn back? I have arranged to speak to the cook before dinner."

Mrs. Green joined them on the stroll back to the house. Her conversation alternated between approving of Fairfax Park and lamenting Miss Stanford's choice in men, which saved Lucy having to think of a single thing to say. At the side door of the house, she bid her companions good-bye and took the back route to the large kitchen at the rear of the property.

Inside, preparations were already under way for dinner, and Lucy waited quietly until the cook's attention wasn't distracted before introducing herself. There was a goodly number of staff in the kitchen, and they seemed very competent despite the lack of a housekeeper. After issuing a series of orders, the cook came to sit with Lucy at the table in the servants' dining hall.

"Mr. Fairfax said I was to speak to you freely Miss Harrington."

"That is much appreciated, Mrs. Holmes." Lucy smiled. "I must compliment you on the dinner last night. It was excellent, as was this morning's breakfast."

"Thank you, miss."

"One would scarcely notice in such a well-run kitchen that the house no longer has a housekeeper. Do you feel the lack of one, Mrs. Holmes? Or do you find yourself equal to taking on all the extra duties yourself?"

"If there was a *proper* housekeeper installed, I would be happy to welcome her."

"As opposed to . . . ?"

"Mrs. Fairfax trying to do the job herself or expecting that nurse, Madge Summers, to do it for her. I'm not surprised that ended in tears, with neither of them knowing how to go on and manage a household."

"Are you saying Mrs. Fairfax expected Mrs. Summers to fulfill the role of housekeeper?"

"She offered her the job in an attempt to keep her sweet and stop her leaving, but Madge would have none of it. And quite rightly so. Everyone should know their place, Miss Harrington, and be grateful and thankful to the Lord for it."

Lucy nodded as one of the scullery maids brought in a tray of tea.

"We are all pleased to see Mr. Fairfax back in his rightful spot, Miss Harrington. Things were never the same after he left." Mrs. Holmes sighed. "He was such a lovely boy."

"I'm sure he will do his best to keep the estate in excellent order for his half brother."

Mrs. Holmes hesitated, her hand poised over the teapot, before she poured. "He's a saint if he does."

"Why would you say that?"

"Because Mrs. Fairfax did everything in her power to keep him from his dying father. She even claimed that Mr. Fairfax propositioned her!" The cook shook her head. "That was the final straw for young Thomas. He left soon afterward, heartbroken that his father believed that woman over him. Not that there weren't rumors about her long before that." She lowered her voice. "Some said she trapped the old master into marriage when she met him at another house where a relative of hers worked!"

Lucy sipped her tea and made encouraging noises.

"She was much younger than him and obviously from a very different social class. When it all came out about Madge being a relative of hers, it all made sense, but at least the old gentleman never knew about that. He was too ill to be bothered by anything except examining his conscience and meeting his Lord and Savior."

"And now Mrs. Fairfax is dead, as well," Lucy said.

"Leaving that poor little boy behind." Mrs. Holmes sighed. "At least the estate is in good hands. I've known Thomas since he was young master Robin's age. He was brought here to live after his mother's death. Mr. Fairfax treated him like a son. We all thought he'd inherit the estate, and then *she* arrived and less than a year afterward gave birth to her son."

"Mr. Fairfax was an excellent land agent for Major Kurland at Kurland Hall. I'm sure he will do even better here, working on an estate he loves. I know he is anxious to set the household to rights and particularly wanted your opinion on hiring a housekeeper."

Mrs. Holmes patted her hair. "He always was a good boy who respected his elders."

Lucy rose and put down her cup. "I won't take up any more of your valuable time, Mrs. Holmes. I know you have a dinner to prepare. Thank you for sharing your opinions on the matter. I shall tell Mr. Fairfax that you are in favor as long as the correct person is found."

"That's right, miss." Mrs. Holmes put the cups back on the tray. "I'm sure he'll listen to you."

Lucy was fully aware that the whole household was buzzing with the notion of her presence there meaning an imminent proposal, but she had no intention of confirming it.

"I do hope so, Mrs. Holmes."

She waited for the cook to leave the dining

room and started to walk toward the main kitchen exit into the interior of the house. A footman came clattering down the back stairs, a tray in his hands, which contained a multitude of broken china and bits of food.

"Damn if she didn't throw the thing at me!" He slid the tray onto the table and rubbed at something on his face, his back to Lucy as he addressed the butler. "I'm not going up there again."

Simmons coughed loudly and bowed to Lucy. "Is everything all right, Miss Harrington?"

"Yes, indeed." Lucy smiled at him, as if she hadn't noticed the odd scene. "I was just going to retire upstairs to dress for dinner."

The footman said nothing more as Simmons escorted Lucy to the correct door and bowed her out of it. As she went upstairs, she considered who might have thrown a tray of food at the unsuspecting footman. Could it have been Miss Stanford? Or was there an old Fairfax aunt secreted somewhere in the house who needed nursing care? If there was, no one had mentioned it to her on her tour.

Her thoughts returned to Mrs. Holmes and her opinion of her dead mistress. Lucy was beginning to feel quite sorry for Mrs. Fairfax. No one seemed to like her. But the revelation that she might have lied to force Mr. Fairfax to disown his own son was horrifying . . . even more o for Thomas Fairfax, who had been stripped of everything he'd loved in one blow.

At her bedchamber door, she paused and went o knock on Penelope's door instead. She found her companion sitting at her vanity, having her hair styled by the maid. She waited until the girl eft.

"Penelope, did your mother ever mention where she first thought she'd met Mrs. Fairfax?"

"I think it had something to do with Mrs. Fairfax visiting Madge. I'm not sure if she came o our home or if Madge told my mother that she had met with her daughter on a day off. Why?"

"Because Mrs. Holmes suggested that Mrs. Fairfax met Mr. Fairfax at one of her relative's homes, while her relative was in service."

"So you think Mrs. Fairfax took advantage of her mother's position in a good household to find herself a rich, older husband?"

"It does sound possible."

"From what we know of her, I suppose it does." Penelope put on her earrings. "It doesn't seem as if her ambition made for a happy marriage, though. She was overawed by polite society and probably terrified of being found out."

"Terrified enough to silence your mother?"

"With her future and the future of her son at stake, I would imagine so." Penelope sighed. "Perhaps she didn't mean to kill my mother and panicked when she did and killed herself."

"And left her son unprotected?" Lucy shook her head. "One thing everyone agrees on is that she was an excellent and devoted mother."

"She left him in Mr. Fairfax's care."

"Which he didn't expect, and he confided in me that she had only recently changed her will to provide for that instance. He was quite shocked to be given guardianship over the house and his half brother." Lucy stared at Penelope. "So perhaps we should let this puzzle go, accept what happened, and move on."

"I suppose you are right." Penelope stood and shook out her skirts. "But what about Mr. Reading and Madge Summers and—"

Lucy held up her hand. "I am going to change for dinner, or I will be late."

"Have it your way, then," Penelope huffed.

Lucy went through to her bedchamber and rang for the maid. She had to stop worrying about this matter. There were other, more pressing issues to consider, such as whether Mr. Fairfax intended to propose to her and exactly what she would say if he did.

"I'm sorry, Major, but Mr. Coleman and the two grooms are both sick."

"Then you can drive me."

"I can't, sir. I have to stay here and manage the stables while everyone else pukes their guts up, sir."

Robert glanced over at the two horses harnessed to the light carriage and set his jaw. It was barely dawn, and his sense of urgency about reaching Fairfax Park had increased through every sleepless hour of the night. "All right. I'll take them myself."

"Thank you, sir. Mr. Coleman suggested taking your valet with you if you need company."

"Thank Mr. Coleman for his suggestion, and tell him I'll be fine."

The stable boy stowed Robert's bags in the gig and held the horses while Robert got in and took the reins. For a long moment he did nothing but stare straight ahead and struggle to breathe. He reminded himself that this was not like riding a horse into battle and that he was in no danger of being trapped under one of the animals.

It didn't help much.

Gritting his teeth, he eased the horses forward and set off.

"Mr. Fairfax?"

Lucy knocked on the half-opened door of the estate office and looked inside. Mr. Fairfax sat at a large oak desk covered in papers and leather-bound books. He looked as if he hadn't slept since his arrival at his former home.

"Miss Harrington, do come in. I fear I have been neglecting my guests." He stood and bowed, his quill pen still in his hand. "I was just about to come in search of you and ask how you were finding Fairfax Park."

She took the seat in front of his desk. "I find it quite delightful, Mr. Fairfax. Despite your worries, you appear to have inherited a loyal and competent staff who are more than willing to continue to work for the good of the family and for you."

"Well, that is a relief." He sighed. "I was worried that my father's wife had alienated the staff and that they were all ready to leave."

"Not at all. I did inquire as to whether your cook and butler thought you needed to employ a housekeeper, and they both believe it is a good idea, but only if you could find someone *suitable*. If you wish, I could draft an advertisement for you to send to the papers and employment agencies."

"I would be very grateful if you could find the time to do that, Miss Harrington." Mr. Fairfax gestured at the piles on his desk. "The house might be running smoothly, but the books are a disgrace. The steward Mrs. Fairfax employed was a scoundrel. I'm having a hard time making sense of some of these accounting methods."

"Did Mrs. Fairfax not check his work?"

"I doubt she would've been able to. Her understanding of accounting and her level of literacy were rather limited." His smile was brief. "My father didn't marry her for her intelligence

She probably had no idea that she was being fleeced."

"But you think you can fix the problems?"

"I have no choice, do I? The only good thing is that the estate has years to recover before it needs to provide Robin with a good income."

"And what of yourself?" Lucy asked. "Forgive me if I sound mercenary, but I assume you intend to pay yourself a salary for all the work you will face."

"I will certainly have to pay myself something." His smile was distracted. "Although, as I intend to live in the house while my half brother grows up, my expenditure will be minimal."

Lucy stood and curtsied. "I will leave you to your books, then, sir. Mrs. Green is suggesting we return to Kurland St. Mary two days after the funeral. Will that be sufficient time for the horses to have recovered?"

"Two days?" He frowned. "I had hoped to enjoy your company for far longer than that. With all his work, I've hardly had a chance to speak to you."

"I quite understand why you have been pre-occupied, and I'm sure the other ladies do, as well. Remember, we came to support your reintroduction to the household, not for our own pleasure."

He came around the desk to her side, his expression rueful. "And I had hoped to combine business *with* pleasure." He took Lucy's hand and kissed it. "Please consider staying longer Miss Harrington. I would be most grateful if you would."

"I'll have to speak to Mrs. Green. I cannot stay without a chaperone. I suspect her decision to return to Kurland Hall rests on whether Major Kurland has succeeded in removing Mr. Reading from the inn."

"Ah, Mr. Reading. I can't say I liked the man. Perhaps you can persuade Mrs. Green to stay here until she receives a letter from the major." He escorted her to the door and opened it. "Then she wouldn't have to risk taking Miss Stanford back into a dangerous situation."

"I'll certainly suggest that to Mrs. Green." Lucy paused at the door. "By the way, is somebody in the house unwell? I saw one of the footmen carrying a tray of food down to the kitchen."

"Not that I know of, Miss Harrington." Mr. Fairfax paused. "Perhaps someone merely decided not to dine downstairs." He smiled. "Now, if I had a housekeeper, I would probably know the answer to your question."

"It is of no matter," Lucy assured him. "Good night, Mr. Fairfax."

He bowed. "Good night, Miss Harrington."

Lucy let him return to work and went back to the drawing room, where she'd left her embroidery frame. As far as she was aware, the only person who had missed dinner that evening had been Mr. Fairfax himself. She supposed it could've been a member of staff who was either indisposed or was an elderly retainer still given a home. But no one had mentioned such a person. As she walked across the main hall, she spoke to the footman stationed there.

"Joseph, are any of the staff sick?"

"Not that I know of, miss."

"I thought I heard that someone was bedridden. Having some skills as a nurse, I wondered if I might be of some assistance."

He shook his head. "That's very kind of you, miss, but everyone is hale and hearty below stairs, thank the Lord." He crossed himself, and Lucy fought the urge to follow suit.

She continued on into the drawing room, where Penelope sat reading a book. As usual, she was probably worrying about nothing, but what if the servants were concealing something or someone from Mr. Fairfax? She had no idea why they might be doing that, but it did seem strange that no one seemed to know who needed a tray sent up to their room.

A yawn shook through her, and she decided to go to bed. In the morning she could always inquire again about the anomaly and would probably find it was nothing more than a figment of her own imagination. She'd also avoided Mr. Fairfax asking her to marry him.

His preoccupation with his work gave her some valuable time to think about what she wanted. But if the staff were concealing something . . . would she want to make such a place her home?

Chapter 20

With the permission of Mr. Fairfax, Lucy spent the day before the funeral with Simmons, the butler, making a thorough investigation of both the servants' quarters in the attics and in the basement. There was no sign of any sick servants or concealed pensioners. Some of the attic space was no longer in use due to the reduction in the need for staff, so Lucy could not claim to have seen the entire house.

She did note another tray of food, which was untouched, on the table in the kitchen as she passed through, but she didn't comment on it. She had a suspicion that interest in the matter might be unwelcome. If the staff were concealing someone from Mr. Fairfax, it would be much better for Lucy to tell him her suspicions and let him deal with it than for her, an outsider, to meddle.

"Miss Harrington?"

She turned from her perusal of the silverware in the drawers to find one of the parlor maids behind her.

"There is a visitor! Mrs. Green asked me to tell you to come *immediately*."

Lucy followed the parlor maid up the stairs to the main floor and proceeded as quickly as she could to the drawing room, where she could already hear raised voices. Had Mr. Reading defied Major Kurland and come to find Miss Stanford?

"Have you informed Mr. Fairfax?" she asked the parlor maid. "If not, go and find him immediately and bring him here."

"Yes, Miss Harrington."

The maid sped off, and Lucy braced herself before she walked into the room, and stopped short.

"Major *Kurland?*"

He looked past Mrs. Green's shoulder and gave her a short nod. "Miss Harrington."

"Why are you here?"

"To tell me that he has ruined my life!"

Lucy spun around to where Miss Stanford was sitting on the couch, a letter clutched in her hand. She was crying.

Major Kurland bowed. "I merely delivered a letter to Miss Stanford from her ex-betrothed, informing her that he has urgent business abroad and cannot expect her to wait for his return."

"You made him write it!" Miss Stanford gulped out the words between sobs.

"I certainly didn't stop him from leaving, Miss Stanford, but he wrote the note without any help from me."

Miss Stanford shot to her feet and cast a glance of great loathing in Major Kurland's direction.

"You have ruined my life." With that, she ran for the door, her sobs echoing down the corridor as she disappeared.

"Well, that went about as well as I expected," Major Kurland muttered. "The bringer of bad news is rarely welcome."

Lucy moved toward him. "What did you have to do to make Mr. Reading leave?"

He held her gaze for a long moment before answering. "I gave him money. What do you expect?"

"It must have been quite a substantial sum in order to compensate him for the loss of Miss Stanford's fortune."

He shrugged. "There were other factors that mitigated the amount I was willing to offer him. He was quite willing to compromise once I'd spelled out those unfortunate consequences to him."

"Then I suppose we should congratulate you."

"Hardly." He looked at Mrs. Green. "Do you think I might sit down, ma'am? My leg is bothering me."

"Of course, Major. I do apologize for keeping you standing for so long. Would you like some tea? I'm sure Mr. Fairfax will be delighted to see you. Do you intend to stay for the funeral?"

"If Mr. Fairfax will have me." Major Kurland tentatively settled himself in one of the chairs, wincing as he bent his left knee. "I certainly don't want to turn around and return home today."

As she went by him to ring the bell, Mrs. Green pressed a hand to his shoulder. "I'm certain Mr. Fairfax will be as pleased as I am to hear that my niece is safe from that scoundrel. Begging your pardon, sir, seeing as he is your cousin, but she is well rid of him. What my sister was *thinking* allowing him to court her daughter, I have no idea."

Lucy sat down, as well, her gaze locked on Major Kurland, who looked tired and in considerable pain. Despite their recent differences, she couldn't deny that his presence added a certain something to her day.

Eventually, he turned to her. "Miss Harrington. Are you well?"

"I am very well, sir."

"Do you have any exciting news to share about your future?"

She frowned at him. "That is none of your business, but no, I haven't."

"Good." He leaned toward her and lowered his voice. "I wish to talk to you alone. Can you arrange that?"

Before she could reply, Penelope and Mr. Fairfax came into the room, and the whole conversation repeated itself as Major Kurland explained his errand and gratefully accepted Mr. Fairfax's hospitality for a night or so.

Lucy stood and curtsied to Mr. Fairfax

"Perhaps seeing as your staff are so busy with preparations for the funeral, I could take Major Kurland to the guest suite next to Mrs. Green's?"

"That would be most kind of you, Miss Harrington." Mr. Fairfax shook Major Kurland's hand. "Dinner is at six. Please join us if you aren't too tired."

Lucy led the way down the corridor and toward the main staircase. She had to slow her steps considerably as the major was struggling to walk even with his cane.

"Did you bring Silas with you?" she asked as they slowly climbed the stairs.

"No. I came alone. There was no time."

"Just with a groom?"

He glared down at her. "What does it matter?"

"There is no need to snap at me. I merely wondered if you needed someone to help unpack your bags."

"I came alone."

Lucy stopped to stare into his face. "You drove *yourself?*"

A muscle flicked in his cheek. "I had no choice. Everyone was sick."

"Then you must be rather tired." There was so much she wanted to say to him, but none of it could be acknowledged, let alone shared. "I'll make sure that Simmons, the butler, sends someone up to attend to you."

She paused before his bedroom door. There

was no one around, and she wouldn't be missed for a while.

"Here is your bedchamber, Major."

"Thank you."

She followed him into the room and leaned against the door as he limped over to the fireplace and turned to face her.

"I didn't come just to deliver Mr. Reading's letter." Her heart gave a curious bump as he stared intently at her. "I know I have given you no reason to hear a word I have to say, but would you please listen?"

She nodded, her hands fisted at her sides, as he took something out of his coat pocket.

"Things don't add up," he said abruptly. "I have a locket that I believe belongs to Mrs. Fairfax but that she refused to claim, I have Bible verses written in an atrocious hand, and Paul spinning stories that I can't quite discount, even though he is a liar and a thief."

"I thought you told me to stop meddling and leave things alone?"

His dark blue gaze held hers. "I was a fool to do so."

"And now you expect me to forget your autocratic behavior and simply continue on as if nothing had happened?"

"Yes." He grimaced. "I mean, yes, please. I would greatly appreciate your company and your insight."

With a deep breath, Lucy left the door and went to sit by the fire. "Tell me everything."

He handed her the open locket, and she studied the portrait of the dark-haired baby. "It certainly does look like Robin Fairfax." She peered more intently at the opposite side. "There are initials engraved here. Something E.F., which would correspond to at least two of the boys' given names." She looked up. "Then why didn't Mrs. Fairfax claim the locket?"

"Presumably, because she knew where it had ended up. If she'd admitted it was hers, we would have realized right away that she'd at least been involved in a physical struggle with Mrs. Chingford that had led to her falling down the stairs."

"I thought you lost the locket. How did you find it again?"

"Dorothea Chingford gave it back to me."

"And what did she have to say about the matter?"

"That she had taken it in case it was needed as evidence of a crime."

Lucy sat back. "So she did see something. Did she elaborate?"

"No, she just insisted that I return the locket to its rightful owner. She ran away before I could question her any further."

"She must have seen Mrs. Fairfax push her mother. There is no other explanation for it. But why wouldn't she tell me?" Lucy sighed. "She seemed afraid."

"That's what I thought. I'm not sure why, when Mrs. Fairfax was already dead and could hardly extract vengeance on her." Major Kurland took back the locket. "I thought Miss Stanford was looking for this when I encountered her in Mrs. Fairfax's old room at the manor."

"Miss Stanford?" Lucy frowned. "I did wonder if she was attempting to help Mr. Reading, but I couldn't understand why he would be so interested in Mrs. Fairfax's death."

"Because he was closely involved with Mrs. Chingford, and he already knew she had poor Mrs. Fairfax in her sights for a spot of black-mail. At first he simply wanted to make sure that Mrs. Chingford hadn't left any incriminating evidence about him after her death. *Then* he decided it might be interesting to pursue Mrs. Chingford's claims about Mrs. Fairfax himself. He heard about the locket from Miss Stanford and thought it might be a valuable tool."

Lucy shook her head. "What an unpleasant individual your cousin is. I am fairly certain that Mrs. Fairfax was Madge Summers's daughter. Both Mrs. Chingford and Mrs. Fairfax employed Madge as a nurse. I suspect Mrs. Fairfax would've been eager to suppress any whispers about her lack of class. Did Mr. Reading ask Miss

Stanford to search for evidence against him in Mrs. Fairfax's room after her death? What an unpleasant gentleman!"

"He did, and he is no gentleman. He insisted that Miss Stanford was more than willing to help him clear his name and that he hadn't actually embarked on his blackmailing of Mrs. Fairfax before she killed herself." Major Kurland gave a short laugh. "As if that somehow made his behavior more palatable to me."

"At least you managed to detach him from Miss Stanford."

"Not that she thanks me for it."

"She will when she comes to her senses and meets a true gentleman." Lucy glanced at the clock and rose to her feet. "I cannot stay here with you for much longer without my absence being noted. You said you came to Fairfax Park to deliver Miss Stanford's letter and for other purposes."

"Yes. I'm worried about Thomas."

"About *Mr. Fairfax?*"

"Paul told me Mrs. Chingford had found out that Mrs. Fairfax was married before and that her husband never returned from the war."

Lucy waited by her chair as Major Kurland stared expectantly at her. "And?"

"She suspected he might still be alive, and that he might even have fathered Mrs. Fairfax's child."

"Good Lord," Lucy breathed. "And you *believe* him?"

"I read Mrs. Fairfax's family Bible. She had name crossed out very heavily in her entry an then *Fairfax* added in a different shade of ink."

The sound of whistling outside in the corrido made Lucy turn and move quickly toward th door.

"Wait!" Major Kurland limped after her. "Tak this. I found it in Mrs. Fairfax's room. I assume the verses were written by the child, but now am not so sure."

"What do you want me to do with them?" Luc whispered frantically.

"Compare them to Mrs. Fairfax's handwriting Tell me what they mean."

Lucy stuffed the paper in the pocket of he gown and opened the door, talking back ove her shoulder. "Good afternoon, Major Kurlanc I'm sure someone will be up to help you unpac momentarily."

"Thank you, Miss Harrington. It was most kin of you to show me the way to my room."

Lucy swung around, smiled as if she had jus noticed Joseph, and opened the door wide enoug for him to get by her as she escaped. "Here i Joseph now, Major. I'm certain he will soon se things to rights."

She escaped down the stairs to the yellow parlo and collapsed on the couch. Was it possible tha

Mrs. Fairfax's death had not ended the tangle of lies and deceit that had bedeviled her life? And if Major Kurland was correct and Robin wasn't a Fairfax, what on earth were they going to do about it?

After dinner, Robert managed to persuade Miss Harrington to walk with him on the terrace while Miss Chingford played cards with Mrs. Green. Thomas had excused himself, pleading an excess of work, and Miss Stanford hadn't come down to dinner, which was hardly surprising. Robert couldn't say he felt guilty about separating his cousin from Miss Stanford, but he didn't like to see her hurt.

He looked down at Miss Harrington, who was wearing a very becoming gown in blue and had arranged her hair high on her head, leaving her long neck and shoulders bare to his gaze. It was a pleasure to see her again, and not as yet affianced to another man.

"I doubt you meekly sat on your hands when I ordered you to stop investigating the matter, Miss Harrington, so what else did you find out?"

"That Madge Summers didn't die in the house fire but was rescued by her neighbors and then spirited away in a coach to no one knows where."

Robert paused to look down into her fine eyes. "Spirited away? You mean she was kidnapped?"

"No. Apparently, she went quite willingly. The

347

family thought she might have been offered a home by one of her previous employers."

"Who somehow heard about the fire and immediately came to rescue her?" Robert snorted. "That seems rather far-fetched to me. One might assume that the person who attempted to burn her house down decided to make sure he finished the job."

"That was my thought, too. But why?"

"Because Madge Summers was a nurse and the mother of Mrs. Fairfax. If anyone knew the truth about Robin Fairfax's parentage, it would be her."

"But Mrs. Fairfax died."

"Perhaps the person who went after Madge Summers didn't know that until he'd already taken her."

"That's possible, I suppose."

They had reached the end of the terrace and slowly turned back. Flickering candlelight spilled out from the drawing room and created squares of brightness in the gathering darkness. Beside him, Miss Harrington shivered, and he drew her shawl closer around her shoulders.

"Do you intend to tell Thomas of your suspicions about his half brother?"

"I'm not sure. I'm reluctant to act on evidence obtained solely from my thieving, lying cousin.' Robert paused beside the doors into the drawing room. "I was hoping we might be able to find some additional proof amongst Mrs. Fairfax's papers or from the staff."

"I can tell you that Mrs. Fairfax wasn't well liked. She was unaccustomed to dealing with a large staff, and I fear she was taken advantage of. I had intended to make a thorough search of the yellow parlor, where she kept her writing desk, but Mr. Fairfax said she rarely wrote letters, being somewhat ashamed of her penmanship."

A shadow moved closer, and Robert took a step back. "Have you read the Bible verses I gave to you yet?"

"Not yet, Major, but I intend to do that before I retire."

"Be careful."

"Of what?" She hesitated. "Actually, there is one thing . . ."

"Major Kurland?"

Robert looked over Miss Harrington's head. "Yes, Mrs. Green?"

"Do you have a forwarding address for Mr. Reading? My niece was asking me. Not that I wish her to communicate with that scoundrel."

"You can tell her that I do not yet know where Paul intends to settle, but she is welcome to inquire later in the year, when he writes to give me his direction."

By the time he'd spoken to Mrs. Green and declined an offer from Miss Chingford to play cards, Miss Harrington had left the room. He had the strangest feeling that what she had been about to share with him was important, but he couldn't think of a way to follow her up the stairs and into her bedchamber and demand answers without causing a stir.

She was definitely up to something. . . . He recalled her determination to read through the Bible verses he'd given her, and suspected she would come down later, when the coast was clear, to investigate Mrs. Fairfax's desk.

Bowing to the ladies and pleading fatigue, Robert went out into the hall and found the butler.

"Simmons, which way is the yellow parlor? Miss Harrington said I would find some writing implements in there."

"That salon is used mainly by the ladies of the house, Major. You will also find pen and ink in the library, which is on the same corridor."

"I certainly don't wish to disturb the ladies. Perhaps you might show me where the library is. I want to make an early start on my correspondence in the morning."

Much later, when the house was quiet and the clock in her bedchamber had struck twice, Lucy eased her way out of the door and took the back stairs down to the yellow parlor. There were still a few glowing coals in the fireplace, so she was able to light a candle and place it on Mrs. Fairfax's desk. The drawers weren't locked, so he sat down, put on her spectacles, and took out what appeared to be Mrs. Fairfax's daybook.

Lucy had one at the rectory for noting down the menus for the week and the tasks that needed to be accomplished on a regular basis for the household to function efficiently. She also used hers to jot down new recipes and comments about the quality of the meat from the butchers or whether they needed to look into finding a new supplier for their dairy needs.

Mrs. Fairfax's book was a testament to disorder and the lack of an organized mind. Her handwriting was almost impossible to read; and her grasp of how to manage a house the size of Fairfax Park, hazy at best. Lucy looked in her pocket to retrieve the paper Major Kurland had given her, and could immediately see that the handwriting was the same.

She squinted at the badly written Bible verses, which seemed to follow a theme of sin and vengeance. The only one she could make sense of was Exodus 4:22–23.

And thou shalt say unto Pharaoh, Thus saith the LORD, Israel is my son, even my firstborn: And I say unto thee, Let my son go, that he may serve me: and if thou refuse to let him go, behold, I will slay thy son, even thy firstborn. Which didn't make much sense . . . Lucy tried to read the verse below, which seemed to be a reference of some kind. "Deuteronomy twenty-one, fifteen and sixteen," Lucy whispered. "I will have to look that one up."

She startled as she heard a crash outside in the hallway. Immediately, she blew out the candle and went to the door, opening it an inch.

"That bloody woman threw the soup at me again!" someone muttered as he went down to the lower level of the kitchen basement. "She don't deserve to be fed."

"That's not your concern, young Frederick, my lad. You just keep your mouth shut until this funeral is over and our guests depart. Then all will be as it should be, you mark my words."

Lucy recognized Simmons's voice, but whom was he talking about? Who was the mysterious captive? And she was fairly certain now that the woman wasn't there on her own free will.

"Take another tray up."

"Do I have to, Mr. Simmons? She's already spoiled my shirt."

"Then it won't matter if you get it spoiled again. Get on with you."

The kitchen door shut, muffling the sound of voices, and Lucy considered what to do. If the footman returned alone, could she follow him up the stairs and discover where he was taking the tray? It might be the only way to satisfy her curiosity on the matter. She hesitated in the darkness at the bottom of the stairs. But what if she was seen? Was there any excuse she could give for being in this particular part of the house in the middle of the night?

The sound of the kitchen door opening below galvanized her into action. She ran lightly up the next flight of stairs and crouched down beside a large Oriental chest on the landing. Within seconds, she heard the rattle of china and the pant of Frederick's breath as he came up the stairs.

He was still grumbling to himself as he carried on up to the next level, which housed the nursery floor and the schoolroom. Lucy listened to the hollow sound of his footsteps, holding her breath as he turned again and continued up toward the attics. She didn't dare follow him, but at least she could attempt to investigate in the morning.

She turned and picking up her skirts, tiptoed carefully back down to the ground floor, letting out her breath as she peered at the outline of the door into the yellow parlor. Her view was abruptly cut off as she collided with an extremely large shape. Before she could even consider screeching, a hand covered her mouth and she was maneuvered out of the doorway and into the parlor.

She broke free of her captor, and he held his finger to his lips.

"Sshh."

Lucy remained still, her gaze fixed on Major Kurland as he listened for any sounds of pursuit. After a long moment, his shoulders relaxed.

"You frightened me!" Lucy hissed at him, on hand still planted over her rapidly beating heart.

"Not half as much as you frightened me. Wha in the devil's name is going on?"

"I think someone is being held captiv upstairs."

"That's ridiculous."

"I *know!*"

He beckoned her toward the two seats by th fire, and she reluctantly followed him over. Ther was very little light in the room, but she didn' want to waste time relighting a candle when sh intended to be leaving very shortly.

"Were you spying on me, Major Kurland?"

"In a manner of speaking, yes." He hesitatec "I wanted to continue our conversation, an I remembered you saying you might come t the yellow parlor to investigate Mrs. Fairfax' desk. As the funeral is tomorrow, I assumed tha when your curiosity got the better of you, yo would accomplish your goal tonight." He gav a ferocious glare. "I *didn't* expect to find yo chasing after footmen."

"I simply wanted to see where he was takin the tray. I had no intention of either chasing hir or following him for long." She rubbed her col hands together. "Did you hear what Simmon said about things being better after the guest leave?"

He nodded. "I assume they have some decrepi

354

nd disorderly family relict locked up until after
ie funeral. I don't condone such behavior, but
 can understand why Mr. Fairfax might have
rdered it."

"I suppose that is possible."

"What else could it be?"

"I'm not sure." Lucy spied the letters spread
ut on the desk and went to retrieve them. "It's
ist that I've been shown every nook and cranny
f this estate, and no one has mentioned any
elatives living here. In truth, the only relative of
Irs. Fairfax who has ever lived here is Madge
ummers, and that ended badly. I wonder why?
)id Madge threaten to expose her daughter's
eception?"

"That we will probably never know. Did you
ind anything in Mrs. Fairfax's desk?"

"Only more evidence that she was barely
terate and struggled to run her household.
he Bible verses were almost certainly written
y her. They all seem to be concerned with
in, particularly the sins of the father, and the
ownfall of firstborn sons."

"Sons?" Major Kurland asked softly. "Perhaps
Irs. Fairfax really was feeling guilty."

"Maybe that's why she came to see Mr. Fairfax
t Kurland Hall." Lucy paused. "And died there
fter bequeathing her son into his care. Perhaps
he knew her secret had been discovered by
Irs. Chingford, and thought that by killing

her, the danger was past, only to discover
that Mr. Reading intended to blackmail her
anyway."

"That is rather a romantical and tragic view of
the matter, Miss Harrington. She changed her
will *before* she came to Kurland Hall. She could
scarcely have known she would encounter Mrs.
Chingford."

"Then she was obviously feeling guilty before
she arrived. Didn't Mr. Fairfax tell you that he
had no idea she had altered her will until the
solicitor arrived after her death?"

"And I told *him* that as Mrs. Fairfax was hardly
expecting to die, she probably didn't think to
mention it or didn't even assume it would ever
come to pass."

"So it is highly likely that Mrs. Fairfax killed
Mrs. Chingford to keep her secrets and then
killed herself when she realized Mr. Reading
intended to use the information against her. I
wonder if it was Mr. Reading who took Madge
Summers from her house? He was staying in
Saffron Walden before he came to Kurland St.
Mary, and could have found her address amongst
Mrs. Chingford's correspondence."

"He didn't mention her to me, but then I
didn't bring her up." Major Kurland sighed. "I
will make sure to speak to him about the matter
when he contacts me. It's possible he left the
poor woman in an inn somewhere, and she will

ventually realize she's been duped and will eturn home."

"I certainly hope so." Lucy hesitated. "Perhaps you should tell Thomas about all of this, Major. If Robin is not the legitimate heir to the estate, perhaps he is."

"I have read through the will, and there is no hereditary title with the estate, and it is not entailed to the oldest male heir. If he'd wanted to, the older Mr. Fairfax could've left the whole lot to Thomas. He did have other property and revenue that would have to go to his legitimate heir, but there is no shortage of money, Miss Harrington. Thomas confided to me that he had expected to inherit Fairfax Park and that Mrs. Fairfax had persuaded his father to cut him out of the will entirely."

Major Kurland sighed. "I think we should wait until after the funeral to suggest anything to Thomas, don't you? Despite everything, Mrs. Fairfax deserves to be buried in peace."

"I agree." Lucy headed for the door. "We should go to bed. The funeral is at midday."

She opened the door and peered into the darkness. All was quiet. Even the noise from the kitchen below had diminished. She tiptoed out, and Major Kurland followed, his cane tapping on the parquet floor behind her.

Lucy had already realized the servants' stairs would be too steep for the major to manage and was resigned to walking up the main staircase with him. In his present mood he was unlikely to accept her disappearing off by herself again. She walked quietly by his side, slowing her step to match his.

There was a faint light under the study door, indicating that Mr. Fairfax might still be working. They started up the wide staircase, which could easily hold six abreast. Lucy was aware of the major's breath hitching with every step. Impulsively, she offered him her arm.

"I don't need help. I'm—"

Even as he snapped at her, his booted heel caught in her skirts, pulling them both off balance. She flung out an arm to grab for the bannister and missed as his considerable weight crashed into her from the side, bringing them both down to their knees on the half landing. A large vase teetered on its stand and fell to the floor.

Below them lights flared and voices emerged. With her skirts trapped under one of Major Kurland's knees, Lucy couldn't get to her feet. Out of the corner of her eye, she saw Mr. Fairfax, the butler, two of the footmen, and a maid converging in the hall and starting up the stairs.

Beside her Major Kurland sighed. "Might as well be hung for a sheep as a lamb. Miss Harrington? Please forgive me."

Leaning forward, he slid one hand behind her

eck, bent his head, and kissed her firmly on the
iouth.

Major Kurland! Are you all right?"
Robert turned to Thomas, who was coming up
ie stairs. "Mr. Fairfax, I can only apologize for
iis . . . unfortunate incident." Beside him Miss
Iarrington made a convulsive movement and
ied to shake off his restraining hand. He kept
er skirts pinned firmly under his knee. "I was
scorting Miss Harrington upstairs and misjudged
ie weakness of my leg when I went to . . . kiss
er good night."
There was silence as Thomas and Joseph, the
ootman, reached them and helped Robert and
ien Miss Harrington to their feet.
Robert caught Thomas's eye. "Perhaps we
ould continue this discussion in your study?"
"Of course, Major Kurland."
Robert took a firm hold of Miss Harrington's
lbow and steered her down the stairs and into
ie study, shutting the door firmly in the butler's
ice.
"You might wonder what I was doing up at this
me of night," Robert continued rapidly. "I was
nable to sieep and took refuge in the library,
'here I knew I would find both the brandy
ecanter and a good fire. Miss Harrington came
ito the library, as well, and was shocked to
ie me there." He glanced at Miss Harrington,

willing her to play along. "I believe she wa looking for a book to help her fall asleep."

"Yes, that's correct, Major Kurland."

She didn't sound quite herself, but at least sh hadn't repudiated him . . . yet.

"Her unexpected presence finally gave m the courage to admit my feelings and ask he to marry me." He cleared his throat. "She wa somewhat surprised and insisted that she neede time to reflect on the matter. I offered to escor her upstairs and made the mistake of giving i to my feelings and attempting to kiss her." H shrugged. "A foolish thing to do, I know, but . . .

"Quite understandable," Thomas said quietly.

"I owe you both an apology. This was not th right time or place to give vent to my feelings. Robert studied Thomas and Miss Harringtor who was resolutely not looking at him. "I do however, stand by my offer of marriage."

"And I will consider your proposal ver carefully, Major Kurland." Miss Harringto curtsied and addressed her next remark t Thomas. "Will you both excuse me? I don't wis to oversleep and be out of sorts for the funeral."

"Of course, Miss Harrington."

She walked out, leaving Robert in th uncomfortable silence. He forced himself to mee Thomas's gaze. "If you wish to call me out ove this . . ."

"I would never do that. I owe you far too muc

shoot you, and to be fair, I wasn't sure if you were honest with me about your feelings for Miss Harrington." His smile was rueful. "I suspect that might be why I've been reluctant to press my suit all along."

"That is very generous of you."

Thomas bowed. "I wish you both a very happy life."

"If I can persuade her that I mean it."

"I'm sure you will, Major. You are a master at getting your own way."

"And we can still remain friends?" Robert searched the other man's face.

"I hope so. I suspect I will be in need of your counsel in the years to come." Thomas came round the desk and shook Robert's hand. "Good night, Major. Please do not worry on my account. The laws of attraction and the arrows of Cupid can fall in the most unexpected of places."

Robert left the study and made his slow way up the stairs; his hip ached with every step. He turned into the corridor that housed the guest bedrooms and caught a hint of lavender soap.

"Major Kurland!"

The whisper came from the velvet curtains that shrouded the large windows looking over the park. He stepped into the shadow and found Miss Harrington with her back to the moonlight filtering through the glass panes.

"Major Kurland, what on earth were you

thinking? All you had to do was say we met i
the library and that I was helping you up th
stairs when you stumbled! Why did you have t
pretend you asked me to marry you, and then *ki*
me?"

Robert brought his hand to rest on the wa
beside her. "Because I wanted to."

Bending his head, he kissed her again unt
she stopped spluttering and kissed him bacl
Eventually, he raised his head and met her gaze.

"You *will* marry me."

"I haven't decided what I—"

He kissed her again, and this time her han
curved around the back of his neck, keeping hi
close.

"You will marry me, Lucy Harrington. W
will discuss the details after the funeral. I wi
ask your father for your hand when we return t
Kurland St. Mary." He eased away from her, an
in a second, she picked up her skirts and ran
the direction of her room.

Robert waited until she reached her door befoi
going into his own room. The rightness of h
decision settled over him, and he permitte
himself a victorious grin.

Miss Harrington would marry him. He wou
not allow her to escape him again.

Chapter 21

The funeral proved mercifully short and was attended only by the staff and guests of Fairfax Park. Young Robin Fairfax stood manfully beside his half brother and seemed to take some comfort in his presence. Lucy struggled to concentrate on the service, when all her thoughts were concerned with the remarkable events of the previous night.

To her consternation, word had spread throughout the household, and she'd had to endure both Penelope's amusement and a lecture from Mrs. Green about her morals. She'd also been informed that Mrs. Green would be writing to her father, so it seemed there was no way out from her dilemma.

And did she seek a way out? After Major Kurland's masterful kisses, she wasn't quite sure what to think anymore. . . .

As the vicar concluded his final remarks, Lucy remembered to look up the Deuteronomy reference in her Bible and placed a bookmark in the correct page so that she could read it after the funeral. The coffin was carried out, and the congregation followed. Mrs. Williams took her charge back to the nursery, and the women went to the house, while the men attended the graveyard.

A light drizzle began to fall, and Lucy was glad to step into the warmth of the hall. She went up the stairs to take off her bonnet and outdoor boots, only to find Penelope waiting at her bedroom door.

"Is something the matter?" Lucy tried to look unhelpful, but Penelope was not deterred and went in the room with her.

"Now that Mrs. Fairfax is safely buried, wanted to ask whether you had reached any further conclusions about who killed my mother."

Lucy sat down to remove her boots. "We think that Mrs. Fairfax killed her because your mother knew she hadn't been honest about her family history."

Penelope's eyebrows rose. "You are suggesting my mother died over a matter of class?"

"It is also possible that Mrs. Fairfax had concealed a previous marriage." Lucy didn't want to expand on that until she and Major Kurland decided what to do about Mr. Reading's claims about the child. "I doubt she *meant* to kill your mother. She said in her note that it was an accident." Lucy's voice trailed off as she considered the letter Mrs. Fairfax had left behind her.

"Dorothea believed it was an accident, as well."

"Then why did she tell Major Kurland that she had evidence of a crime?"

Penelope shrugged. "She was afraid."

"Of what? For goodness' sake, you might as well tell me the truth now. As you said, Mrs. Fairfax can hardly care."

"Dorothea saw them arguing, and then Mrs. Fairfax shoved our mother rather hard. I don't think either of them had noticed they were at the top of a staircase. Mrs. Fairfax ran one way, and Dorothea ran the other. She glanced down the stairwell before she left and saw our mother lying quite still." Penelope sighed. "The silly goose also thought she saw someone else down there with her, and that's why she was afraid."

"Someone else at the bottom of the stairs?" Lucy thought back to Dr. Fletcher's comments that Mrs. Chingford's neck could have been broken in the fall or that someone might have strangled her. "How odd."

"As you said. Not that it matters anymore." Penelope stood up. "I'm glad that I know what happened to my mother. I did not like her, but she deserves to rest in peace. I suppose Mrs. Fairfax paid her own price for her crime."

"I suppose she did."

Deep in thought, Lucy barely managed to register Penelope's withdrawal. Major Kurland had mentioned seeing someone leaving from the lower level at the wedding. . . . Was it possible that both he and Dorothea had seen the same person? A person who might have strangled Mrs. Chingford to ensure that she didn't survive her fall?

"But why?" Lucy whispered.

She glanced down at her Bible, which had fallen open at the page she had marked earlier and began to read aloud.

"If a man have two wives, one beloved, and another hated, and they have born him children, both the beloved and the hated; and if the firstborn son be hers that was hated: Then it shall be, when he maketh his sons to inherit that which he hath, that he may not make the son of the beloved firstborn before the son of the hated, which is indeed the firstborn."

Lucy rose to her feet. She had to go back down and be polite to the vicar and socialize with the other guests. After that, she would wait until the house was quiet and go and search the attic for a locked door. She suspected that would be the only way to establish the truth for her sake, for the Chingford sisters, and most importantly for poor Thomas Fairfax.

"I am coming with you."

Lucy stared at Major Kurland. "You are incapable of being quiet."

His brows drew together. "You are not going

alone. I will bring my pistol and protect you."

"From a woman who has been locked up and who probably will be delighted to be free?"

"I am still coming."

Lucy sighed. "Then meet me on the top floor, beside the servants' stairs, at midnight."

"You believe Madge Summers is locked up here, don't you?"

"Who else can it be?"

"But why would Thomas condone that?"

"Perhaps he knows what Madge believes and doesn't want her telling all the guests about his half brother's potential illegitimacy."

"One might think he would want that information to be as public as possible so that he could stake his claim on the estate."

"You forget, he is illegitimate himself, Major. Mayhap he wishes to treat the matter in a more private and sympathetic manner."

"That might be true." Major Kurland looked impatiently around the room. Miss Stanford was standing with Mrs. Green and doing her best to ignore him; Miss Chingford was expending all her energies on consoling Thomas, which was to be expected now that he was back on the marriage mart. "I do wish we could just confront him with our evidence rather than skulk around in this underhand manner."

"If the lady in the attic isn't Madge Summers, you have my full permission to approach Mr.

Fairfax in whatever manner you like," Lucy said firmly.

"Yes, Miss Harrington." He bowed and moved away from her. "I will most certainly do that."

After the funeral breakfast, Robert took the opportunity to rest his leg and have a long nap, which made the prospect of tiptoeing round the house at midnight slightly less daunting. He *was* worried that his damned knee would let him down again, but he wasn't prepared to let Miss Harrington face the "captive" in the attics alone. The fact that she'd accepted his decree meant that she was probably more aware of the danger than she had admitted.

He put his black funeral garb back on, had a subdued dinner with the other guests, where vague decisions were made as to when the party intended to leave, and was now waiting impatiently in his room for the house to settle down. His fingers twitched, and he wished he could smoke one of his cigarillos, but he didn't want the smoke to linger on his clothes while he hid with Miss Harrington.

"Hide-and-seek is a children's game," he muttered to himself as he made sure his pistol was primed and ready for use before carefully placing it in his coat pocket. "Let's hope it remains that way."

Eventually, it was time to make his way up

to the attics and find Miss Harrington. He took his time, avoiding the main staircase and the odd scurrying maid, and slowly gained the top floor. It took a moment for his eyes to adjust to the darkness of the low-beamed interior, with its sloping roof. There were three doors on either side of the corridor and one at the end.

A hand touched his sleeve, and he almost jumped until he realized it was Miss Harrington, intent on pulling him into one of the rooms. It proved to be a small bedroom bereft of any adornment other than a small bed, a rolled-up straw mattress, and a lumpy pillow.

"We can wait in here," Miss Harrington whispered close to his ear. "From what I've seen, one of the servants usually checks on her around midnight."

Robert took out his pocket watch and squinted at the hands. "Fairly soon, then. What is your plan for getting into the room if it is locked?"

"I'm sure we can think of something."

"I'm sure we can."

Silence fell as they both listened to the murmurings of the house as it settled down below them and the wind whistling through the trees in the park.

"Did you intend to marry Thomas?"

"I certainly thought about it."

Robert frowned into the darkness and tried

to sound fair. "He would make any woman an excellent husband."

"Indeed he would."

He let another minute slip by, but she said nothing more. "Do you regret my presence here then?"

"Why should I?"

"Because you were thinking about marrying Thomas Fairfax. You came here to see if this place suited you."

"That wasn't the only reason I came here."

There was a hint of amusement in her voice which made him wary. "I assumed the other reason was to get away from me."

"It might surprise you to learn that I didn't think of you at all. I was anxious to discover what had happened to Mrs. Fairfax, and I reasoned that the best way to understand her was to visit her home."

"Ah." He reached for her hand and found it waiting for him. "I should have known that finding the answer to a puzzle was far more interesting than worrying about the deficiencies of men."

She sighed. "I did worry, but I was determined to discover whether Mrs. Fairfax murdered Mrs. Chingford. At least I know that, although it seems wrong that your meddling cousin gets to walk away from a tragedy."

"It's not the first time he's done that. I live in hope that one day his mistakes will catch up with him. Rest assured that I have made it clear that when retribution strikes, I have no intention of lifting a finger to save him."

"Good. He doesn't deserve it, and he certainly doesn't deserve to inherit your estate."

"Another good reason for marrying me, Miss Harrington. We can produce a bushel of brats to keep the land and title in our branch of the family forever."

"Major Kurland, you cannot describe your future children as *brats*. . . ." She stopped speaking and pointed to the door, beyond which Robert could clearly hear the sound of feet clumping up the stairs.

The footsteps went past them, and Robert eased forward to peer through the crack in the door at the end of the corridor, where the footman was unlocking a door.

"Now then, missus. None of your tantrums. I've come to collect your—"

There was a crashing sound and then some cursing, which made Robert wince, coming as it did from a woman, followed by the hasty sound of retreat.

"Bloody woman! The quicker Mr. Fairfax gets rid of her, the better!" The footman disappeared down the stairs, muttering to himself.

Robert waited another ten minutes before cautiously opening the attic door and beckoning Miss Harrington out into the corridor.

"Let's try the door," he whispered.

They crept toward the end door, and Robert bent forward to check for an exterior lock but found instead the key already inserted in the lock. He pointed it out to Miss Harrington.

"Do you think the footman forgot it?"

"Possibly. If he did, we'd better be quick." Robert turned the key, which had obviously been oiled, and the latch slid free.

"Let me go first," Miss Harrington said.

He reluctantly agreed, thinking that from what he'd heard, if the woman locked in the room *had* a gun, she would already have used it on the hapless footman.

Miss Harrington gently knocked on the door. "Mrs. Summers? May we come in?" She pushed the door open as she spoke to reveal an elderly woman with a chair leg raised like a weapon above her head. "We wish you no harm."

"Who in the Lord's name are you, and where are Thomas Fairfax and my daughter?" Madge Summers demanded.

Robert bowed. "I'm Major Kurland, and this is Miss Harrington. We've been looking for you since your house burned down."

"For what purpose?"

"To tell you that your daughter is dead." Miss Harrington took over the conversation. "She came to see Mr. Thomas Fairfax, who had been working on the Kurland estate, and died

372

after suffering a head injury during a carriage accident."

"I don't believe you. Why didn't anyone tell *me?*" Madge Summers drew herself up to her full height and lowered the chair leg. She wore a serviceable dark brown dress with an apron over her skirts, and her graying hair was drawn back in a bun. "Is Thomas back, then?"

"He is here. Have you not seen him?"

Before the words were out of Miss Harrington's mouth, Madge was pushing past her and Robert, her gaze fixed on the open door. "I bloody well have not! My house burned down, and the Fairfax carriage came and picked me up. He *tricked* me into coming here! Just wait till I get my hands on him. . . ."

"But—"

Robert had put out a hand to prevent Madge from leaving when she stopped of her own accord and stared at something over Robert's shoulder.

"There's no need to come and find me, Mrs. Summers. I am right here. The footman brought up another tray and found the door ajar and reported it to me."

Thomas stood in the doorway, a lantern in one hand and a pistol in the other. "What exactly is it you wish to speak to me about?"

Robert reached out and carefully drew Miss Harrington closer to his side, his pistol hidden in the fold of her skirts. There was no way out of the room apart from through Thomas, and he doubted they were going to be allowed to leave quite yet.

Thomas continued speaking. "I do apologize if you are annoyed with me, Mrs. Summers. I thought it better to keep you safe until after the funeral and the departure of my guests."

Madge took a threatening step toward him. "What happened to my Emmy?"

"As Miss Harrington has probably told you, she died after a carriage accident. She unintentionally took a fatal dose of laudanum to relieve her headache and passed away in her sleep."

"I don't believe you. She was coming to visit *me*. She wanted to make up."

Thomas sighed. "I'm sure she was, but—"

"Was that her funeral today? Why didn't you tell me and let me attend? What did you do to her, and where's my grandson? What have you done with *him?*"

As Thomas moved farther into the room, Robert took a step toward the door, bringing Miss Harrington with him.

A hint of annoyance flashed across Thomas's face. "Mrs. Summers, your grandson is perfectly well and is currently asleep in the nursery after a rather stressful day."

"Emmy would want me to be with him."

"And so you shall be," Thomas said soothingly.

"As I said, I thought it best if you didn't attend the funeral. I know how awkward it would be for you to mingle with your betters, and your daughter would've hated anyone to know you were her mother." He put the lantern down and held out his hand. "Will you forgive me for keeping you here and allow me to reunite you with your grandchild?"

Madge raised the chair leg again. "I don't trust you. Emmy didn't trust you, either."

"Then why did she change her will and leave Robin in my sole charge?"

"She would never do that. You are lying!"

For the first time, Thomas looked directly at Robert. "Major Kurland, can you confirm that Mrs. Fairfax changed her will?"

"I can confirm that she did. I spoke to her solicitor after her death."

Madge shook her head. "You must have forced her to do so."

Thomas raised his eyebrows. "Why on earth would I have done that? We were barely on speaking terms when I left. It was something of a surprise to me, too."

"I'll wager it was, seeing as how much you hated my daughter for giving old Mr. Fairfax another son—a legitimate one, and not a bastard like you. You did everything you could to tear them apart, didn't you? Even pretending to fall in love with my Emmy, but she saw through you, she knew she couldn't trust you, and she told me so many times."

"Things changed. She obviously decided to trust me, after all." Thomas was no longer smiling and looked white around the mouth. "Now, do you wish to come and see your grandson or not?"

Madge backed up two more steps. "And have you murder me on the stairs? I don't believe a word of this. All I know is that Emmy was afraid of you and feared for her life. That's why she begged her husband to send you away. All those accidents young Robin had! They all stopped when you left."

"You are mistaken, Mrs. Summers. The only person determined to destroy any relationships was your daughter. I lost *everything* because of her."

"And you deserved to lose everything, making up to her, turning her head, bedding your own father's wife!"

Miss Harrington gasped and pressed her fingers to her mouth. Thomas went still.

"That is a lie. She was the one who put herself in my bed and then told my father I'd forced her!"

"Because she was afraid of you! She knew that if she didn't get rid of you, then neither she nor her child would live." Madge snorted. "And now that you've gotten rid of her, how long before you start on the boy?"

Robert cleared his throat. "Mrs. Summers, hose are serious allegations. Do you have any proof?"

"I have the letters she wrote to me, telling me what was going on. I was here and saw a lot more than he realizes when I was in charge of the nursery."

"The last letter Mrs. Fairfax wrote . . . ," Miss Harrington said. "I picked it up from the floor after Mr. Fairfax finished reading it. It was written in a perfect hand." She swallowed hard. "Did she even *write* that note? Only Mr. Fairfax saw it and read it out loud to us."

Thomas turned toward them. "Miss Harrington, you cannot possibly believe the ranting of this old woman! That's why I had to keep her under lock and key. She is ill and insane."

"Did you write that note, Thomas?" Robert asked. "It is a perfectly reasonable question. If you forced Mrs. Fairfax to confess to a murder she did not commit, what else might you have done?"

"I have done nothing," Thomas snapped. "This is ridiculous. *This* is why I kept Mrs. Summers away from you all."

"Because she knew the truth?" Robert asked before turning to Madge. "I wonder what else she knows. Is it true that Mrs. Fairfax was married before?"

"Yes, sir. That is correct."

"Is it also true that no record of the first husband's death exists?"

"He died fighting in France. A lot of men never came home from there or were ever given a proper Christian burial."

"That is highly possible. I was there myself. But did he perhaps return after Mrs. Fairfax had unknowingly remarried?"

"Why on earth would you think that, sir?" Madge looked flabbergasted. "Who put such notions in your head? Was it Thomas?"

"No, it was someone else entirely." Robert exhaled. "I'm beginning to believe he was misled. I was informed that Mrs. Fairfax's marriage was bigamous, and her child by default illegitimate."

For a moment there was silence. Robert focused his attention on Thomas, who had gone very still. "Were you aware of this, Thomas? Did Mrs. Chingford perhaps share that particular piece of gossip with you at the Stanford wedding? I can imagine what you must have thought if that proved to be true. Young Robin was no better than you, which would mean the unentailed estate would have to be divided between you and him and the rest passed on to a legitimate heir."

Thomas frowned. "I don't understand what you are implying, Major."

"But you must. Why did Mrs. Fairfax come to see you at Kurland Hall? What was she really hoping to achieve? You told me she wanted you to return to Fairfax Park to manage it for her son."

"That's the *truth*."

"But she was afraid of you and had driven you away once. Why on earth would she ask you back?"

"I don't know!" Thomas made a violent gesture with his pistol, and Robert tensed. "She *begged* me to come back."

"Did she tell you her son might be illegitimate?"

"Of course not! If I'd known that, I would never have—" He stopped speaking.

"You would never have persuaded her to take too much laudanum and written a note for her, confessing to pushing Mrs. Chingford down the stairs?"

Madge cried out, the sound ragged in the small room.

"You cannot prove that." Thomas held Robert's gaze. "She *did* push Mrs. Chingford. That's the truth. Miss Dorothea Chingford saw her."

"But you were the one who made sure Mrs. Chingford was dead, weren't you? You were the only one allowed to blackmail your stepmother."

Thomas shook his head. "This is all merely conjecture. I am surprised at you, Major Kurland."

Miss Harrington had moved closer to Madge and put a comforting arm round her. "I think you are lying, Mr. Fairfax. I agree with Mrs Summers. How long will young Robin las under your guardianship before you find a way to dispose of him, as well?" She looked over a Robert. "We cannot let him hurt the boy."

"For God's sake! I have no intention of hurting the boy!" Thomas snapped. "There will have to be some adjustments to the estate because of hi illegitimacy, but I don't see why we can't live in harmony together."

"You are convinced Robin is not your father' son, then?" Robert asked.

"Mrs. Fairfax suggested to me that he was not *That's* why she came to see me after altering her will. Mrs. Chingford's foul gossip only con firmed what I had already guessed—that Emily' marriage was bigamous, and her child the son o her previous husband."

Thomas smiled. "There is no case to answer Major. Mrs. Fairfax accidentally killed Mrs Chingford and then took her own life out of guilt I will continue to be in charge here, as my fathe would've wished, until Robin comes of age Then the estate will be divided between us." He hesitated. "Can we not leave it at that?"

"Dorothea Chingford saw you," Robert said.

"I don't understand."

"She saw you at the bottom of the stairs, beside Mrs. Chingford's body. That's why she's been so afraid. She tried to warn me, but I didn' understand until now." He felt in his waistcoat pocket and took out the battered locket. "She asked me to bring this back to Mrs. Fairfax."

Madge made a lunge for the locket. "That's mine. Emmy said she would get it repaired for me in London."

"I believe she was wearing it when she pushed Mrs. Chingford. It was found wrapped in Mrs. Chingford's fingers."

Madge took the locket and carefully opened it. "Mrs. Chingford was always a liar and a gossip. I hated working for her. She used to read all our letters. I didn't realize that until it was too late and she knew all our secrets. But she didn't allow the truth to stand in the way of a bit of gossip or blackmail." She looked right at Thomas. "You murdered my daughter because you thought she'd come to tell you that your father wasn't Robin's father?" Her face contorted. "You were half right. Robin isn't your father's son. He is *your son*. You've been planning on killing your own bastard."

"No!" Thomas shook his head and took an unsteady step back. "*No,* that can't be right. She—" The pistol in his hand wavered, and his mouth twisted. "You are lying!"

"Why would I lie? You've killed my daughter. The only thing I can do now is make sure you don't kill her child, as well!"

Thomas pointed the pistol straight at Madge.

"Be quiet, you stupid old bitch. Shut your mouth!"

Robert leapt forward to knock Thomas's pistol hand up toward the ceiling, and Miss Harrington flung her arms around Madge and pushed her to the floor. The confined space exploded with sound. Before Robert could regain his balance, Thomas turned and ran from the room. Plaster from the ceiling continued to fall, coating them all in fine white powder and making Robert cough.

A shriek from Madge made Robert look up.

"Miss Harrington is hurt! Help her, Major Kurland!"

Robert immediately knelt beside Miss Harrington, who appeared to be bleeding. In shock, he took out his handkerchief, gathered her in his arms, and pressed it against the wound in her skull, where something sharp had laid a bloody, furrowed path.

A babble of voices erupted behind him. Without letting go of Miss Harrington, who remained unconscious, he shouted above the noise.

"Find Mr. Fairfax! Keep him away from the nursery, and fetch a doctor!"

Madge struggled to her feet, her face white. "I'll go to the nursery. I won't let him harm my boy."

"Be my guest." Robert handed her his pistol and she left the room. "Simmons, are you there?"

"Yes, Major Kurland."

"Mr. Fairfax has a gun. Take two of the footmen and try to apprehend him before Mrs. Summers finds him. Lock him up somewhere secure and call the local magistrate."

"But *why,* sir?"

"Simmons, just do as I say!" Robert roared, using every note of his commanding voice. His knee was beginning to ache, so he sat on his arse and kept hold of Miss Harrington, balancing her on his lap. The smell of blood was making him ill and reminding him of too many battlefields and lost friends and . . . He took a deep, steadying breath. He was not going to lose Miss Harrington. He would not countenance it.

Eventually, she opened her eyes and winced. "What happened?"

"Thomas tried to shoot Mrs. Summers, and your head got in the way."

She tried to bring her hand up to her face, but he gently stopped her fingers and held on to them. "You'll have a scar, but I think you will live."

"Good," she murmured. "I have a headache. Can you take me home now, sir?"

He carefully placed a kiss on her nose. "That, my dear, will be my pleasure."

Chapter 22

Robert nodded at the footman stationed outside the small parlor. "I'll see Mr. Fairfax. Please don't let anyone else in, and lock the door behind me."

"Yes, sir."

Robert found Thomas seated at a small table. His bruised face bore the signs of the scuffle to prevent him absconding, and his coat was ripped at the shoulder. He looked up as Robert approached him, and shot to his feet.

"Major Kurland, sir, you *have* to help me. This is not what I intended to happen. Please, believe me, I—"

Robert held up his hand and sat down. "I have a few questions to ask you purely on my own account."

Thomas subsided into his seat. "I suppose you think the worst of me now, just like everyone else."

"I certainly think you made some extremely foolish decisions."

"But my intentions were good!" Thomas said earnestly. "Mrs. Fairfax was not capable of running this estate. All I wanted was the opportunity to live here and help my . . . my half brother."

"Your son," Robert said gently. "Is that perhaps why Mrs. Fairfax came to see you at Kurland Hall? To tell you the truth?"

"Then why didn't she tell me *all* of it?" Thomas said. "She hinted at things and then asked me to return and manage the estate. I had no idea that she had changed her will and had made me Robin's guardian. When she got into the altercation with Mrs. Chingford at the wedding, I had just left her. I heard Mrs. Chingford fall down the stairs behind me and went back to see if she was truly dead."

"And strangled her. When you did that, you realized you had an opportunity to persuade Mrs. Fairfax to do what you wanted by threatening to reveal her part in Mrs. Chingford's death."

"*Yes,* but if she had told me the truth, I would never have thought of it. Or needed to do anything." Thomas sought Robert's gaze. "Can't you see?"

"Oh, I think I see. With Mrs. Chingford out of the way, you would no longer have to fear her spreading her stories about Robin's parentage. And Mrs. Fairfax was so afraid of discovery, she would be willing to do whatever you told her."

"You make it sound so . . . mercenary," Thomas said quietly. "But I can assure you, I didn't plan for Mrs. Fairfax to push Mrs. Chingford down the stairs."

"But you were more than willing to take advantage of it," Robert said. "And what about Mrs. Fairfax's death?"

Thomas dropped his gaze to his hands. "She was consumed with guilt over what had happened to Mrs. Chingford. I tried to reason with her, but she was determined to confess. I couldn't allow her to do that." He sighed. "She knew I strangled Mrs. Chingford."

"I'm not sure that she did. The only person who mentioned seeing another figure at the foot of the stairs was Dorothea Chingford."

Thomas groaned and buried his face in his hands. Robert waited patiently for him to look up.

"You wrote the confession for Mrs. Fairfax, didn't you?"

"I thought it would end things—that everyone would accept what had happened, and I would be free to go and reclaim Fairfax Park."

"And eventually inherit the estate after poor Robin suffered a terrible accident."

Thomas swallowed hard and whispered, "You think I'm an out-and-out murderer, don't you? But they all lied to me. If I'd only known the truth, I would never have had to take advantage of the circumstances that occurred."

"That's no excuse, Thomas." Robert stood and looked down at Thomas's bowed head. "Two women are dead because of you and your choices.' I have no sympathy for you at all."

He bowed and turned to the door before remembering something else. "And what of Miss Harrington? Did you truly intend to marry her, or was your interest in her feigned to prevent her from speaking out?"

"I would have married her, Major. I have a great deal of respect for her," Thomas said. "If we had married, I would've been able to prevent her from meddling in what no longer concerned her."

Robert snorted. "Miss Harrington was born to meddle, and thank God for it. You would've had to dispose of her to keep her quiet." He turned away from the defeated figure at the table and made his slow way over to the door. "The local magistrate will be here soon. I'll advise him to take you to the county town and hold you here."

There was no reply, and for that, he was deeply thankful. His ability to maintain his temper in the face of Thomas's inability to see anything but his own selfish needs was waning. Mayhap Thomas *had* taken advantage of the circumstances, but he had done so without regard to the sanctity of human life.

And he had been more than willing to add Miss Harrington to his list of victims.

Robert slammed the door behind him, startling the footman on duty.

"The magistrate will be here shortly, Major."

"Good. Let me know when he arrives so that can speak to him."

"Mrs. Green is busy writing letters in the yellow parlor, so you may come in and see the patient Major Kurland."

Robert nodded at Miss Chingford as she opened the door. "Thank you."

Miss Harrington was sitting up in bed, her hair was braided to one side of her head, and she had large bandage on her forehead. She still managed to look quite formidable.

"Good morning, Miss Harrington, Mrs Summers."

The old nurse sat by the fire, knitting, and barely acknowledged his presence. She had taken up residence in the nursery with Mrs. William and had kept young Robin away from all the upheaval.

"Did you find Mr. Fairfax?" Miss Harrington asked.

Robert took the seat next to her bed. If he wasn't mistaken, his betrothed was going to have a black eye before the day was out. He decided not to mention it.

"He was apprehended in the stables, trying to saddle a horse. I've sent for the local magistrate who is away from home."

"Did you speak to Mr. Fairfax yourself?"

"I did." Robert sighed. "I can't help but feel a little sorry for him. He seems to be incapable of understanding what he's done. He kept saying that if he'd just left well alone, he would have come back to work for Mrs. Fairfax at Fairfax Park, discovered Robin was his son, and settled down into an unconventional but satisfying relationship, managing the estate for both of them."

Miss Harrington's lips thinned. "I have no sympathy for him whatsoever. Don't forget he probably strangled Mrs. Chingford and deliberately helped Mrs. Fairfax overdose herself on laudanum."

"In his opinion, he was merely taking advantage of the opportunities that suggested themselves to him. I asked him whether he had anything to do with the carriage wreck, and he denied all responsibility for that. He did admit that he was able to use Mrs. Fairfax's condition after the wreck to his benefit. I suspect the carriage incident was my cousin Paul's attempt to unsettle me. He hoped to come in and run the estate for his poor crippled cousin and probably attempted to make sure I never got out of bed again."

"Mr. Reading was staying in Saffron Walden, wasn't he?" Miss Harrington sighed. "Poor Mrs. Fairfax."

"I don't have much sympathy for her, either.

If only she'd told Thomas the truth from the beginning."

"And lost all the social advantages her marriage had given her and her son?" Miss Harrington shook her head. "She was far too afraid to do that."

After a quick glance in Madge's direction, Robert reached out and took Miss Harrington's hand in his. "At least you didn't marry him."

"I had no intention of doing that." She hesitated. "What will happen to him now?"

"It is up to the local justice of the peace. I'll present him with the evidence we have and leave it up to him."

"Will he be brought to trial?"

"I'm not sure. As Thomas said, all these things are difficult to prove, especially when both of the main witnesses are dead."

"Then he might get away with murder?"

"Yes." He squeezed her fingers. "I can use my influence to make sure he is persona non grata in society. I have already suggested that if he survives an investigation, it would be in his best interests to leave England."

"I hope he takes your advice."

"I don't think he will have any other option. I will also make sure that young Robin and the estate are protected from Mr. Fairfax. The solicitor I met at Kurland St. Mary is due to arrive here tomorrow."

"When will we be able to leave Fairfax Park?"

He brought her fingers to his lips and kissed them. "Within a week, I think, although you could leave earlier, if you so desire."

"I'd rather stay and see it through to the end," she said resolutely.

"That's exactly what I would expect you to say." He cleared his throat. "I will be speaking to your father when we return."

"As to that . . ." She searched his face. "You do not *have* to marry me, you know."

He held her suddenly shy gaze. "I want to marry you. Will you have me?"

"Yes, I will."

He smiled at her and stood up. "Then everything is settled. I might not be the most even-tempered man in your life, but I swear no one will love and protect you better."

She brought her hand to her flushed cheek and simply stared at him. Satisfied that he had for once confounded her into silence, Robert winked and made his way out of the bedchamber. His smile faded as he contemplated what lay ahead for Thomas Fairfax, but he would not let the other man's mistakes destroy his current sense of happiness.

Happy.

Robert stopped in the corridor and considered that foreign emotion before whistling and going down the stairs to deal with the demoralized staff.

Every man made his choices in life, and for once he was content with his. Thomas Fairfax had overreached himself and, in Robert's opinion, deserved to lose everything—especially Miss Lucy Harrington.